**A/F**
**Aug & Sept**
**2005**

## DATE DUE

| | |
|---|---|
| 1087 | SEP 0 2 2005 |
| 2257 | SEP 2 6 2005 |
| 1316 | OCT 1 7 2005 |
| 1023 | DEC 2 6 2005 |
| 1871 | APR 2 1 2006 |
| 1571 | JUN 0 9 2006 |
| 1011 | OCT 0 4 2006 |
| 1952 | JAN 1 6 2007 |
| 1164 | FEB 2 0 2007 |
| 2118 | MAY 1 0 2007 |
| 2384 | SEP 0 7 2007 |
| 1892 | JAN 2 1 2008 |
| 1693 | FEB 1 6 2010 |
| | |
| | |
| | |

# BY MARIAH STEWART

# DEAD
# END

# DEAD END

*A Novel*

## MARIAH

## STEWART

BALLANTINE BOOKS

*New York*

Copyright © 2005 by Marti Robb

All rights reserved.

Published in the United States by Ballantine Books, an imprint of The Random House Publishing Group, a division of Random House, Inc., New York.

BALLANTINE and colophon are registered trademarks of Random House, Inc.

ISBN 0-345-48381-2

Printed in the United States of America on acid-free paper

www.ballantinebooks.com

2 4 6 8 9 7 5 3 1

FIRST EDITION

Book design by Dana Leigh Blanchette

*I have been blessed to have had
the most wonderful, incredible women
in my corner for ten glorious, fun-filled
years. Love and thanks to my personal
dream team—Kate Collins, Linda Marrow,
Gina Centrello, and of course,
St. Loretta the divine.*

Talk of devils being confined to hell, or hidden by invisibility! We have them by shoals in the crowded towns and cities of the world.

Talk of raising the devil! What need for that, when he is constantly walking to and fro in our streets, seeking whom he will devour.

Anonymous

# DEAD
# END

# PROLOGUE

*Cortés City, Santa Estela*
*Central America*
*December 2002*

An unhealthy dampness clung to the shacks of corrugated tin and rotted wood in the poorest section of a poor city. Beyond the mean dwellings, the river moved lazily to the ocean just a few scant miles away. Between the windowless shacks and the river stood a series of ramshackle warehouses—long abandoned by the banana trade—and several decaying docks where only the most dangerous or the most desperate dared to venture after the sun went down.

A street fair earlier in the evening had lured the residents of the shacks to the town center some blocks away, where reggae had blended with salsa and hip-hop to flavor the night. At this late hour, however, even the most die-hard revelers had staggered home, drunk and exhausted, leaving the unfriendly streets to the rats and little else.

The rattle of the old panel truck as it made its way toward the docks might have drawn attention had not the local population celebrated themselves into a stupor. Slowing as it came to the alley between the last two warehouses, the truck jerked to a stop, but its engine remained running. Within minutes, a black SUV with tinted windows pulled boldly behind the truck and made a half U-turn. The drivers of both vehicles got out and conversed in hushed tones, their gestures speaking more loudly than their words, as they negotiated a mutually agreeable amount for the truck's cargo. Finally, a deal struck, the driver of the SUV motioned toward his car, and several more men got out. One carried a briefcase. The others carried rifles and made a semicircle around the driver of the SUV.

The truck's cargo door began to rise as flashlights were trained on the opening. No fewer than forty children, stunned in terrified silence, turned their heads to avoid looking directly into the beams as the lights made their way from one dazed young face to the next.

A lone witness watching from the shadows between the buildings debated what action to take. The children—boys and girls, the youngest of whom appeared to be no more than five or six, the oldest perhaps twelve or thirteen—were obviously all headed for slavery or would be filtered into the international child-sex trade before the end of the week. Whichever hardly mattered at that moment to the observer, who knew only that something had to be done, and quickly. But he was wise enough to recognize that caution had to rule. There was one of him, and at least six of them, perhaps more inside the truck.

He'd come upon the scene by accident as he'd made his way to the last dock, where he was to be picked up by a small boat and whisked away to a larger craft, upon which waited the helicopter that would take him to a small airport in Mexico. From there, he'd be shuttled back to the States. His mission—totally unrelated to the scene unfolding around him—was now complete, and he was expected to give a full report to his superiors at Quantico at eight o'clock the next morning.

From downriver, he could hear the first hum of the boat's motor and knew that he had to make a decision, and fast.

The driver of the SUV directed one of the men to shine the light onto the contents of the briefcase, and as he did so, his face was illuminated as well. The man in the shadows had more than enough time to study the well-lit features. A thin face, sparse dark hair that receded from his forehead, making him appear older than he probably was. Round dark eyes, small and wide set. A nose made flat by at least one run-in with a well-aimed fist. A humorless mouth.

The sound of the boat came closer, though the men in the alley appeared not to hear over the drone of the truck's engine. The man in the shadows counted the rounds in his gun.

He heard a faint shuffle behind him and flattened himself against the wall of the warehouse, his gun drawn, hoping he wouldn't have to fire and call attention to himself. He raised the gun as another shadow eased around the corner where he himself had earlier emerged, then lowered it as he cursed softly.

"Jesus! What the fuck are you doing here?" he growled.

"I might ask you the same question," the newcomer whispered.

"Are you on this? You're working this?"

"Yeah. Been following them for weeks. No one told me you were part of the operation."

"I'm not. I'm supposed to be picked up in about three minutes down on the dock. I'm to brief the director in the morning on—" He caught himself. "On another issue."

"Well, I suggest you get yourself down there, or you're going to miss the boat."

"You're on this, though, right?" He grabbed the newcomer by the arm. "You know what's in that truck, right? You know what's going down here, what's going to happen to those kids? And you're going to take care of it?"

"Hey, relax. I said I was on it. Don't worry, they'll never get the truck out of the alley. We're just waiting for the deal to be completed, then we'll get them all."

"You have backup . . . ?"

"More than enough. Go on, man, get going. Don't miss your boat. The engine's cut, they must be right down at the shoreline. But I'd suggest you go out the way I just came in, down through the little stretch of woods to the water."

"That's one ugly son of a bitch, down there. Don't let him get away."

"Don't worry." There was a pause, then he asked, "You saw him? Saw his face?"

"It's a face I'll never forget. See you back in the States," he said as he slipped into the darkness.

The man remaining in the alley leaned back against the wall and exhaled, a long tired breath laden with anxiety. He wiped the sweat from his forehead with both hands and wondered what the hell he was going to do.


The man with the receding hairline and the flat nose took an envelope from inside his jacket pocket and passed it to his companion, whose eyes darted around the outdoor café.

"Not to worry. No one here cares what we do," he said as he signaled for the waiter to bring another coffee.

His companion merely nodded.

"All right, Shields," the man demanded, "out with it. What's on your mind? Not having second thoughts about our little bit of commerce, are you?"

"Someone saw you last night."

"What do you mean, someone saw . . ." His small eyes grew even smaller. "Saw me?"

"When I came around the building, someone was there, watching you."

"And you left his body where?"

"It's not quite that simple."

The waiter silently traded the old cup for a new one and disappeared back into the café.

"Explain to me what is complicated about getting rid of a witness."

"It wasn't just any witness. He's with the Bureau and he's . . ."

"He's an agent? Another agent saw me with a truckload of kids . . ."

"I told him I was on the case. I told him I was handling it. He doesn't know who you are."

"What the hell was he doing there? That's your job, to make sure that no one else in the Bureau noses around."

"He was on his way to a pickup, on his way back to the States. He just happened to be getting picked up on the docks at the same time you were concluding the deal."

"And the reason you didn't kill him . . . ?"

"If he hadn't made the boat, there'd have been five or six coming ashore to find him. He was supposed to be meeting with the Director this morning. There was no way he wasn't going to be missed immediately."

"All right." The man took a sip of his coffee and tried to calm his thoughts. "You're certain he saw me?"

"Yes."

"Okay. We can handle this. He doesn't know my name, he doesn't know you're involved."

"He thinks I'm shutting the operation down."

"Well, that's fine. You're due back in the States in another few weeks, right? You were reassigned?"

His companion nodded.

"So, you find him, you take care of him then. I'm due back in two months. I can't run the risk that he'll recognize me, Shields. I want him gone. Permanently." The index finger of his right hand tapped methodically on the table. "You know him, right? You know where to find him?"

"Yeah, I know him. And finding him won't be a problem." He rubbed his hand over his mouth, which had gone dry. "He's my cousin."

1

Lyndon, Pennsylvania
August, 2005

What could possibly be going through a man's mind at the moment
he decides to take the life of a child?

Detective Evan Crosby stared down at the twisted body of
Caitlin McGill and wondered.

The young girl's blank eyes stared endlessly at the sun, her mouth
open in its final scream. Her thin arms stretched outward, bent
at the elbows, to form perfect Ls. Her feet turned in, toes touch-
ing.

"Pigeon-toed."

"What?" Evan turned his head slightly, though his eyes were still
on the girl who lay at his feet.

"We used to call people whose feet turned in like that pigeon-toed," one of the crime-scene investigators noted. "How old was this one?"

"Not even fourteen," Evan replied.

"Just like the last one." The CSI shook his head. "Crazy. Just plain damned crazy. She was a real cute kid."

"They were all cute kids."

"This is what, the third? Fourth? In the past two months?"

No one responded to the question, which was rhetorical. Everyone on the scene—from the Avon County, Pennsylvania, detectives to the CSIs to the local police to the medical examiner—knew exactly how many others there'd been since the first of May.

Four.

Jamie Kershaw.

Heidi Fuhrmann.

Andrea Masters.

And now Caitlin McGill.

All between the ages of twelve and fourteen. All pretty girls who attended one of the many private schools that flourished in the Philadelphia suburbs. All with dark red stains down the front of the white cotton shirts that were standard school-uniform attire.

All of them barefoot.

"What's up with that, anyway?" Joe Sullivan, Evan's onetime partner at the Lyndon Police Department, came up the hill from the playground and stopped three feet behind Evan. "Whaddaya suppose he's doing with their shoes?"

"Your guess is as good as mine."

"Poor kid." Sullivan shook his head. "What's your old lady say about it?"

"I haven't had a chance to talk to her yet. She's been away." Evan let the "old lady" comment ride. He'd had that conversation with

Joe on more than one occasion. It had never done any good—Joe was Joe and wasn't about to change.

"Guess they keep those FBI profilers pretty busy, eh?"

"Never a shortage of psychos, Joe, you know that." Evan nodded to Dr. Agnes Jenkins, the Avon County medical examiner, as she hurried past.

"Can't remember anything like this, though. But at least he left them where they'd be found quickly." Sullivan's voice was flat, emotionless.

The M.E. bent over the body and began her ministrations. Evan looked away. Over the past eight weeks, he'd had more than his fill of young girls who'd had their throats slashed. He took a few steps back, then turned and went back to his car. The crime scene would be turned over to him once the M.E. was finished, but for now, he'd use this time to check his phone messages, return those calls he could. Start the paperwork on this latest homicide. Get as much work done as he could while he could. It had all the makings of another very long night.

It was well after three in the morning when Evan arrived at his townhouse in West Lyndon. Bone weary, he left his car parked out front, and bleary-eyed, let himself in through the front door. He ignored the pile of mail on the hall table—when had he put that there?—and pretended not to see the blinking red light on his telephone. Messages could wait. He was simply too tired to deal with anyone or anything.

Too tired, too, to make it up the steps, so he let himself drift backward onto the living-room sofa, fully clothed. He'd just closed his eyes when he heard the soft footfall on the stairs. Dismissing it as little more than wishful thinking on his part, he continued to sail toward sleep.

"Evan?" a voice called from the doorway.

More wishful thinking, surely.

"Evan." The voice, gentle, filled with concern, drew closer.

Soft hands caressed his arm. He sighed and smiled in his state of almost-sleep.

"Evan, don't sleep down here. Come up to bed." The voice was in his ear now.

He reached out and touched skin.

"Annie."

He felt her weight as she sat on the edge of the sofa and leaned over him, her lips pressed against the side of his face.

"When did you get here?"

"About nine." She snuggled next to him, and he felt himself relax for the first time in days.

"Why didn't you call me?"

"I heard on the scanner that another body had been found. I didn't want to disturb you. I figured you'd be home when you were finished with what you had to do."

"How long can you stay?"

"I'll be in town through Tuesday. Have you forgotten that my sister is getting married on Friday?"

"Oh, shit. I did forget." He stared up at the ceiling. How could he have forgotten that?

"It's okay. I'm here to remind you. Thursday night, rehearsal dinner. Friday night, wedding. Saturday, sleep until noon. Saturday night, just me and you. Sunday through Tuesday, I'll be staying with my niece, until Mara and Aidan get back. Not much of a honeymoon for them, but at least they'll have a few days to themselves."

"Rewind back to Saturday. Saturday sounded real good." It had been weeks since they'd had a night together alone. There'd been something every weekend for the past month. Four weeks ago, it had been Mara's wedding shower. The past three, either Annie or Evan had been working.

Maybe on Saturday night they could have dinner at their fa-vorite restaurant, he was thinking, then catch a movie. Or maybe they'd just stay at home, just the two of them. That sounded even better.

She lay against him, her head on his chest. His fingers trailed lightly through her soft blond hair.

"How old was she?" she asked softly.

"Thirteen. Almost fourteen."

"Same as the others?"

"Yes."

She fell silent, and he knew that she was working it through. As a psychologist and one of the FBI's most skilled profilers, Annie—Dr. Anne Marie McCall—couldn't help but sort through the pieces.

"Shoes?"

"Missing," he told her through a fog of fatigue. "Just like the others."

"Odd trophy," she murmured.

"I wanted to ask you what you thought about that."

"Tomorrow." She sat up. "We'll talk about that tomorrow. Right now, you think you can make it up the stairs?"

"Doubtful."

"Okay."

She stood, and cool air replaced her warmth. His hand searched for her in the dark, but she had already moved out of reach.

"Where are you going?"

"I'll be right back."

Moments later she returned. He felt the soft flow of a blanket drift over him, the comfort of a pillow under his head.

Bliss.

"Move over." She slid under the blanket and wrapped her arms around him, her body molded to his in the dark.

"Annie . . ."

"Shh. Tomorrow. There's nothing that can't wait until the morning."

He wanted to say something, but his tired brain had stopped communicating with his mouth. Effortlessly, he sailed off into the darkness, where he dreamed of endless closets filled with small bloody shoes that frantic mothers tried to match into pairs.

"Evan! How's it going?"

A hand slapped him on the back, and Evan turned to find Will Fletcher, a friend of Annie's from the Bureau, leaning against the bar.

"Some wedding, huh?" Will gestured around the tent with one hand, the other hand wrapped around a glass of champagne.

"Yeah. Beautiful. Glad the weather held for Mara and Aidan. The reports this week weren't too promising." Evan declined the flute offered by a tuxedoed young man and opted for a pilsner of beer.

"That's one beautiful bride." Will nodded at Mara, who, with her tall, handsome groom, was making her way around the room.

"No argument from me," Evan agreed.

"Great idea, don't you think, to have Annie and Julianne give the bride away?"

"Well, since Mara's parents aren't alive, having her sister and her daughter there for her was a really nice touch."

"The kid—Julianne—looks like she's survived her ordeal pretty well."

For a moment, Evan had forgotten that Will had been there when Julianne had been returned after spending seven years living under an assumed name with her father, Jules Douglas. Unable to forgive Mara for having divorced him, Jules had done the one thing he knew would hurt Mara the most. He took their five-year-old daughter, and disappeared.

After years of tracking, the FBI was finally led to the Valley of the Angels, a Wyoming ranch that was part of the network of one self-proclaimed evangelist who called himself Reverend Prescott, whose mission in life was to "rescue" young drug-addicted runaways from the streets, only to clean them up and sell them to the highest bidder on the Internet. Jules's mathematical wizardry had come in handy when it came to cooking the reverend's books. Jules was currently in prison awaiting trial for kidnapping and a host of other charges related to his work at the Valley of the Angels. Julianne had been present when her father was arrested, just a few days after she'd been reunited with her mother. All in all, it had been one hell of a year for everyone involved.

"From all accounts, Julianne seems to be doing just fine. She seems to be accepting Aidan as a stepfather—Mara would have postponed the wedding if she hadn't been able to handle it—and Annie has been keeping tabs on her. She thinks Julianne's doing great." Evan's searching eyes found Annie, halfway across the tent. He willed her to look at him, and eventually, she did. She smiled and winked, and continued her conversation with one of the guests.

Will said something else, and Evan nodded and excused himself.

The band was starting to play an old ballad from the forties and he wanted to dance with Annie, wanted to feel her arms around him, wanted to feel her pressed against him. He smiled at the person she was chatting with—a man he vaguely recognized as someone from her office—and took her hand.

"It's time to dance with your guy," he told her as he led her to the dance floor.

"Gladly." She moved into his arms and swayed with him.

"What's with this forties music?" he asked.

"Mr. Shields asked them to play it."

"He asked them to play the last two sappy songs. Since when does the father of the groom get to submit his own playlist?"

"Since no one has told him he couldn't."

Out of the corner of one eye, Evan watched the Shields clan gather. They were all now, or had been at one time, in the FBI. Aidan, the groom. Connor, his older brother and best man. Thomas, their father, and Frank, their uncle and Thomas's brother, both now retired. The cousins—Frank's kids—Andrew, Brendan, Grady, and Mia, the lone female in the family. Two generations of FBI, eight in all.

But of course, there had been nine. It was the ninth Shields— Thomas's middle son, Dylan—who was on everyone's mind right then.

"Annie!" Grady shouted over the heads of the other dancers. "We need you!"

Evan thought he'd felt her stiffen slightly, but she smiled and kept on dancing.

"We're about to drink a toast to Dylan, Annie"—Brendan made his way through the crowd and took Annie's arm—"and we can't do it right without you."

Annie appeared slightly uncomfortable, as if unsure what to do, but did not protest when Brendan tugged her along.

"Evan, do you mind . . . ?" she asked.

"You go on," he said. "It's okay . . ."

"If you're sure . . . ?"

"Sure." He shrugged, and watched her disappear into the crowd.

A few minutes later, Thomas Shields asked the band to stop playing so that he could propose a toast to his son.

Not Aidan, the groom. But Dylan, the one who'd been killed in an undercover drug deal gone bad more than two years earlier.

Dylan, everyone's favorite, the best of the Shields brothers. Best athlete. Best student. Best friend. Best agent. The golden boy whose memory would forever remain untarnished to those who had known and loved him.

Dylan, who had been engaged to marry Annie.

Evan signaled the bartender for a beer, then leaned back against the bar and took a long drink while listening to the tributes, one after another, being paid to the fallen hero.

"If they keep this up much longer, they'll turn the wedding reception into a wake," he muttered.

"What?" The man next to him leaned forward, thinking Evan had been addressing him.

"I said, nice that they're remembering Dylan," he said dryly.

"Oh, hell of a guy. Damn shame, what happened to him." The man shook his gray head. "Just a damn shame. And him all set to marry that pretty little Annie McCall. Broke her heart, the day he died, I can tell you that. Just a tragedy."

The man appeared to wipe a tear from his face, and Evan fought an urge to roll his eyes.

"Friend of his, were you?" the man asked.

"Ah, no. We never met. I'm actually a friend of the bride."

"Then you must know Annie."

"Yes, of course. I know Annie."

"They sure do love her, don't they?" He nodded to the cluster that the Shields family made on the opposite side of the room. "But then again, what's not to love about Annie, right? Damn shame she had the love of her life snatched away from her like that."

Evan's stomach began to knot. He put the beer down on the bar and started to excuse himself, but his companion kept talking.

"Makes it worse for everyone, not knowing, you know."

"Not knowing what?"

"Not knowing who pulled the trigger. Never did find the shooter. I think that would have helped everyone, if they had closure, you know?"

"I'm sure the Bureau investigated thoroughly."

"They did, but nothing came of it. Sometimes it happens like that. It's not always like it is on those TV shows, you know."

Evan knew.

The eulogies finally over, the band began to play again. Evan looked around for Annie, but found her still surrounded by the Shields family. When he saw Mara standing along the edge of the dance floor chatting with a girlfriend, he put his beer down and made his way to her.

"May I have the honor of dancing with the bride?" He held out his arms.

"I thought you'd never ask." Mara smiled and joined him on the dance floor.

"Beautiful wedding, Mara," he said.

"Oh, thank you. I'm so glad it didn't get humid. You know how it gets here in Pennsylvania in the summer. It can really swelter."

"Well, you lucked out, all around." He moved her around the dance floor in time to the music. "Everything is perfect."

She nodded somewhat absently, and he caught her looking over his shoulder.

"What?" he asked.

"We should be leaving soon, but I'm afraid it's going to be hard to tear Aidan away from his family."

"On his wedding night? I doubt it."

"It's been a difficult day for them—for Aidan and his dad and his brother and the rest of them. This is really the first big family event since Dylan died, and they're all missing him so much." Her eyes flickered, and she looked up at him. "Probably not so easy for you, either, but for a different reason, right?"

He shrugged.

"The Shieldses are a tough group, Evan," Mara said, as if that were all the explanation necessary.

"Honey," he said softly, "it's your wedding. They should let you have your day and not turn it into a memorial service for a man who's been dead for more than two years."

Her cheeks flushed, and he instantly regretted his words.

"I'm sorry, Mara. I shouldn't have . . ."

"It's okay. And you're right. I know I should say something, but they are just a little intimidating when they're all together. And I don't think any of them ever got over him dying like that, the way he did. I know Aidan is still having a lot of issues because of the way he died."

"Look, how about if I go on over there and see if I can get Aidan's attention."

"That would be great. Thanks, Evan. Maybe just let him know that he needs to watch the time, and that I'm ready to leave whenever he is."

He left Mara with the same friend she'd earlier been chatting with and somehow managed to breach the edge of the circle that was gathered around Thomas Shields and his two sons. Between Aidan and Connor sat Annie, looking very much a part of the clan. Evan managed to catch Aidan's eye and mouthed that Mara needed to talk to him. A quick glance at his watch reminded Aidan why. He nodded and excused himself quietly. Evan stepped back to let him pass, pausing, trying to decide the best way to get Annie's attention. But she was absorbed in a story Grady was telling about one time when they were younger and he'd had the bad judgment to challenge Dylan to a pitching contest, the prize being Grady's new bike. Dylan, who'd been scouted by several pro baseball teams as a senior in college, had all but taken his cousin's head off with his fastball and, at the end of the exercise, had driven off on Grady's bike, whistling "Take Me Out to the Ball Game."

Evan stepped back and away from the crowd. Still on the fringes, he watched Annie for a few more minutes, but she never glanced his way. He walked out of the tent toward the parking lot and disappeared into the night.

He drove around for forty minutes trying to decide what to do. When his phone rang, he answered on the first ring.

"Crosby."

He listened for a moment, then turned his car around in the next parking lot.

"I'm on my way."

He headed for Belle Mead, a small town four miles away, where another young girl lay dead, and tried to ignore the fact that his first reaction had been relief of sorts for having been provided with an excuse for having left the wedding.

He knew that it was Annie he'd left behind, and that sooner or later he'd have to deal with that. For now, he could simply tell her he'd been called away, and rather than making a scene at the wedding, he'd thought it best to just slip out quietly. Surely she'd understand. She was, after all, with the FBI.

She's also a shrink, he reminded himself, and more likely than not would see right through that smoke screen.

Well, so be it. He'd deal with it.

And sooner or later, they'd both have to deal with the fact that while Dylan Shields was gone, he sure as hell wasn't forgotten.

3

Anne Marie sat at the red light and speed-dialed Evan's cell phone for the fourth time. He always had his phone with him, and it was always turned on. Why wasn't he picking up?

Maybe he's in a meeting and has the volume turned down. Or maybe he's at a crime scene and can't take the call. She glanced at the clock on the dashboard. It was almost two in the afternoon. He could be home, sleeping. Maybe he'd been out on a case all night and had only been home for a few hours. Not unusual for a homicide detective to play catch-up during the day if he'd been up for more than twenty-four hours.

She'd find out soon enough. She was less than six miles from West Lyndon and Evan's townhouse.

She closed up her phone and tossed it onto the passenger's seat, and tried to ignore the uneasiness that had been haunting her since she'd looked for Evan at the wedding and found that he was gone.

That had been three days ago. She hadn't heard from him since, despite having left several messages for him on his home, office, and cell phones.

Not a good sign. Definitely not a good sign.

As she turned the corner onto Evan's street, she was surprised to see his car parked out front. Annie pulled into the space behind his and turned off her engine. Walking alongside then in front of his car, she placed her hand on the hood. It was cold. The car had been there for a while.

*Okay, so I was probably right about him sleeping.*

She slipped the key he'd given her three months ago, when their relationship passed from occasional to steady, into the lock. Assuming that he was in fact asleep, she opened the door and quietly entered the townhouse then paused in the foyer. From the basement, she could hear music. Loud blues, which grew louder with every step she took in the direction of the steps leading downstairs.

"Evan?" she called.

"Yo!"

Well, if nothing else, he was awake.

She descended the steps into the long, narrow space Evan had been working on for the past year. His goal was to have a fully operational family room—complete with wide-screen TV, a bar, and a built-in stereo—before next Christmas. For months, he'd barely had time to work on it. Today, he appeared to be determined to make up for lost time.

In the center of the room, Evan stood over a table saw. At his feet, a pile of two-by-fours was stacked unevenly. He turned on the saw and proceeded to cut first one, then another, of the lengths of wood until they were all of a uniform size. Annie sat on the third step from the bottom, watching the pile grow, making mental bets with herself as to how many minutes would pass before he would turn around and talk to her.

Finally, she stood up, unplugged the saw, and turned off the radio.

"Why, yes, I was able to find a ride home from the wedding, nice of you to inquire."

"Any one of a dozen people would have been more than happy to see you home on Friday night. I knew you'd have no problem getting a ride." No longer able to cut, he started to stack the wood in an obsessively neat pile, an attempt on his part, she knew, to concentrate on anything other than her.

"That's it? That's all you have to say?" Her eyes narrowed. "You knew someone else would take me home after you dumped me?"

"I didn't dump you. I got called out."

"Not another . . . ?"

"Yup."

"Same as the others?"

"The same—but different this time."

"Are you going to elaborate?"

"Same MO. Throat slashed. Vic is the same age as the others, but no one seems to know who she is. No ID. No one's reported her missing. And she's Hispanic. The others have all been white, reported missing before the bodies were found. This girl, it's like she came out of nowhere. I'm not sure what to make of that."

"You're sure it's the same guy?"

"Like I said, same MO. Same cause of death, the missing shoes—"

"Any chance of a copycat?"

"We never released the details, no one outside the investigation knows about the shoes."

"I realize this is an important case, but you could have taken one minute on Friday night to tell me you were leaving."

"I couldn't have gotten to you even if I'd tried."

"What's that supposed to mean?"

"It means you were in the Shields zone. No outsiders allowed."

"That's ridiculous."

"Is it? I did come over to the table, but I couldn't get through the throng. Couldn't even get your attention, you were so caught up with whatever story whichever Shields was telling at the time."

"If I didn't know you better, I'd think you were jealous."

"Maybe you don't know me so well, after all."

"Are you serious? You're jealous?"

"Let's just put it this way, Annie. It's really tough having to compete with a dead man for your attention. Especially when that dead man was, by all accounts, an absolute paragon of—"

"Stop it, Evan. Just . . . stop it."

She turned her back and started toward the stairs. She got up to the second step and turned back to him.

"I will say this one time, so listen up." She took a deep breath. "If you are waiting for me to tell you that I did not love Dylan, you are going to be very disappointed. I did love him. I loved him with all my heart. I planned to marry him and grow old with him. When he was killed, I thought I'd never feel that way about anyone, ever again. I accepted that."

"Annie . . ."

"Don't. You started this, you will let me finish."

She came down off the steps.

"The first time I met you, I knew how I was going to end up feeling about you. Don't ask me to explain it because I can't. But I met you, and I thought, Well, now, how about that? Lightning can strike twice, apparently. Then we began dating, and for a time, I was confused, because I wasn't sure I understood how anyone could be lucky enough to find that kind of love more than once. And I knew that I loved you, pretty much right from the time we started seeing each other. There was just something in you . . . something so good and honest, something that just spoke to my heart." She took a long breath.

"Don't take this the wrong way, but there was something else I saw in you that I saw in Dylan as well, and I don't mean this to sound as if I'm comparing you to him. I'm not. It wasn't that you were alike. It's more in the way he cared about what he did. It might sound corny, but he took the whole business of fighting crime very seriously. He was always on the side of the victims, always stood for those who couldn't stand for themselves. I loved that in him. I saw all those same things in you—that same determination, that same dedication—and I loved it in you, too. I really felt that in spite of what had happened, I would have my happily-ever-after. With you."

Evan rubbed the back of his neck, then shoved his hands into his pockets. He just didn't know what to say.

"I'm sorry that you felt left out on Friday. I have to be very honest with you—I did feel uncomfortable, after a while, the way Dylan's family was turning my sister's wedding into a sort of memorial service. But you have to understand that this is a very close family. In some ways, they are still trying to come to grips with Dylan's death. His father will probably never accept it. He's still reeling from it. I feel bad for all of them. It hasn't been easy."

"You didn't seem to be protesting too much when I saw you."

"What was I supposed to do, Evan? Tell them all to just get over it, to get on with their lives?"

"You didn't have to sit there all night and be part of the wake. It looked to me that you fit right in."

"I did not know what else to do, Evan. I did not know how to gracefully walk away. They see me as a link to him. Especially Thomas. Dylan loved me; they have to love me, too. If he hadn't died when he did, I'd have been one of them."

"You are one of them."

"This is a family that has been shattered by a death they believe wasn't supposed to happen. It makes it all the more difficult for them to accept because they still don't really know what happened that night. That wound is still festering. That one of their own was murdered, and none of them—none of the big bad FBI Shieldses—has been able to bring his killer to justice."

"Someone else said something like that, someone I was talking to near the bar. He said that the FBI still didn't know what went wrong."

"True. And it haunts everyone, everyone who knew him."

"Are you haunted by him, Annie?"

"Not *by* him, maybe, but *for* him, I guess. I wish I did know what happened that night. I wish I did know who killed him, and why. I wish there could be justice for him. It was set up to look like it was part of that undercover drug deal, but no one ever thought that felt right, and no one has been able to come up with an alternative that makes any sense, either."

"What didn't feel right? It's not unusual to have an undercover op go bad."

"The dealers Dylan and Aidan were meeting didn't arrive until after Dylan had been shot. They pulled into the alley just after, and of course, the agents in the building across the alley opened fire, and—"

"So you're thinking if the dealers had been onto the op, they wouldn't have shown up at all. If anything, they'd have sent their henchmen to kill Dylan and Aidan and simply disappeared."

"Exactly. But these men came to the buy, just like they'd planned. And they all denied having known that Dylan and Aidan were law. They all swore they had no clue."

"Of course they'd deny it. No one in his right mind admits to setting up the FBI."

"True. But no way, if they'd shot an FBI agent minutes before, would they have shown up at all. That's just plain stupid, and these guys have been at this a long time. They're far from stupid." She shrugged. "And that's what's so hard to accept for everyone. Dylan's killer got away with murder, and no one has the slightest idea who he is. That's what keeps it raw, keeps it stuck in everyone's craw. Not knowing why, or who."

"Does anyone really think they'll ever answer those questions?"

"Realistically, no. But they'll never stop asking, never stop talking about it."

Evan shook his head somewhat vaguely.

"What?"

"I'm sorry for what happened to him, I swear I am. But I can't fight them for the rest of my life, Annie. There are just too damned many of them. Your sister married into the family; they're always going to be around." He took a deep breath. "I'm always going to feel as if I'm sleeping in a dead man's bed. I'm just not sure how long I can go on doing that."

"Oh God, Evan, I had no idea you felt that way. I'm so sorry. I'm sorry I can't change the situation," she said softly. "But I can't change what was or what is. I'm so sorry, for both of us. I was hoping that you and I . . ."

Her voice trailed off and she made a gesture—a sort of "I give up" flutter of her hands—before going up the steps and directly to the front door. Once in her car, she sat quietly for a few moments, trying to compose herself, fighting back the tears that had been threatening to fall, trying to stop the hollow feeling inside her from spreading, but it soon engulfed her. With a sense of sorrow and regret, she put the car in gear and headed toward the airport. It was going to be a long trip back to Virginia.

Evan sat on his back steps, his forearms resting on his thighs, mindlessly peeling the label from his bottle of beer, dropping the little scraps of paper at his feet. The deck he'd started building in the spring was just as he'd left it two months ago, mostly frame, some little bit of floorboard. Incomplete, like the basement.

Like his life.

Well, he'd almost had it all, hadn't he? The girl, the job, the future he'd always dreamed of. Then, of course, he had to go and let that green-eyed monster take over his intellect, had to go and open his big mouth. Well, that was the end of that. Shit, he must have sounded like a bratty adolescent who'd caught his girl walking with another guy to her locker.

He blew out a long breath that was filled with exasperation and self-doubt. He had some big decisions to make, and he'd have to make them now, before things between Annie and him got any worse.

Like they could get worse.

He went inside, dropped the empty beer bottle into the glass recycling bin, and got himself another, then went back outside. He walked the deck frame, balancing carefully as he followed the narrow supports that would eventually be covered with flooring.

If I get that far.

He stood at one end, the end where he'd planned on building steps that would go into the narrow backyard. A few months ago, back in the early spring, he and Annie had stood out here and discussed flower beds. She'd been excited about the prospect, and they'd spent an afternoon talking about how he would go about digging beds around the entire perimeter of the yard so that she could plant her favorites—roses, peonies, hollyhocks. All the staples of an old-fashioned garden, she'd told him, just like the one her mother had planted in the tiny yard of their twin home in Philadelphia's University City back when her father was a professor at Drexel. Annie's cheeks had flushed with the joy of that memory, and her eyes had sparkled at the prospect of re-creating her mother's garden.

Evan had dug up one section that weekend, a short piece across the back face, and the following day, Annie had gone to the nursery and bought three peonies, which they'd planted together.

"The man at the nursery said that they won't bloom for a few years, but that's okay." She'd smiled up at him. "We can wait them out together. Just think how much we'll appreciate those first flowers when they finally bloom . . ."

That had been the last time they'd worked on it. The responsibilities that came with both their jobs had intervened. Now Annie's garden lay before him, just one more loose end in his life. Just one more thing he'd started, but never got around to finishing.

Evan put the beer down on the back-porch steps and went into his garage. He emerged a minute later, carrying a shovel. He went straight to one side of the fence, walked off a depth of three feet, and began to dig. When he finished with one side, he began to dig along the other, until the entire fence was framed with a newly dug bed.

He stood in the middle of the yard, panting slightly from exertion. If she came back, the garden would be ready for her to plant.

He leaned upon the shovel handle and asked himself just how likely it was that she'd come back.

"Fat chance, Crosby," he muttered aloud. "Why would she?"

*Because she loves me.* His inner voice spoke without hesitation.

Dragging the shovel, he walked back to the porch, took a long swig of lukewarm beer, and told himself something he already knew.

*The ball is in my court. First, I need to decide how I feel about her.*

*Do I love her? Yes.*

*Do I want her? Yes.*

*How far am I willing to go for her?*

*As far as it takes . . .*

But how, he wondered, could they plan a life together, with the specter of her dead fiancé standing between them?

As long as questions about Dylan's life remained unanswered, Evan knew he and Annie could not move forward, could not plan a life together. It was as simple as that.

"Okay, then. So that's the bottom line." He muttered the words aloud, acknowledging what had to be done.

Maybe he'd known all along. Maybe Friday night had just brought it all into focus.

He dialed Annie's cell phone and was disappointed when he got her voice mail. Taking a deep breath, he began.

"Annie, I'm sorry. I acted like a fool. A very immature fool. I'm trying to put myself in your place, and I guess maybe I'd feel the same way. If something happened to you . . . well, I doubt I'd ever rest until I found the truth. I'd owe you that much. Just as you owe Dylan. So. We need to talk."

He paused, then added, before he hung up, "I love you, Annie. With all my heart. I'm not willing to spend the rest of my life without you. If finding Dylan's killer is what we need to do in order for this thing to work between us, then let's do it. Let's try to figure it out so that Dylan can be at peace. And so can we . . ."

He tried to think of something else to say, then realized he'd said it all. He disconnected the call and slipped the phone back into his pants pocket. There was still another hour or so of daylight. The local nursery was only ten minutes away. Maybe he'd have time to pick out a rosebush or two.

On his way to his car, his phone rang.

"Crosby." He smiled, anticipating the sound of her voice.

"Evan, we need you. We've found another body . . ."

"Where?" His adrenaline began to flow, and Annie's garden was, once again, forgotten.

4

It was four in the morning before Evan had a chance to check his messages. His message to Annie had been received—apparently well received, since she'd asked him to return the call, regardless of the time.

"Hi." She answered the phone on the third ring, her voice heavy with sleep.

"Hi."

"You still on the job?"

"Yeah." He glanced around at the crowd of law enforcement personnel that seemed to grow by the minute.

"Like the others?"

"Like the others, but different. Same difference as the last one."

"She's Hispanic. No ID. And no one reported her missing."

"Right. 'Course, maybe by morning, we'll have gotten a call. Someone might be looking for her by now, or maybe someone thinks she's at a friend's house . . . there could be a hundred maybes when you're dealing with a kid, you know?"

"I know. I saw your chief on TV yesterday."

"The press has been all over this. It's national news. The grandfather of one of the victims is an ambassador."

"I saw him on CNN."

"So did I. He had some harsh words for the D.A."

"Yeah."

The awkward pause he'd been avoiding settled in. It was now or never.

"Look, Annie, I . . . I had this idea. I'm thinking that, well, I'm thinking maybe we should take one more look at Dylan's death. I'm thinking you're right, to want to clear this thing for him. And I have to be honest with you, looking at this from a strictly selfish point of view, I'm thinking it's going to be that much harder for you and me to move forward with our own relationship while there's still this long, dangling thread in your life."

He hesitated, expecting her to break in, but she remained silent, so he went on.

"So, maybe just one look, to see if, I don't know, maybe something will jump out at us. Then, maybe, you and I . . . well, then maybe we can see where we are . . . where we both want this thing to go . . ."

Evan was pacing along a berm at the edge of the clearing where the latest body had been found. "I know the Bureau's best has been on this, so I guess it sounds presumptuous for me to even suggest it—"

"I don't think it's presumptuous at all," Annie said softly.

"You don't?"

"No. You're a great investigator. And there's always the chance that a fresh eye might see something everyone else has missed. But are you sure you want to spend your time on this?"

"I'm sure that I want this to work between us. I'm sure that the only way that's going to happen is for you to feel that you've done everything you can to do right by Dylan's memory. The way I see it, as long as Dylan's murderer is out there, you're always going to be looking for him. Not that I blame you. I understand why it's important. But it just seems to me that in order for you to move on with your life, you need to know that everything that could be done has been done."

"That's very insightful."

"And you thought you were the only one in this relationship with a little psychology know-how," he joked, knowing there was a vast difference between his three undergrad psych courses and her doctorate. "There's no guarantee that this case will ever be solved. But I think it's worth one more look."

"Thank you." Her voice caught. "Dylan deserves to have his killer brought to justice. I know Aidan and Connor and a bunch of his cousins have looked at the case, but not one of them was able to uncover anything new. So chances are, nothing will change. But one more look—sure, it's worth the time. I'll be in the office tomorrow. I'll see what I can get my hands on."

"Can you send me a copy of whatever you find?"

"I'd rather bring it up this weekend."

"Even better."

"But you're swamped with your case. I'd better send copies of the reports overnight. That way, when we finally do get together, you'll have had time to read them through. Maybe something will pop out at you."

"Sounds like a plan."

"Evan, I can't thank you enough. For understanding. For putting your own feelings aside—I know this has to be hard for you."

"Not nearly as hard as the thought of losing you."

"You wouldn't have lost me over this. My loving you is separate from wanting what's right for Dylan."

"I know that, but I also understand that you'll never be completely happy as long as you feel he's not at rest, Annie. I know your Irish soul."

"It's his Irish soul that worries me. I just need to know it's found peace."

"We're going to do our best."

"One thing you need to know . . ."

"What's that?"

"I am happy with you, I've been happy with you. And I do love you. Without reservation. Regardless of the outcome, I will never forget that you offered to do this, with the case you're already working on. I don't know any other man who would be as sensitive as you are to this whole thing with Dylan."

The crime-scene technicians had finished processing the scene and signaled that they were waiting for him.

"Annie, I have to go. You get those reports and send them up; I'll find the time to look them over. Then we'll talk . . ."

Dan Crimmons, the Prattsville chief of police, was walking up the hill toward him. Evan knew he'd have a million questions about the crime scenes in Lyndon and the other parts of the county where bodies had been found. In the distance, he could see the lights from the cars parked along the road. Newspaper, magazine, and TV reporters and their cameramen were gathering again.

Evan switched off his phone and walked down the hill to meet Crimmons, thinking that his instincts had served him well. Annie wouldn't be completely at peace until Dylan was. He would give it his best effort.

It hadn't been false modesty on his part to say that he felt a bit presumptuous, taking on something that the Bureau's finest had already looked into. Dylan's brothers and cousins were all known to be top-notch agents. What were the chances he'd succeed where they had all failed? If it helped Annie to know that they'd done their best, and that helped her to move on, what did they have to lose?

Nothing at all, he reassured himself as he walked down the hill, his hand extended in greeting to the chief.

"Chief Crimmons, I see the sharks are right on the scent. How many officers do you think you can spare to keep the press from getting anywhere near the crime scene . . . ?"

Annie scooped the folder into her arms and strolled casually back to her office. It wasn't that she was doing anything wrong—she did sign out the file—but she was just a little reluctant to advertise the fact that she was looking over the records relative to Dylan's death yet again. People might think she was obsessed.

She read through the now-familiar reports, looking for something, anything, that might catch her eye. But there was nothing out of the ordinary. She'd read through the accounts of the agents who were present that night, including Aidan, who had been badly wounded and at one point, early on, wasn't expected to make it. Thank God he did, Annie thought. Losing Dylan had been hard enough. Aidan had been her friend long before he'd become her brother-in-law.

The alarm on her watch reminded her that she had a lecture to deliver to a group of agents-in-training at two. She closed the file and pushed it to one side of her desk, then grabbed her purse from the back of her chair.

"Hey, Annie, how's it going?" Brendan Shields poked his head in through the doorway.

"Great, Brendan, thanks. I was just on my way to—"

"Was that a great wedding or what? And Mara was just the most beautiful bride. Dylan would have been pleased to see his little brother married to your little sister. Funny, isn't it, the way that worked out?"

"I guess it worked out the way it was supposed to."

"Nice guy, that detective you were with, by the way. A couple of the guys said they'd worked a few cases with him up in Pennsylvania, said he was top-notch."

"Evan Crosby. He's good, yes. I've worked with him, too."

"Well, good luck with him, if that's the way it's going for you and him. God knows you're due for something good, Annie."

"Thank you, Brendan. That's really very nice of you."

"Hey, is that the file on the McNamara case?" He looked beyond her to her desk. "I just stopped down at the records room and Angie told me she'd signed it out to you yesterday."

"The McNamara file is in the trunk of my car. That"—she nodded toward her desk—"is Dylan's file."

Brendan raised an eyebrow.

"Evan and I were talking the other day, and we thought we'd give it one more look-see." She shrugged as if the idea had little merit. "We just thought maybe . . ."

"Maybe this time something might jump out at you?"

"I guess. I know it's a long shot."

"You know we've all looked at that file so many times it's a miracle we haven't worn the ink right off the pages."

"I know. I guess we just thought maybe fresh eyes . . ."

"Hey, sure, why not? Can't hurt. God knows we weren't able to come up with anything. Good luck with it."

"I've got to run," she told him, "but if you walk out with me, I can give you the McNamara file right now."

"Great. You have everything you need here?" He turned off the light, then followed her into the hall. "By the way, you don't happen to know where my cousin Connor is, do you?"

"Über-agent Shields? No." She laughed. "No one ever knows where Connor is, Brendan. You know that. He comes in, gets his secret assignment, and leaves before anyone even knows he's been in the building."

"Yeah. The ultimate secret-agent man. No one was happier than

Connor when the Bureau expanded its operations after 9/11. I think he was the first from the Bureau to apply. He just eats up that covert stuff. My sister, Mia, made the comment the other night at the wedding that maybe he should have joined the CIA."

"Very funny. Did you try his cell phone?"

"No. Grady was looking for him this morning; I was just wondering if you knew if he was still in town."

"Sorry. I haven't seen or heard from him since Friday night. But if by some chance I do, I'll let him know to call Grady."

"Good enough. Well, you're going to have to push the speed limit to get down to Quantico on time as it is, so let's hope this is one of the days when the elevator actually works." He poked the down arrow.

"I'll be fine, as long as the traffic doesn't back up somewhere along the way." She watched the elevator lights descend slowly from the upper floors. "Or the elevator doesn't pass us by."

The elevator pinged as the doors slid open, then pinged again as they closed. It took less than forty-five seconds to reach the lobby. Annie, who detested elevators, counted off every one.

They passed through the lobby to the parking garage, where Annie had parked three cars in from the stairwell.

"You were here early," Brendan noted.

"I had to be. I'd left the notes for my lecture in my office. Don't ask me where my head was."

She unlocked the trunk of her car and reached in for the file she'd been studying in the hopes of coming up with a profile for the killer who'd been terrorizing a small town in Idaho.

"Any thoughts on this one?" Brendan asked as he tucked the file under his arm.

"He's young and he's angry. Probably was in the service, my guess, right out of high school. I'd put my money on an early discharge, not necessarily honorable. He has definite issues with women." She slammed the trunk lid. "I can send you an e-mail with a copy of my full evaluation when I get home tonight. My notes are all there."

"Great. Appreciate it." Brendan kissed her on the cheek. "You take care, Annie. And listen, if it's what you want, I hope that all works out with . . ."

"Evan."

"Sorry. His name slipped my mind, honest to God. That wasn't intended as an insult."

She smiled as she got into the car. Brendan and his sister, Mia, were probably the only members of the Shields family for whom that might be true. Andrew and Grady had made no effort to disguise their disapproval of Annie showing up at a Shields wedding with another man.

"Call me if you have any questions after you get my memo," she told him as she started her car.

"Will do." He stepped back from the car as she pulled from the parking spot. Annie waved as she headed toward the exit.

The highway ahead was clogged as a result of an unfortunate combination of volume and a three-car accident. Annie debated taking an alternate route, one that would take her through several small towns and would cost her at least forty minutes in time. She weighed the known delay against the uncertainty of the tie-up on the highway, and opted for back roads.

It was turning out to be a wonderful, sunny day. At times like this, she wished she'd chosen the convertible over the sedan she'd recently bought, but she opened the sunroof, rolled down the windows, and slipped Enya into the CD player. The sun on the top of her head soothed, as did the music. She felt herself relaxing for the first time in days.

Well, it had been an unusual week.

First, there'd been the wedding, and all that it entailed. It wasn't every day your sister got married.

Annie thought back to Mara's first wedding, to Jules Douglas.

"I never did like that pompous ass," Annie muttered, recalling how her first reaction to Jules had been right on the money. "Slick little bastard."

But Mara had fallen for him, and nothing Annie could say had opened her sister's eyes. In the end, Annie recognized as fact, when someone is hell-bent on making a mistake, sometimes you just have to stand back and let them.

And what a mistake it had been. From early on in their marriage, Jules had betrayed his wife with an endless string of his college students who'd fallen for him in the same way Mara had. By the time Mara had discovered his affair with a fellow faculty member, their daughter was five years old. Mara asked for and was granted a divorce. The day after it was finalized, Jules took Julianne and disappeared for seven long, agonizing years.

Well, he wouldn't get that chance again. Even with his plea bargain to testify against Reverend Prescott, they were going to keep his sorry ass behind bars until he was so old he wouldn't even remember his name.

Any of them, she thought dryly, recalling that Jules had taken several aliases while on the run.

She stopped at a red light and watched a young woman casually push a stroller across the street. Life in these small towns . . . Annie smiled to herself. Everyone takes their time.

And why not? We spend too much time hurrying along, not noticing our surroundings, not—

The light had turned green, and the driver of the pickup behind her apparently wasn't of a small-town mind. This was a reality she understood. She pulled away from the light and wondered if the accident on the interstate had been cleared away yet. She turned on the radio and scanned for a news station.

Her finger paused on the station where Bono sang about "one love." Dylan had been a huge U2 fan and had loved that song. Hearing it never failed to bring back the memory of a drive they'd once made to the Outer Banks, when he'd played the CD over and over so many times she finally threatened to toss it out the window as they crossed the Wright Memorial Bridge.

Thoughts of Dylan led inevitably to thoughts of Evan.

Initially, Annie had been surprised at Evan's reaction to Dylan's seeming presence at the wedding. After all, it was Dylan's brother who was getting married, and the first gathering of the clan after Dylan's death—except for his funeral. It was bound to be emotional. But after looking back on the night, on the way events had unfolded, she had to admit that things might have gone a bit far. Not might, she told herself. Did. Thomas Shields simply could not move past his pain. When she'd realized that Evan had left, she had secretly suspected that the Shieldses' focus on their fallen brother could possibly have had something to do with it.

But she'd been genuinely surprised at Evan's suggestion that they take one last look at Dylan's death. While she refused to delude herself into thinking that they'd solve the case, the fact that Evan understood, that he made the gesture, endeared him to her even more. She hadn't been exaggerating when she'd told him that finding him, realizing that she could find love again, had stunned her. She'd not even considered looking, assuming that she'd spend the rest of her life alone. She had pretty much made her peace with that. No one, she'd figured, had the right to expect that kind of total love, total devotion, more than once in a lifetime. It had shocked her to learn it could happen—and that it had happened to her.

She was so deep in thought that she missed the call on her cell phone. She picked it up and looked at the screen. Connor. Speak of the devil. She hit the automatic-dial number and he answered on the first ring.

"Hey, sorry. I missed your call by about one ring," she told him. "Where are you?"

"Now, you know that if I told you, we'd have to kill you."

She smiled at the overused quip, which, in his case, could be true.

"Did you talk to Grady? I saw Brendan this morning. He said Grady was trying to reach you."

"We spoke. He just wanted to know if I'd be around this week."

"Are you?"

"No. I won't be around for a while."

"Okay, I won't even ask."

"Thank you."

"So what's up?"

"I just wanted to congratulate you and Mara on the wedding. You did a great job putting it together. Everything was just terrific, Annie."

"Thanks, Connor. I never realized how much work a simple wedding could be. But we did manage to pull it off. Everyone seemed to have a good time."

"Well, that's another thing that I wanted to talk to you about. I think I need to apologize on behalf of all the Shieldses for having maybe misdirected some of the focus."

"Meaning?"

"You're sweet, Annie, but I know you know what I'm talking about. Too much Dylan, too little Aidan. We owe him an apology, too."

"I doubt he felt slighted."

"Knowing Aidan, no, I'm sure he didn't. But looking back over the night, one thing seemed to lead to another . . ."

"It's okay, Connor."

"I just feel a little embarrassed about it."

"Connor Shields, international man of mystery, sheepish? Puh-leeze."

He laughed.

"Anyway, it's done. Don't give it another thought."

"Must have made things uncomfortable for the new guy."

*Ah,* she thought. *That's what this is really about.*

"Evan was fine with it."

"That why he left early?"

"He's a homicide detective, Connor. He got a call . . ."

"Oh. Okay. Just wanted to make sure we didn't somehow mess that up for you."

"Not at all. As a matter of fact, he's made an incredibly generous offer."

"What's that?"

"He thinks we should take another look at the circumstances surrounding Dylan's death."

A long silence followed. Finally, Connor said, "Why would he do that?"

"He understands that something inside me will be unsettled as long as Dylan's killer has gotten away with his murder."

"And he thinks he's going to be the one to solve it? Is he aware that it's been investigated more than once? That we've all looked into it?"

"He knows all that, Connor. And he's not going into this thinking he's going to show anyone up, or that he's going to take one look at the file and say, 'Aha! I know who the killer is!' I think it's his way of showing me that he respects Dylan's memory and wants to give it his best shot."

Another silence.

"He must be quite a guy, this homicide detective of yours."

"He is, Connor."

"Then tell him if he needs anything, if he has any questions, to talk to me."

"I'll do that. Thanks."

"Listen, I have to run. You take care, Annie, and remember, if you need anything . . ."

"I will. It was great talking to you, great seeing you on Friday."

Her emotions unexpectedly got the better of her and she felt her throat tighten. "You take care, Connor, wherever you are, whatever it is you're doing. You take care of yourself."

"Will do. See you, Annie . . ."

She dropped the phone into her purse and bit her bottom lip. She couldn't help but worry about him. She always did. For men like Connor Shields, there was no telling where or when—or from whom—the danger might come.

A finger of cold crawled up her neck, and she shivered, then shook it off. Connor had faced a thousand dangers during the ten years he'd been with the Bureau. Surely he'd emerge from whatever obscure corner of the world he was now in, unscathed as always. She wondered what it was that made him thrive on the danger, that kept him accepting the most perilous assignments.

That well's too deep for me, she told herself as she passed a tractor trailer when the road expanded from two lanes to four. Leaving Connor's psyche for another day, she slipped a cassette into the dash to play back a taped session of a lecture she'd given to the last group of agents-in-training to refresh her memory. She had less than an hour before she was to speak, and needed to focus now on her speech.

Annie tucked away all thoughts of Connor and Dylan and even of Evan. She had work to do.

5

Luther Blue checked his Rolex and decided that it was none too early to make a call. If he was up, everyone should be up.

He dialed and waited.

"Shields."

"I know who I called, thank you," Luther said dryly.

"What's up?"

"You tell me."

"Tell you what?"

"Tell me what I want to hear."

"It's too early to play games, man."

"Tell me if I'm going to run into your cousin Connor when I arrive at headquarters this morning."

"No. No, you definitely will not run into Connor."

"So you are telling me you took care of the problem?"

The pause was just a beat or two too long.

"You didn't do it, did you?" Luther tried to keep his temper under control.

"I honest to God haven't had an opportunity."

"A good agent doesn't wait for opportunities. He makes them."

"Look, he was around this weekend, but the entire family was there. My dad, his dad, my brothers, my sister. He was never alone. There was just no chance to—"

"This is just more of the same to me, Shields. I'm really tired of hearing it. As far as I'm concerned, you created this problem, one, by bumbling into him in that alley down in Santa Estela—what, two fucking years ago? And two, by not taking care of him right then and there." The anger began to build. "You're telling me in two fucking years, there wasn't one time you could have taken him out?"

Silence.

"Shields?"

"I heard you, man, I—"

"You're just so much bullshit, you know that? Do I need to remind you who works for who here?"

"No. No reminder necessary."

"Then tell me how you're so certain I won't be coming face-to-face with him at any time soon?"

"He's out of the country."

"Where?"

"No one knows, except maybe the guy he reports directly to, and the Director."

"So how do you know he won't be around?"

"I talked to him yesterday. He said he'll be gone for at least three, probably closer to four, weeks."

"Did he say anything about that deal in Santa Estela?"

Another pause.

"Shields?"

"Not recently."

"What the fuck does that mean?"

"He asked about it when I saw him the first time, maybe a month, two months after that night. The night he saw you. I told him it had been taken care of. That everyone had been arrested and the authorities were ID'ing all the kids to send them home. He was concerned about that."

"He never followed up?"

"Why would he?"

"Oh, maybe if he saw me walking through the office, it might shake his memory."

"I told you. You're not going to run into him. He's gone for probably a month."

"You don't seem to understand my situation here, Shields. I am at a real disadvantage. I don't know what this guy looks like. I could be standing next to him in an elevator, or passing him in the hall, and he could be remembering me, and I won't even know it. You have any idea of how vulnerable that makes me?"

"He's never seen you at HQ, he'd have said something to me, but—"

"I'm tired of looking over my shoulder, you understand me? I've spent the last two years looking over my shoulder, and I'm goddamn tired of it. Every new assignment here in the States, I'm holding my breath, wondering who I'm going to be working with, who I'm going to run into. Well, I've been reassigned back here for a while. I do not want to have to be concerned about this again." Luther took a deep breath, tried to calm himself. He knew that when he got really upset, his voice had a tendency to grow shrill. He hated when that happened. "When he gets back here, I want him taken out. No *ifs, and*s, or *but*s, you hear me? No excuses. Take care of him. I'm done with this shit, Shields."

"Okay, I hear you."

Luther checked the date on his watch. August 9.

"I want him gone within a week of his stepping foot off the plane, hear?"

"I heard you."

"Hear this." In spite of his best effort to maintain control, Luther could feel the anger, the need for control, rising in him rapidly. "By the fifteenth of September, one way or another, there *will* be one less Shields on the federal payroll, and frankly, at this point, I don't care which of you it is."

He hung up before the agent could respond.

Dumb son of a bitch. It's that old, blood-is-thicker-than-water crap. Connor Shields was lucky he was out of reach right now. For two cents, Luther would take care of him himself. If he knew where he was, and what he looked like.

Luther had connections everywhere. Unfortunately, he didn't know where Connor was. He'd just have to be patient and wait for Connor to come to him.

Patience was not one of Luther's virtues.

He sipped at his coffee, then put the cup down slowly and forced himself to concentrate on the breathing exercises they taught him in anger-management class. Sometimes it helped, sometimes it didn't.

Today it did. When the waitress returned to ask him if he'd like another cup, he smiled and declined like a gentleman.

A gentleman who, at midnight tonight, would receive a fresh shipment from a very small, very poor Central American country where the chief export was its children, and its import was the money sent back by the workers who had fled illegally to the United States to work as laborers.

Luther took out the wish list he'd compiled from his roster of usual clients and studied it carefully.

Four of the older girls, between the ages of ten and twelve, were to go directly to a lovely Tudor-style house in a northern New Jersey suburb. At this most unlikely-looking brothel, they would replace four girls who were being sent to a house outside of Philadelphia, where they would be traded for four girls who would move on to D.C.

"Keep 'em moving, keep 'em confused," he told the owners of the houses. "And keep the product fresh. Make sure there's always something new. That's the way to build up that repeat business."

And when the girls reached their midteens, worn out in mind, spirit, and body?

"You just dispose of them. You can't send them back to their families." He'd given this speech to all of his customers at one time or another. "Look, you got a cop or two on your payroll, right? Of course you do. Now, if I were you, when the girls just don't have it anymore, when they start losing that fight, I'd give 'em to the cops, a little reward for their loyalty. When they're done with the girls, they can take care of them. Trust me, no one knows how to get away with murder better than a cop."

He drained the coffee in the cup and left a ten on the table with the bill for his breakfast. Once outside in the swelter of an early August Virginia morning, he paused and took a deep cleansing breath, just as he'd been instructed to do.

To have a good day, keep the anger at bay.

It had become his mantra. Not that it always worked, but today, it was good enough to take the edge off. He got into his car and prepared for his meeting.

Then it was off with the Rolex, on with the Timex.

Damn, but he loved that gold watch with the diamonds, loved the feel of it on his wrist, loved the way it looked, so classy, so expensive. With a sigh, he dropped it into its box and placed it in his briefcase.

He had yet to meet the FBI agent who could afford a watch like that. The watch, the house in Myrtle Beach, the condo in Manhattan, the apartments in Paris and London—all real estate in his mother's name, of course—the new Jaguar . . . who could live like that on what the government paid?

He wondered idly how his good friend Agent Shields spent his share of the money they'd made since he'd recruited him three years ago. He hoped Shields was as smart about it as he himself had been. Maybe he should have a chat soon, find out where it was stashed. In the unfortunate event that something should happen to his good buddy, shouldn't someone know where to find the cash?

After all, in their line of work—legitimate as well as illegal—an untimely accident could occur at any time.

And as far as Luther was concerned, Connor Shields was headed for an accident, as soon as he'd taken care of one little loose end.

Maybe sooner.

6

Annie sat cross-legged on the floor of her apartment, the contents of the thick file stacked around her in piles. Police reports here, photos of the crime scene there, autopsy report and photos on the edge of the coffee table.

In her hand she held the master list of the contents of the file. She'd read through the reports of Dylan's death many times, but this time she thought she'd put them in the same order in which they appeared on the list. It would be easier for Evan, who'd be taking his first look at the records this weekend. It would go a lot faster if he could just follow along and check off each report as he read it. Unfortunately, the file had been taken apart and read by so many people over the past two years, nothing was where she'd expected it to be.

The photos were easy to put in order. They were numbered in chronological order. The witness statements were a little more challenging. It seemed that few of them had been returned to their rightful place.

No time like the present, she told herself as she proceeded to search the file for the first report on the list. She found it near the bottom of the stack. She checked it off, then went on to the next. Three hours later, she had most of the reports where they should be. There were three, however, she'd not been able to find.

One was a report attributed to Connor Shields. She frowned, trying to recall if she'd previously seen a report from Connor in the file. She didn't think she had. And why would there have been a report from Connor? Hadn't he been out of the country at the time of Dylan's death?

If he hadn't been there, hadn't been involved, what could he possibly have contributed to the investigation?

She was tempted to call and ask him, then thought better of it. Who knew where he was, or with whom? Better to send an e-mail that he could read at his leisure.

She opened her laptop and typed her message.

TO: CShields00721
From: AMMccall00913
RE: Report
Hey, Connor—Just a quick question. Brought Dylan's file home tonight, it's all out of order (too many hands in this pot over the past couple of years)—quite the mess. Started trying to organize, using the master list as a guide. Found all but three items in file, including a report that was attributed to you. Could I ask you about the nature of your report? Do you remember? Did this

reflect directly on the op, or did this deal with
identifying Dylan at the M.E.'s office, maybe? Am
confused, since I was not aware you had been involved in
this op in any way.

Just curious—would like to tidy up the file, as well
as try to find some closure. I guess we all would like
that.

Annie

She turned her attention back to the file and its master list, which continued to guide her in her quest to put the file in perfect order before sharing its contents with Evan. Some minutes later, she heard the *ping* that announced in-coming email. She leaned over the computer to see who the correspondence was from and was surprised to see that Connor had responded so quickly.

To: AMMccall00913
From: CShields00721
Re: Yours
Hey, Annie—You're sure that report isn't stuck inside
another folder or something in the file? Definitely turned
it in. Didn't contribute a whole hell of a lot to the
investigation. They just wanted me to confirm that I had
been pulled from the op at the last minute and that
Dylan substituted for me and why—how that whole thing
had been set up. All before-the-fact stuff. Nothing
that shed any light on the events later that night.

Anything I can help you with, any other questions, I'm
here.

Connor

Annie read the e-mail, then reread that one line over and over. *They just wanted me to confirm that I had been pulled from the op*

*at the last minute, and that Dylan substituted for me and why—how
that whole thing had been set up. All before-the-fact stuff . . .*

Annie stared at the screen. Connor had originally been part of
this operation? Dylan had been sent at the last minute as a substitute
for Connor? Why had she not heard this before?

Or had she? In the dense fog of confusion and pain she'd been
trapped in for weeks after Dylan's death, had someone mentioned
this?

Maybe.

She doubted it, but then again, there was much from that time
she couldn't remember. She was hard-pressed to remember Dylan's
funeral, had little recollection of the viewing, and none whatsoever
of the graveside services, though certainly she'd been there. Maybe
someone had mentioned that Connor originally had been slated for
this assignment, and the information had been lost in the midst of
her grief. She couldn't honestly say she hadn't been told. On the
other hand, she couldn't say she had.

She drummed her fingers on the side of her laptop, trying to determine the importance of this new information.

She dialed Evan's number and was grateful that he picked up on
the second ring. She told him about the e-mail from Connor, then
said, "I'm trying to decide how—or if—this changes things."

"I guess the only way to answer that is to know what else Connor had been involved in back then."

"You mean, if he'd been involved in something someone might
have wanted to kill him for?" She laughed roughly. "That's every assignment Connor's ever been on."

"Look, why not just ask him if there was anything going on back
then that sticks in his memory."

"Even if there was, he wouldn't be able to tell me."

"Maybe not, but maybe it's something he can look into himself.
You won't know if you don't ask."

"True. Maybe I'll just e-mail him . . ." She opened her laptop and debated on how best to put forth the question.

"Good idea. Bring it all with you this weekend and we'll toss it around a little more."

"How's your case going?"

"Not well." His voice dropped with something more than disappointment. "In the past week, we've had three victims. I was going to call and ask for your opinion on this. Have you ever known a serial killer to target different types the way this guy is? I mean, two distinctly different types of victims? This guy is going back and forth between the pampered and privileged to girls who haven't even been reported missing a week after we've found their bodies. It just doesn't make sense to me."

"It is odd. And no, to answer your question, I've never heard of a case like this one." She pondered the facts he'd given her. "Maybe I should take a look at the files while I'm up there this weekend. Can you get me copies of all of them? It will give me something to do while you look over Dylan's file."

"You show me yours, I'll show you mine?"

"Something like that." Annie smiled.

He laughed.

"We're going to be all right, aren't we." It wasn't a question.

"We *are* all right," he told her.

He appeared to be about to say something else, but his thoughts were interrupted by a click on the line.

"Hold up, Annie, I have a call coming in." He put her on hold.

Moments later, he was back.

"I have to go," he said, and she knew by the tone of his voice he was wanted at a crime scene.

"I'll see you Friday night, then," Annie told him. "I'll be flying up, then I'll rent a car at the airport."

"You sure you don't want me to pick you up?"

"You might be tied up. I'll just go to your place, and you'll get there when you get there."

"I'll see you then," he said as he hung up. "I love you, Annie."

"I love you too, Evan."

Later that night, Annie opened her laptop and checked her e-mail. Amid several from the office, there was one from Connor.

To: AMMccall00913
From: CShields00721
Re: Missing Reports
Forgot to ask—what were the other missing reports?

Annie went in to the living room and opened the file, searching for the note she'd made, then returned to her laptop to respond.

To: CShields00721
From: AMMccall00913
Re: Missing Reports
One was written by SA Melissa Lowery. The other is a diagram of the crime scene drawn by SA Lou Raymond.

Connor's reply was almost instantaneous.

To: AMMccall00913
From: CShields00721
Re: Missing Reports
Special Agent Raymond killed in car ax almost two years ago. Heard Missy Lowery quit the Bureau but don't remember when.

Annie stared at the e-mail as it appeared on the screen, and a little chill sneaked up her spine.

*Don't look for something that isn't there*, she reminded herself. *People die in car accidents every day. Agents quit the Bureau every day.*

She began to type.

To: CShields00721
From: AMMccall00913
Re: Missing Reports
Thanks for the info. BTW, I noticed there's no reflection
in the file that you had been set for this assignment
originally—other apparently than the report you wrote,
which is missing. Seems odd to me. Just out of
curiosity, was this widely known? That you were on this
op? And called off at last minute?

———

To: AMMccall00913
From: CShields00721
Re: Missing Reports
It was no secret that Aidan and I were running this—
don't know who knew that Dylan stepped in for me when I
got called out. What are you thinking? That I was
intended target?

———

To: CShields00721
From: AMMccall00913
Re: Missing Reports
Well, it did cross my mind. Can you think of anything
you might have been working on back then that could have
made you unpopular in the wrong places?

———

To: AMMccall00913
From: CShields00721
Re: Missing Reports
You're kidding, right?

———

```
To: CShields00721
From: AMMccall00913
Re: Missing Reports
```
That's what I thought you'd say. Would you let me know
if anything comes to mind, maybe something . . . odd or
strange that happened that made you think twice? Sorry
if I sound off-the-wall. I just don't recall having
heard that you were slated for that night. Strange no
one else mentioned it.

She hit *send,* then waited. And waited. But there was no further reply from Connor that night. Nor was there e-mail from him waiting for her in the morning.

She'd touched a nerve, no doubt, and felt a stab of regret. If Connor started to question if the bullets that killed his brother had been intended for him, he'd have one hell of a time forgiving himself.

Then again, knowing Connor, there'd be no question that he'd put his own personal feelings aside to search for the truth.

Annie turned off her computer, content with that knowledge, for now. If the truth had been buried with Dylan, there was no one more likely to help her ferret it out than Connor.

Annie stepped out of her office and began the long walk to the elevator, made longer this afternoon by the heavy files she juggled in both arms. One had come just that morning from a police department in Michigan that had requested a profile on a killer who was targeting homeless men. The other was Dylan's.

She turned the corner and stopped in her tracks. Thirty feet down the hall, near the conference room, a group of men in dark suits were gathered. All tall, dark haired, well built.

All Shieldses.

Andrew, Brendan, Grady, and Aidan.

From the back, they were nearly identical. Oh, some were a bit taller—Aidan and Grady were a few inches shorter than the other two—but even someone who knew them all as well as she did could have a tough time telling them apart from the back.

From this angle, any one of them could have been Dylan.

She had no idea how long she'd stood there, staring, before Aidan turned and saw her.

"Hey!" he called to her, his mouth curving into a wide smile. "My favorite sister-in-law! I was just on my way to see if you were in your office when I ran into this motley crew."

The group walked toward her, and her stomach knotted. They were all so damned alike. Brendan and Aidan even walked the same way.

"Good to see you, Aidan." She turned her cheek for him to plant a kiss. "I just left voice mail for Mara. I wanted her to know I'd be out of town for a few days."

"Business or pleasure?" Grady peered around his brothers to see her better.

"A little of both. I'm going to Lyndon, Pennsylvania, to see Evan, but he's in the middle of a case he wants me to look over."

She stole a quick peek at her watch.

"I have to get going or I'll miss my plane. See you all later. Aidan, tell Mara to call me when she's free."

The men stepped aside and allowed Annie to pass. She waited for the elevator, anxiously tapping her foot. She should have left at least a half hour ago.

*Maybe the plane will be late,* she found herself hoping.

"Annie, hold the elevator."

She caught the door with her foot and held it open for Andrew.

"Thanks, Annie." He entered the car and hit the button for the lobby. "You are going to the lobby, right?"

She nodded and shifted the files.

"Here, give me one of those." Andrew took the nearest file from her arms.

"Thanks. I was just starting to think I might lose that one."

He glanced at the label.

"I heard about this case. Catherine Cook was just sent out on it. What's the count up to now, seven homeless guys?"

"Eight, as of this morning." She watched the light follow the floor numbers, then stepped back when the elevator stopped at the third floor and the doors opened.

Two women in summer business suits smiled absently as they entered the elevator. No one spoke until they arrived at the lobby.

"Which level is your car on?" Andrew asked Annie.

"I'm right outside the door."

"You must be a real early riser, to have gotten a spot at the door."

"Early enough." She smiled and reached for the file.

"I'll walk you out."

He followed her across the lobby, then held the door to the parking lot open for her.

"Give me the other file," he said when they got to her car and she began to search her bag for her keys. "I'll hold them while you open the car."

"This is Dylan's file," Andrew said softly after glancing at the label.

"Yes." She unlocked the door and tossed her bag onto the passenger seat.

"How many times have you read through this?" he asked.

"Lots. You?"

"Lost count." He looked past her, toward the exit. "Every time I think, I wish I had been there. Maybe I could have done something . . ."

"There was nothing anyone could have done. Aidan was there, and he couldn't save him."

Andrew merely shook his head.

"Andrew, when was the last time you looked at this file?"

"A couple of weeks ago," he admitted. "We were all sitting around at Aidan's bachelor party, talking about how much we missed Dylan, and I just felt—I don't know, compelled, somehow, to take another look. I guess I always somehow hope this time it will end differently." He shrugged. "Of course it never does."

"Do you happen to remember seeing a report from an agent named Melissa Lowery?"

"Not really. I remember her, though. Didn't she leave the Bureau a while ago?"

"Not long after Dylan died. She was on the backup team that night."

"Maybe she had a tough time dealing with it." He cleared his throat. "She wouldn't have been the only one."

"Any idea where she is now?"

"No. I didn't really know her. I only know her to say hi."

Annie opened the back door, then turned to take the files from Andrew. She placed the files on the backseat, then got into her car and started the ignition.

"By the way, Andrew, did you know an agent named Lou Raymond?"

"Yeah. What a waste. He died in a car crash out near I-95 a couple of years ago."

"That's the one."

"He was on one of the exit ramps coming off 95 into Maryland. Three or four in the morning. Word was he apparently fell asleep or something and the car hit the guardrail, then went out of control and flipped over. At least, that's the story that was going around at the time. Best I recall, there were no witnesses."

"No other cars involved?"

"Not as far as I know. It was called in by a tractor-trailer driver who came across the scene at some point after it happened." He cocked his head to one side. "Did you know him?"

"No. I just saw his name in the file—Dylan's file—and was curious, that's all. The master-file list notes that Raymond had sketched the crime scene, but there's no sketch in the file."

"You mean the sketch that shows where everyone was at the time of the shooting?"

"I'm not sure what it was. I haven't been able to find it. Likewise a report written by Melissa Lowery."

"I worked maybe two or three cases with Lou when I first got out of training. He always drew things out, made it part of his report. He'd show where everyone was stationed, parked, standing, whatever. Put his whole account in pictures. It was pretty interesting, actually." Andrew appeared to think for a minute. "I don't remember ever seeing sketches that Lou drew in this file. Not ever. And like I said, I've gone through it a couple of times. Can't say I remember a report from Lowery, either, but that doesn't mean it wasn't there. At some point, they must have fallen out."

"Must have." She put the car in gear. "Thanks for carrying the files for me."

"Anytime." He stepped back to allow her to back out of the parking space. "Tell what's-his-name I said hello."

"It's Evan," she told him. "His name is Evan . . ."

"Sorry." He shrugged, much as his brother had a few days earlier, and waved to her as she drove off.


"So, you think this guy is targeting homeless guys because he thinks he's on some kind of a mission to clean up the streets?" Evan sat on the sofa, his bare feet propped on the coffee table.

"I think he has a vigilante mentality. Look, check out this letter he sent to the local papers." Annie found the newspaper and read, " 'The city belongs to the people who pay the taxes that pay the police and the firemen and the city workers. I'm a street cleaner, just like them.' "

"Ugly." He frowned. "Who thinks like that?"

"Some misguided soul in Denton, Ohio." She yawned and closed the file cover. "How about your case, you ready to talk about it now?"

"I don't know what else to tell you that you haven't already read for yourself. I'm finding it confusing as hell."

"It is confusing, but I still think you're looking for two different people, Evan."

"The killer is doing exactly the same things, in exactly the same manner. Rape the girl, slash the throat. Dump the body. Steal the shoes. The murders are identical."

"Except for one very important difference. The victims. And you know what I always say." She poked him in the ribs with her pen.

"Yeah, yeah. Know the victims, know the killer."

"Are you humoring me?"

"Nope. That's what you always say. And you're usually right; at least, in my experience with you, that's held true. I just don't see how it could be two different killers. Especially since we haven't released any of the details about the crimes. I just wish we had something—hair samples, DNA, something—that we could use to confirm one way or the other. We've kept the MO, the signature, all of the important things, under wraps. And as far as I know, there haven't been any leaks."

"Well, someone is talking. The second killer has to be someone close to the investigation."

"You realize what you're saying?" He bristled. "The only people close to the investigation are the cops working the case. I've known all these guys forever, since I joined the force in Lyndon. I've worked with every one of them at one time or another, either as a county detective or as a Lyndon cop. I can't believe that any of these guys would kill a kid."

"Someone's killing them, Evan. And you of all people should know that killers don't look like killers. They look like the rest of us."

"I can't argue with that, but I just don't see any of these guys killing little girls. I couldn't even narrow the list down to a few likely suspects, Annie."

"It'll be the person you least expect. It always is," she said almost absently as she made notes on the yellow legal pad.

"So, you almost finished with your analysis?"

"Almost." She nodded. "I won't be too much longer. I want to get this e-mailed to the chief of police tonight."

He sat up and began to lay the photos of the murdered girls side by side across the table.

"Those are your vics?" She looked up from her notes.

He nodded and continued setting out the pictures in order of the girls' deaths.

Annie put her notes aside and sat next to him, studying the photos.

"It's not the same guy, sweetie," she said softly.

"Annie . . ."

"Look at these girls in their school uniforms, at the way they project such innocence. Now look at them through his eyes, at the way he's left them, defiled. He's ruined them. He's taken something clean and pure and ravaged it. He's stolen from them. He has tremendous power over them now. He's definitely feeling very proud, very smug. He's stolen something precious, and no one can stop him. No one is *powerful* enough to stop him."

"You think this is mostly about power for him?"

"It is only about power. My guess is he works a low-level job where he's in contact with people whom he perceives as socially and economically superior to him."

"We all come in contact with people like that."

"This is daily, this is close contact on a daily basis. He resents that he's placed in a position of inferiority, of subservience, when he knows he's morally and intellectually superior to all of them. That he's forced to work for them, that his livelihood is dependent on people he thinks are less than he. That they can't see his brilliance marks them all as fools. This is how he retaliates. He's showing *them* who has the power. He's showing them who's really in charge."

"And you don't see that here?" Evan tapped on the photos of the last three victims.

"Not at all. Where are the symbols of purity, of innocence? He's tried to make them look the same as the others, I think in an effort to fool the police. To make you think this is all the work of the same man. So far, he's succeeding."

"You feel that strongly about this?"

"There is no question in my mind." She studied his face. "I'm sensing a lot of resistance here, Evan. Why so reluctant?"

"If I take this in to the office, I have to be able to convince the chief of detectives that there are two killers, not one, out there targeting young girls. Yet I have no DNA, no trace, nothing, to distinguish the crimes."

"Want me to write a memo or something outlining why?"

"Sort of like a note from my mother to give to my teacher?"

"You're the one who's pressing here."

"Maybe a memo would help," he conceded. "And keep in mind that right now there is no link. We're still waiting for the lab results from the first two vics."

"What's taking so long?" She closed the file and set it on the table near the photos.

"It's a small lab, only a few techs. They're doing their best, but this is not the only open case in the county right now."

"Why not send what you have to the Bureau's lab?"

"What's the timetable there?"

"Depends on who's asking." Annie grinned.

"Suppose you asked . . ."

"We'd have the results in a week, maybe better."

"And if I asked?"

"What year is it now?"

"So how do we get you involved?"

"I write that memo, you give it to your chief, tell him we can get the evidence expedited if only he asks. I can take it from there."

"You have friends at the lab?"

"You betcha."

"What's your take on this possible second killer? You're pretty specific about the first one; how do you peg this other killer that no one sees but you?"

"I'm still working on that." She stood and stretched, then took his hand and pulled him to his feet. "I thought maybe I'd sleep on it."

"Excellent idea. I think I'll sleep on it, too." He tugged her toward the steps leading up. "I'm thinking maybe between the two of us, we should be able to come up with something . . ."

8

Evan sat on the edge of the desk in the medical examiner's office, reading through the autopsy report of Caitlin McGill and last night's unnamed victim, and waited for the M.E. to finish washing up.

"So the throats were definitely slashed with different blades?"

"Definitely." The county M.E., Agnes Jenkins, washed her hands at the sink in the far corner of her office. "Not even close. The knife used on the schoolgirls was thin and finely sharpened. The knife used on the unidentified girls was thicker, duller. Different width."

"What do you think of two different killers?"

She reached for a roll of paper towels to dry her hands.

"I think it's highly likely. As a matter of fact, I'd bet on it. The schoolgirls—let's call them the group-one victims, just for the purpose of this conversation—had been, for the most part, still in possession of their hymens before the attacks. Not so the unidentified girls—the group-two vics, if you will. Internal examination showed that these girls were no novices."

"Prostitutes?"

"That, or they were real party girls." She frowned. "They were pretty young, though. Hard to tell for certain; their teeth weren't well cared for and two of them showed evidence of old healed fractures. And all three of them were small, physically. I'd guess from poor nutrition at some time in their life, most likely early childhood."

"Semen?"

"Not in or on any of them. Both guys wrapped up first." She rolled up the paper towel and tossed it into a nearby trash can. "It will be interesting to see what we get back from the lab, don't you think?"

"I've asked the chief to okay a transfer to the FBI lab, just to speed up the process. Our county lab is way behind and just isn't willing to expedite this case over any others in the pipeline."

"That would be Jeffrey Coogan." She named the head of the lab and made a face. "He's not much of a team player. You'll never get him to put one case aside to work on another. He's so goddamned anal. Everything in strict order."

"He's not happy about giving up the samples, but the chief leaned on him good and hard. I suspect the D.A. might have made a call as well."

"Sometimes you just have to talk tough with the assholes, Crosby." She grinned. "Anything else I can do for you?"

"You could get me a copy of the autopsy report on our latest victim."

"As soon as Mary Ellen out there finishes transcribing my tape, it's yours. I'll have her call you and you can stop back and pick it up."

"Thanks. I appreciate it."

"And you'll get me a copy of the lab results as soon as the FBI gets them to you?"

"Absolutely." He hopped off the desk and started to the door.

"Sounds like a deal." She smiled and turned to answer her ringing phone. "Oh. There was one more thing. Our unidentified girls all had tattoos on their left hips."

"Tattoos?"

"Little stars. Somewhat crudely made, but they were definitely stars. Three tiny stars, right below the waist at the top of the hip on the left side. What do you make of that?"

"Stars?" Annie asked.

"Right. I'm faxing you a photo right now. Can you see if it matches up with anything in the Bureau files? I tried to scan it into our computer, but once again, the computer is giving me the finger. Some glitch in the firewall, they're telling me."

"Go ahead and fax it down, let me take a look."

"It should be there any minute." Evan paused, then said, "Dr. Jenkins agrees that we're dealing with more than one killer."

He reiterated the gist of his conversation with the medical examiner.

"Prostitutes? Fourteen-, fifteen-year-old prostitutes?" She thought for a minute, then said, "Well, that would make sense, wouldn't it? Maybe they were tattooed by whoever is putting them out. Then again, they could be gang members. That's just as likely, don't you think? Maybe the stars identify them as a member of a specific gang. Or maybe they mark them as the property of a gang."

"It's worth looking into, but I have to tell you that I haven't heard of anything like that around here. I'll check with Philly, Trenton, Scranton, Camden, Newark, New York—maybe someone will have seen this before."

"If they were prostitutes, it would explain why you haven't received missing persons reports. If it's a gang thing, though, you might still have parents involved somewhere. The girls would most likely live at home. If that's the case, someone should be looking for these girls, Evan. Still no calls?"

"None. And we've told the dispatchers from every community to call us the minute anyone inquires about any one of these kids, but there's been nothing. I'll put out inquiries up and down the East Coast, though. See if someone, somewhere, is looking for them."

"I think the tattoos might help us track them." She bit at a cuticle, something she almost never did. "I just can't help but think that somewhere, someone is crying their eyes out over these girls. Someone has to have missed them. These kids have names, they have families somewhere."

"Well, maybe one of us will get lucky and we'll find out where that somewhere is."

"Let me make a call or two and get back to you."

Annie was searching her desk drawer for the office directory even as she hung up. She found the number she was looking for, dialed, then waited.

"Fletcher."

"My favorite computer geek." She sighed dramatically.

"My favorite profiler." Will Fletcher laughed. "How's it going, Annie?"

"Good. You?"

"Terrific. Great wedding, by the way."

"You and Miranda seemed to be having a good time." She paused, then added, "Especially Miranda."

"Hey, my girl does love to party. Never met a band she couldn't dance to."

"And dance, she did."

They both laughed, then Will said, "But you didn't call to talk about Miranda's happy feet."

"Actually, I was hoping you could give me a hand with something."

"This have anything to do with you and Evan looking into Dylan's death?"

"How'd you know about that?" she asked. "Oh. I almost forgot. The word is that Will Fletcher knows everything. Word is that you have mysterious sources."

"Not so mysterious. I saw Brendan yesterday. He mentioned it."

"Evan and I are taking a look at the circumstances surrounding Dylan's death, but this has nothing to do with that."

"Doesn't matter. I'm happy to help, either way."

"Actually, this has to do with a case Evan is working back in Pennsylvania."

"Those young girls that have been murdered?"

"If you know that, you probably know that they have three victims that are similar but unrelated."

"I heard a rumor, but no details. Tell me."

She did.

"So you're looking to identify the tattoo."

"For starters, yes. I can fax you a picture of them." She reached over and studied the faxed image again.

"When do you need an answer?"

"As soon as you have one."

"Let me get to work on it and get back to you. I assume if I get a hit, you want all available information?"

"Absolutely."

"I'll see what I can do."

"Thanks, Will. Give me your fax number."

She wrote it down, then programmed the number into the machine next to her desk.

"It's on its way."

"I'll be waiting for it."

How did anyone ever get anything done without all of this modern technology? she wondered as she fed the picture into the machine.

*Well, they got it done, it just took a lot longer.*

Evan's fax fed through the machine and the buzz assured her the operation was completed. If anyone could trace that tattoo, it was Will Fletcher, whose skills were legendary in the Bureau. She had full confidence that if the tattoo had been entered into the system, Will would find it. She mentally moved on to the next task on her list of things to do.

Find Melissa Lowery.

9

Chris Malone, chief detective, Avon County, was staring out the window, a sheet of paper in his hand, when Evan knocked on the doorframe. Malone turned to look over his shoulder.

"Come on in, Crosby."

"What's up?" Evan entered the office and leaned over the back of a leather wing chair.

"Same thing that's been up. The D.A. has the entire county on his back over this killer who's running around, snatching the daughters of some of our leading citizens off the street, and we're all being toasted in the press."

"Yeah, the parking lot is full of news vans. I had to park down on Fourth Street again this morning."

"Well, get used to it. None of them are leaving until this is over. Did you see this morning's paper?"

He walked to his desk and held up the front page of the county's tabloid. LOCAL LAW ENFORCEMENT STYMIED. HOW MANY MORE VICTIMS WILL THE KILLER CLAIM?

He turned the page and opened it to the lead story on page three and read the screaming headline. " 'Will Your Daughter Be Next?' "

Malone tossed the paper onto his desk in disgust.

"And up until this morning, we didn't have one fucking clue."

"What happened this morning?" Evan asked.

"This." Malone handed him the sheet of paper he'd been holding. Evan studied it for a full minute before reacting.

DEAR CHIEF OF DETECTIVES MALONE,
I SAW YOU ON THE NEWS TONIGHT. YOU SAID THAT YOU
FOUND THREE MORE VICTIMS OF THIS GUY WHO IS
KILLING GIRLS IN AVON COUNTY. WELL, THAT WOULD
BE ME. AND I AM TELLING YOU THAT I DID NOT KILL
THOSE OTHER GIRLS, THE ONES YOU FOUND IN THE
WOODS. THAT IS SOMEONE ELSE'S WORK, IT IS NOT
MINE. STOP SAYING I KILLED THEM ALL. I KNOW WHO
MY GIRLS WERE AND WHERE I LEFT THEM. THESE
OTHER GIRLS, I DON'T KNOW WHO THEY ARE OR WHO
KILLED THEM. IT WAS NOT ME.
AND ANOTHER THING. WHAT DO I HAVE TO DO TO
GET A SPECIAL NAME FROM YOU GUYS? YOU KNOW,
LIKE THE BOSTON STRANGLER, OR THE GREEN RIVER
KILLER. I THINK I HAVE EARNED A SPECIAL NAME. I LIKE
THE SCHOOLGIRL SLAYER. I THOUGHT SOMEONE AS
SMART AS YOU WOULD THINK UP A NAME. SINCE YOU
DID NOT, I HAD TO MAKE UP MY OWN. I THINK IT IS A
GOOD ONE. I HOPE YOU LIKE IT. YOU'LL BE USING IT
OVER AND OVER. JUST NOT FOR THESE OTHER GIRLS.

WHY WOULD I WANT TO KILL A BUNCH OF NAMELESS
NOBODIES? HOW COULD YOU BE SO STUPID TO THINK
THOSE OTHER GIRLS WOULD INTEREST ME?
    SIGNED,
    THE SCHOOLGIRL SLAYER

"You think this is legit?" Evan asked.

"What do you think?"

"He seems pretty indignant that we would assume that the other
vics were his. Like somehow he's above them." Evan read from
the letter. "This whole last part, about those other girls being nobodies . . . he clearly thinks they weren't worth his time."

He handed the letter back to Malone. "As if one girl's life was
more important than another's."

"He's certainly implying that."

"I spoke with Dr. Jenkins a little while ago, right after she finished the autopsy on our last unidentified vic," Evan told him. "She
says the weapon used to kill the schoolgirls is not the same weapon
used to kill our as-yet-unidentified girls. She thinks that the physical
signs point to a high level of sexual activity on the part of the girls
who still haven't been reported missing, no such activity on the part
of the others."

"So she's seeing two distinct types of victims, two different
killers."

Evan nodded.

"I also took the liberty to discuss the case with one of the FBI's
profilers, Dr. McCall, and she—"

"The same Dr. McCall who accompanied you to the D.A.'s fund-
raiser last month?"

"Ah, yes." Evan had forgotten that Malone had met Annie at a
party to raise money for the district attorney's reelection campaign.
"Right."

"What was her take on all this?"

"She feels pretty strongly that there are two different killers. She's working up a report for us."

Malone pointed to the letter, which was still in Evan's hand. "Think she'd be able to look at that and give us her thoughts? Any chance we could meet with her? If nothing else, we can tell the press we've brought in the FBI."

"I can ask her. You may have to go through the Bureau, and they'll probably want to send some of their own agents to work the case."

"I've already resigned myself to bringing them in. It's a tough call, since there are so many police departments involved. On the one hand, it looks like we've got every PD in the county on this, and this guy is still dancing around us. Doesn't look good, you know what I mean? Looks like we have no confidence in our local people." Malone reflected on this for a moment, then added, "On the other hand, if we're being outsmarted at every turn by this guy, and we don't ask for help, we look like stubborn fools. At this point, I feel we need all the help we can get. I hate to say it, but without a suspect, without any leads—hell, we don't even know where he's killing these girls. We're just finding them where he leaves them."

"I'll call Annie and see when she's available." Evan couldn't help but be pleased at the prospect of working with Annie again, even if it was only for a consult. He hadn't been able to see his way clear from this case to figure out when they could spend time together. The thought of even one night with her was a gift, despite the tragic circumstances.

"One more thing. Jenkins noted that each of the three unidentified victims had three stars tattooed on her left hip."

Malone's head snapped up.

"Gang members?"

"Maybe. Maybe a pimp, branding his property."

"Any history on these tattoos?"

"I didn't recognize them and couldn't find anyone who did. I already faxed the photos of the tattoos to the FBI. Apparently, there's someone on staff who's really an ace at tracking down stuff like this. Annie says if it's in the system, they'll find it."

"Good move. And you already sent the samples from the lab down there as well?"

"I did, as soon as the lab director agreed to release them. Thanks for stepping in there."

"Coogan can be a hard-ass. Sometimes you just have to remind him who's in charge. In this case, it would be the county D.A. He had no problem getting Coogan to see things his way."

"Whatever it took. I'll just be happy to see a little solid evidence. It's frustrating to gather all those samples, all that potential evidence, then have to wait weeks to see what's what," Evan admitted.

"In this case, a few weeks could mean the difference between life and death for another young girl. Or two. The killer has definitely put us on notice. He's not finished."

"What are you going to do with the letter?" Evan pointed to the paper in his hand.

"I've already sent the original to a handwriting analyst at the FBI—you're not the only one with contacts, you know."

"How do you propose to respond?"

"Well, I was hoping Dr. McCall might have some thoughts on that."

"I'm sure she will. But in the meantime—"

"In the meantime, I've sent letters to every school in the county, advising parents and school officials that until this guy is caught, no one's daughter is safe. Your kid goes no place alone, checks in with the parents, and reports any suspicious activity. Anything, from anyone. And if she's not home when she's supposed to be, the first call the parents make is to their local police department."

"Tough talk."

"Can't be tough enough. This guy has killed five young girls—all daughters of well-off, influential county residents, so that just adds to the colossal heat we're taking. This last girl was the daughter of the next-door neighbor of one of the town supervisors in Broeder."

"I heard about that." Evan nodded. "My sister's fiancé is the chief of police down there."

"Right. Sean Mercer. He's got the local politicians and a passel of reporters crawling up his butt over this, so of course he's crawling up mine. Not that I blame him, but it isn't as if we aren't trying to track this guy. We just don't have much to go on."

"How much are you going to make public?" Evan asked. "Are you going to let it be known there are two killers? Are you going to release the letter to the press?"

"Not yet. Right now, I don't want to change the status quo. I'd really like to wait to see what Dr. McCall has to say. Maybe she'll have some insight into whether silence or publicity is to our best advantage. I don't want to throw something out there only to have it bite us in the ass later on. Let's get the best advice we can before we act. For now, just proceed as you were. Keep the letter under your hat, for now. And let's sit on this two-killer thing until after I've spoken with Dr. McCall." Malone drew a hand through the thinning hair on top of his head. "The one thing I do want is every department in this county on alert. I know everyone's been on this, Crosby; don't jump on me. But I want every available man on the street."

"Chief, it's impossible to cover all these private schools. They're in this county, they're over in Landro County. There's no way we can cover all these kids."

"No, but we can cover them when they get back to our jurisdiction. So far, he hasn't hit any town in Landro County. He's confined his work here, in Avon. That could mean something, maybe not. Who the hell knows what this guy is thinking, what sets him off, what makes him go after one girl and not another? For now, the best we can do is to warn parents to keep their eyes on their kids and make them understand the danger, that to a certain degree they are going to have to be responsible for themselves and for their friends."

"Let's hope the lab results are back soon and give us something. Right now we have nothing."

"And he knows it. Bastard knows that right now he has us chasing our own tails, and he's enjoying it," Malone told Evan. "Let's see what we can do to ruin his fun before he kills again."

At Annie's suggestion, Malone made his request for FBI assistance directly to John Mancini, who headed up a special unit within the Bureau to handle sensitive cases. John personally reviewed the files, which had been messengered to him overnight, before assigning three of his top agents to the job.

"Shouldn't take you more than a day or so," he said to Annie while authorizing her to provide an analysis of the killer's psychological profile to the chief of detectives in Avon County. "What's on your calendar right now?"

"The Ohio case. A case out in Michigan. Something that came in last night from Oregon; I'm taking that with me to read on the plane. I have a meeting in Seattle next Tuesday. Otherwise, I'm okay."

"Great. See if you can shed some light on this case." John pushed his chair back from his desk, his habitual nonverbal notice that the meeting had concluded.

Annie stood and gathered her bag and her briefcase, noting that John's job was clearly taking its toll.

"You okay, John?"

"As okay as I've ever been, I guess."

"Genna okay?" She asked, referring to John's wife of two years.

"She's fine." His eyes narrowed. "What's with the interrogation?"

"You just look a little tired, that's all."

He laughed. "When have I not been tired?"

"You just look a little more worn-out than you normally do."

"It's just the job, Annie. But I appreciate your concern."

"Maybe you should be the one going to Pennsylvania and out of here for a few days."

"Well, actually, I'll be doing just that. Genna's got that cabin out on that lake up in the northeastern corner of the state, you know. We're supposed to go for a week, starting on Tuesday."

"Do it. Make it your priority. Don't let anything come between you and that time off, John. Seriously. I can't remember the last time I called this office and you were on vacation." Her voice softened. "You need the time, John."

"You been talking to my wife?"

"Just looking out for you, pal."

"I appreciate the sentiment," John told her. "You keep in touch, and have a safe trip."

"You, too."

She left John's office and headed straight for her own on the seventh floor. She was gathering up files she'd left on her desk when Brendan Shields appeared in her doorway.

"Hey. Where's the fire?" he asked.

"Oh, I'm on my way to Pennsylvania to look into that serial killer they have on the loose, and I need to take some of these notes with me." Where was the file she'd started with her own notes on Dylan's case? She checked her briefcase and found she'd already tucked it away.

"I heard Mancini's sending a couple of agents up there," he said. "I heard Miranda Cahill, Mike Hoffman, and Kevin Muller were going."

"Oh, great. I love working with all of them. I should check with Miranda and see when she's leaving. Maybe we can fly up together."

"She's in Maine right now. I think she's heading down there tomorrow."

"Word travels fast around here."

Brendan shrugged. "I had lunch with Will a while ago. Miranda called him while we were eating."

"I can't believe how incestuous this place is. And how quickly news travels." She laughed and added one more file to her briefcase. "Gotta run."

Brendan backed into the hall to allow her to pass.

"See you when I get back." She stepped around him and started down the hall, then stopped and turned around. "By the way, do you know an agent named Melissa Lowery?"

"Name sounds familiar, but I can't place her. Why?"

"She was on the scene the night Dylan died, but her report is missing from the file."

"You sure?"

"Positive."

"It probably dropped out at some point, or got stuck to something else and misfiled. Happens all the time."

"Anyway, I was just wondering what was in the report, if she might remember what she'd written, but no one seems to know where she is."

"I can ask around, see if anyone knows."

"Thanks, Brendan." She smiled and resumed her quick trot to the elevator, calling to the woman who was just about to enter the car, "Hey, could you hold that for me, please . . . ?"

Anne Marie sat on the black leather sofa in the office of the Avon County district attorney and read through the letter she'd been handed almost immediately upon entering the room.

"This is what we're dealing with, Dr. McCall," the District Attorney, Art Sheridan, told her. "We think this is, in fact, from the killer, but we want your opinion. On the author of the letter as well as on the contents."

Annie took her time reading, then read it through a second time.

"I agree this is from your killer. There's so much going on here . . ." she told the men who had gathered in the office and appeared to be waiting for some revelation from her. "But this isn't like a psychic reading. I need a little time to think this through. But I can tell you up front, I do believe it to be genuine. He fancies himself as very intelligent, very much in control of this situation; he's very cocky about having you all on the ropes, and is quite proud of that. Yet, at the same time, he's telling you a great deal about himself."

"Such as . . . ?" Sheridan asked hopefully.

"This is not a very young man. I'm thinking he's in his late twenties, perhaps his early thirties. He's not well educated, but he believes he's quite smart and is annoyed that everyone doesn't recognize his brilliance. He's in a low-level job—I think he has been for years, which is why I think he's in his thirties—a job that makes him subservient, and he hates that feeling. He knows he's better than everyone else, so he's smug, even as he's humiliated by the menial tasks his job requires of him." She looked up at Sheridan. "I wrote a preliminary profile for Detective Crosby. This was all in that memo."

"Anyone have that memo?" Sheridan looked around the room.

"I have it." Malone passed it to Sheridan, who glanced at it, then asked, "How come I didn't get this?"

"I, ah, sent you a copy," Malone told him. "It might still be in your interoffice mail."

"In any case"—Sheridan gestured to Annie—"continue, Dr. McCall."

"You're looking for someone who does menial work for a lot of people who are much better off financially than he is, or who comes into contact with such people on a regular basis. He resents what they have, doesn't understand why he hasn't been able to make as much or to have the kind of life that they have. His resentment is deep-seated and has been building inside him for a long time. He thinks he's as worthy as they—more so, actually—but they don't recognize this. They probably don't see him at all. So he's forcing them to look at him, to stand in awe of him, by taking something precious from them, something they value greatly, to prove to them how much control he has over their lives. He's stealing their daughters, defiling them, taking their lives. And flaunting what he's done." She looked from one man to the other. "He will not stop. He will keep on going for as long as he can."

"Are you saying this is socially motivated, that this is a class thing . . . ?"

"If you want to use those terms, Chief Malone, but this goes so much deeper than that. Look here, in his letter. He's incensed that you would think that he would be bothered with these other victims, these nameless girls. He's infuriated that someone is trying to copy what he's done, but even angrier that this copycat killer has targeted girls that *he* feels are so beneath him. It's bad enough that someone is copying his style, but to have the deaths of these girls who he feels are inferior and therefore so unworthy of his attention—well, he's just not going to take that. Uh-uh. He wants you to make sure the public knows his standards are much higher than this copycat. And he wants this copycat caught."

She held up the letter.

"See here, what he's telling you. 'Why would I want to kill a bunch of nameless nobodies? How could you be so stupid to think those other girls would interest me?' "

"He's going after girls whose families are well-known," Malone murmured.

"We already knew that," Sheridan reminded him brusquely.

"But now we know why. That's his game. If I understand Dr. McCall correctly, this is his way of shoving it to people he feels look down on him."

"Not only in the sense of retaliation, but in showing them that ultimately, he can control them, not the other way around, that he can impact their lives in ways they'd never have imagined," Annie told them. "Look for someone who's worked a menial job for a long

time, ten years or better, in a place where he'd come into daily contact with the victims' families. A country club, golf course, restaurant, a pool company, landscaping company . . . some business that
would attract the well-to-do or the influential from the community."

"Green Briar Country Club. It's the only country club in the
county. Only golf course, as well," Malone offered.

"See if the victims' families were members," Sheridan told him.

Malone reached for the telephone, made a call, then hung up.
"I've got someone on that. We should have a list of members within
the hour. I also requested that contact be made this morning with
the parents to find out who they used for landscaping, if they have a
pool or handyman—all the possibilities Dr. McCall just talked
about. We'll see if we get any matches."

He turned to Annie.

"Any chance we can pick your brain on this second killer while
we have you here? You have any thoughts on him?"

"I think it's all staging," Annie said. "He's tried to make his victims look as much like the others as he could. He's copying the other
killer's style because he wants to go unnoticed. He wants these girls
dead, but isn't making a statement, the way the first killer is. I'd be
willing to bet the shoes he took from his victims were tossed into the
trash. Unlike our first killer, who is keeping them in a special place
and treating them like treasures. These other killings were more like
executions than murders that involved any passion or fulfilled any
need or fantasy of the killer."

"Why would someone want to execute a fourteen-year-old girl?"
Malone murmured.

"Because she knows something that the killer doesn't want anyone else to know, or has seen something he didn't want anyone to
see," Annie suggested. "Or because she's in his way. Possibly she's
served a purpose and isn't needed anymore. She's disposable, for
whatever reason, and so he disposed of her. Having a serial killer in
the area preying on young girls was simply a matter of convenience

for him. He figured he'd just piggyback onto that, make his kills look the same. And at first glance, they do."

Malone swore under his breath.

"Yes." Annie nodded. "My thoughts exactly."

"Dr. McCall, there are details about the killings that were not released to the public. That still haven't been released to the public."

"Like the fact that the girls' throats were slashed and their shoes were taken?"

"Yes."

"Well, as I said to Detective Crosby, either someone connected with the investigation is leaking information . . ." She paused.

"Or someone connected with the investigation is the killer." Sheridan finished the thought.

He and Malone stared at each other. Finally, Malone broke the silence.

"I can't even begin to imagine a suspect from that pool. We've got the entire Lyndon police force, we've got county detectives. We've got Broeder police, we've got Chapman PD, the D.A.'s office. How the hell do you narrow that down?"

"Someone is going to have to." Annie looked from one man to the other. "Identifying the girls—knowing who they are, what brought them together with their killer—will help lead you to him. I have someone at the Bureau trying to identify the identical tattoos these girls had. Right now, that's all we have to go on. Within twenty-four hours, we should have reports back from our lab on the trace from both groups of victims. Hopefully, we'll have something that will lead us in the right direction. Until then, do what you can with what you have."

"First order of business is getting our hands on the membership list from Green Briar," Malone noted.

"Which is more direction than we had an hour ago," Sheridan reminded him. "Let's see where that takes us . . ."

———

"What a treat this is." Annie glanced around the handsome dining room at the restaurant, which overlooked the small man-made lake nestled in the heart of the beautifully manicured golf course.

Evan nodded. "Lots of dark wood, lots of flowers. It's a pretty classy place."

"Well, the room is lovely, and the view spectacular, but I was referring to the fact that you and I are actually having dinner together in the middle of the week."

"And even more surprising, it isn't cold pizza out of the fridge at two in the morning." He took a sip of wine. "It is pretty nice, isn't it."

She laughed. "You are a master of understatement."

He refilled her glass and set the bottle off to one side of the table.

"What a coincidence that you chose the Green Briar Country Club for dinner tonight." She lowered her voice. "Don't think you're fooling me. I know you're dying to go into the kitchen and start interrogating the busboys."

"All in good time." He smiled at the waitress who served their salads.

"You wouldn't."

"If I had a better idea who I was looking for, sure. We just haven't narrowed things down enough yet. But sure. If I knew for certain our guy worked here, I'd be in there in a heartbeat." He grinned. "Of course I'd wait until after dessert."

"But you have confirmed that all of the victims' families were members here."

"Yes, but we also confirmed that they all bought their pools from Kava's and three out of five bought their groceries at Marshall's and had them delivered." He pushed the croutons aside on his Caesar salad. "And we're still trying to figure out how many of these families had their yard work done by the same landscaper and used the same handyman."

"He's there, though, Evan. I can feel him." Her voice dropped even lower. "You're going to find him in one of those places, and you're going to find him soon."

"You sound awfully sure of yourself."

"I am sure of myself. Sometimes I'm not so sure. Sometimes I give it my best guess, and sometimes I'm right, but I've been wrong, too. This time, I know I'm right."

"Well, then, I think we should drink to a speedy resolution." Evan refilled his glass.

Annie touched the rim of her glass to his, then took a sip.

"Here's what bothers me, though," she told him. "You will get this guy, and you will get him soon. The other one—the one who killed the girls with the tattoos—he's a different duck altogether. He's going to be hard to find. Tracking him down is going to take your best skills. Your best use of the available science."

"You really think he's a cop?"

"I think he's most likely a cop or someone close to one of the investigating departments." She tapped her fingers on the stem of her glass. "You might want to ask Sheridan to bring this investigation strictly into the county, have only your people handle it from here on out."

"Less chance of a cover-up if it's a cop." He nodded. "Of course, that means I'll be stepping on a lot of toes."

"But there'll be a greater chance for justice for those three girls. For them and their families."

"That's the bottom line, isn't it? Finding out who these girls are and helping to bring closure to their families." He took another sip of wine and added, "Someone needs to pay for what he did to them."

"If we can identify the significance of the tattoos, there's a good chance we'll be able to determine where these girls came from. Then maybe we can figure out who they are and how they got from there to here."

"It should only be so easy."

"Easy? Not on your life." She tilted her glass in his direction. "But I promise you, the payback will be huge. When you look into the eyes of the parents of these girls and tell them the man who did this to their daughters has been captured and will be punished, that their daughters can rest in peace, you will know it was worth every hour you spent, every bad lead that you followed, every toe you stepped on along the way."

"I can't argue with you. I'll speak with Malone in the morning, see if he agrees, see if he wants to talk to Sheridan himself or if he's okay with me taking the lead here."

"What are the chances he'll toss this to the Bureau as part and parcel of the other investigation?"

"I'd be real surprised. I think he's going to keep this totally separate, and frankly, I think he should. For one thing, we all believe the killings are not related. For another, he'll want to assure the more prominent citizens that the deaths of their daughters merit the attention of the FBI. These other girls, maybe not. Which is okay with me. I want to handle this case myself."

"What will you do if Sheridan doesn't want to bring that investigation into the county?" she asked. "What are the chances he'll want to permit the local departments, the locals where the bodies were found, to work the individual cases?"

"If I know Sheridan, he's going to weigh this very carefully from a political angle. If he thinks there's a chance his office can track this guy down and make a collar, he'll jump at it. If he thinks it's a long shot, he'll put me off until he thinks we have something."

"Then we'll have to get him something." She leaned back in her seat to permit the waitress to serve their entrées. "And we'll start with the tattoos. As soon as we get an ID on them, you'll have something to take to him. In the meantime, you have all the resources of the FBI at your disposal. Use them."

"Sheridan hates the FBI, you know."

"I know." She grinned. "But it's going to make him look really good if he can hold a press conference and assure the county movers and shakers that he's brought in the best the feds have to offer to take this killer down." She pounded her fist lightly on the table for emphasis.

Evan laughed at her attempt to mimic the D.A.

"That's all good for tomorrow's agenda, but no more shop-talk. Tonight is ours, and I want to enjoy every minute of it with my girl."

"Well then, let's eat up and head home early." She smiled and toyed with her fork. "The night, as they say, is still very, very young . . ."

11

"Dr. McCall, I'm surprised to hear from you so soon." Art Sheridan had grabbed the phone as soon as he heard who was on the other end of the line. "Should I be encouraged?"

"A little optimism is always good," Annie replied. "And in this case, warranted. I have the lab results from the Bureau. I'd like to go over them with you. When would be a good time?"

"How soon can you get here?" He sat up straight in his chair, hopefully anticipating a break in this god-bloody-awful case. Praying for one.

"Fifteen, twenty minutes."

"You're still in town, then. Terrific. I'll be waiting. Okay if we have Chief Malone and Detectives Crosby and Weller in on this?"

"Certainly, whomever you feel you need. You might want to include the three agents the Bureau sent up as well," she replied. "I'll see you soon."

The D.A. buzzed for his secretary without bothering to hang up the phone. "Lois, I need Malone, Crosby, and Weller here in fifteen minutes. No excuses."

He stood and went to the window to look out. Those damned news vans were everywhere. Outside the courthouse, in the parking lots, down the side streets. He knew a press conference was overdue, but he had nothing, not one bone to toss to the reporters who badgered his every move once he stepped out of the safety of his office. They followed him home, had even followed him to his son's softball game last night. He knew he owed them, but wasn't about to speak until he had something real, something legit. He'd seen too many D.A.s make asses out of themselves on television by calling conferences when they had nothing to talk about but yesterday's news. He wasn't going that route. Never let it be said that Arthur M. Sheridan wasn't smart enough to learn from the mistakes of others. When he called the press in, he'd have something solid. End of story.

Still, he was hoping that day was close at hand. He was up for re-election in November and was looking forward to blowing out the competition, a man he'd gone to law school with and had never liked.

"Sanctimonious ass," he muttered to himself. The mere thought of his rival always brought out the worst in him. Now, *he* would be just the type to call a premature press conference just to get his pretty face on national TV one more time. Well, Sheridan wasn't going to play that game.

The D.A. just hoped that whatever the FBI had was something he could use, and use now. The pressure was mounting daily. Even his wife had gotten into the act, since their children attended the same private school as one of the victims.

"Honestly, Art, I'm afraid to show my face at Northgate. Every-one wants to know what you're going to do about this monster who killed the Fuhrmann girl. Everyone's scared."

"Everyone should be scared," he'd told her at the time. Christ, like we're dragging our feet here . . .

"What's going on?" Chris Malone stuck his head through the doorway.

"Come on in. Where are Crosby and Weller?"

"Crosby's on his way in, Weller is right behind me."

As if on cue, Jacqueline Weller tapped on the door, then entered without waiting for an invitation. She was tall, plain, humorless, and a decent detective with lofty ambitions. She'd been at the job three years longer than Evan and had earned the respect of everyone in the county. Those who knew such things whispered her name as a possible successor for Sheridan once he moved up the ladder.

"Jackie, take a seat." Sheridan motioned to the five matched chairs that had been arranged in a semicircle around his desk. "We're going to be joined by Detective Crosby and the profiler the FBI sent us. Apparently, she's received the results from their lab and is eager to share with us. I'm hoping she's going to be bringing us good news."

"I suspect she'd merely fax it if she didn't have something solid," Malone observed. "She doesn't seem to be the type to waste her time."

"May I come in?" Annie rapped on the door much as Jackie Weller had done.

"Dr. McCall." Sheridan walked from behind his desk to greet her. "I can't tell you how happy I am to have you back here so soon. I'm hoping you have something good to share with us."

"I think I do."

"Have you met Detective Weller?" The D.A. smiled. Next to the petite profiler, who was always meticulously dressed, Weller looked like an unkempt Amazon. Sheridan wondered if Crosby knew just how lucky he was.

"I have. How are you, Detective?" Annie offered her hand.

"I'm hoping I'll be better once we hear what you have to say."

"Were you able to get in touch with Agents Cahill, Hoffman, and Muller?" Annie asked pointedly.

"Ah, no. I thought, since time was so short, I'd let Detective Weller here pass along whatever information you might have."

"I see," Annie said.

"Ah, here's Detective Crosby." Malone tilted his head in the direction of the door, where Evan stood.

"Come on in, Evan. We're just about ready to start. Take a seat there"—Sheridan pointed to the remaining unoccupied chair—"and let's see what Dr. McCall has for us."

"I think you might want to copy these so everyone has their own." Annie held up the folder containing the lab reports.

Malone left his seat and reached for the folder.

"I'll take care of it," he told her, and left the room.

"Just so you know"—Sheridan addressed Annie—"I'm treating these murders as two separate cases. We're going to work on the assumption that we do in fact have two different killers. Detective Weller is going to be in charge of the Schoolgirl Slayer killings; Detective Crosby will lead the investigation of the unidentified victims. As far as the public is concerned, however, this is one case. Maybe if this second killer thinks he has us fooled, he'll get careless."

He turned to Evan.

"Just remember this was your idea, when Jackie solves the big case and gets all the publicity." Sheridan's idea of a joke.

"Jackie brings that guy in, she is more than welcome to the publicity." Evan turned to her as Malone came back into the room. "Hey, this case could make you a star."

"Right," she said without smiling. "And the book deal could make me rich."

Before anyone could comment on that, Malone started passing out the lab reports.

"Dr. McCall, if you'd like to start . . . ," Sheridan said.

"Just a few things of note," Annie told them. "First of all, we have recovered several areas of trace evidence. On all your victims, Detective Weller, the lab found traces of maroon carpet fibers. The fibers were matched to carpeting used by several auto manufacturers—specifically Ford and GMC—between 1992 and 1999."

"Any particular models?" Weller asked.

"No. They used this pretty much across the board. But we're checking to determine if this color carpet was used exclusively with any exterior colors. We'll narrow it down as much as we can. In the meantime, there is more . . ." Annie turned to the next page in the pack. "On these same victims, the lab found snippets of grass."

"Grass?"

"Grass, Chief Malone. Green grass. Which fits quite nicely with our theory that the killer is a laborer. I understand you've narrowed the field down a bit, Detective Crosby?"

"We've determined that three businesses were common to all of the victims. Green Briar Country Club, Sweet Summer Pools, and Davison's Lawn and Garden. All employ workers who would come into contact with mowed grass."

"Wait a minute, I thought this was my case," Detective Weller said crisply, the only animation she'd shown since she arrived.

"It is, as of this morning," Evan responded pleasantly. "I went through all of the businesses and services the victims might have had in common last night. I found that some were used by two or three of the victims' families, but only these three were utilized by all of them."

Jackie Weller turned to Annie.

"Anything else that pertains to my case?"

"Actually, I think the rest of the report is pretty much self-explanatory. Most of the remaining trace I'd like to address right now concerns the three unidentified girls."

"If I might be excused, then?" Weller looked at the D.A. "I'll need to talk to the agents who came up yesterday, fill them in."

"Of course. Go right ahead." Sheridan nodded. "Just keep in touch. We'll want to know the minute you think you have a viable suspect."

"Will do." Detective Weller grabbed her bag, said her good-byes, and left the room in a blur.

"Now, what else do you have for us?" The D.A. turned his attention back to Annie. "You said you have information pertaining to the other girls?"

"Hair from three different men and a dog."

"Three men and a dog?" Malone leaned forward slightly to look at her, his brows raised.

"Right. Pubic hair from two of the men, head hair only from three. Dog hair from an as-yet-unidentified breed. The lab is still working on that."

"So three guys are involved; only two had sex with the girls?"

"Looks that way. The hair we found on all three victims is the same. Same three men. Same two pubic hairs."

"So what's this other guy doing, watching?" Malone frowned. "With his dog?"

"Don't know. But the third man has been close enough to the vics to leave a little bit of himself with each of them," Annie told him.

"Any other trace? Carpet fibers like the others?" Sheridan wanted to know.

"No carpet, no fabric fibers of any kind. I'm wondering if he wrapped them in plastic before he transported them from where they were killed to the place where they were left."

"Maybe that's the third guy. Maybe he just moved the bodies."

"You said the lab was still working on the dog hair. Can they even determine the breed of dog?" Malone asked.

"It will take a little longer to get a match, but yes, they can. Of course, it may well be that the girls came in contact with the dog someplace else. No one's saying a dog was on the scene. The dog could have belonged to the girls. The evidence just tells us that at some point, all three of these girls came in contact with the same dog, or with something that had dog hair on it."

"Three guys—one of whom may or may not have a dog—two of whom rape and murder these three girls, while another guy only handles the bodies, maybe only to move them?" Malone rubbed the back of his neck. "Anyone else think that's odd?"

"There is one other thing," Annie told him. "All three of these girls had dirt under their fingernails and in the tiny creases of their feet. Dirt with the same composition. We're checking to see if the dirt samples check out with the areas where the bodies were found, but I'm betting they don't. We already know that the girls were killed elsewhere and dumped where they were found. There's no evidence of struggle, nowhere near the amount of blood there'd have been if their throats had been cut right there at the drop site. So they must have been taken someplace, someplace where they were raped and murdered, then moved to these other areas where they were found."

"Someplace where they would be easily found. Posed, like the other girls, their shoes missing." Sheridan noted.

"That little detail is key," Evan reminded them. "Since no one knows about the shoes . . ."

The statement hung there between them.

"Okay, let's accept the fact that someone near to the investigation is involved in this." Sheridan finally broke the silence. "From here on out, no information about these unidentified girls gets released to anyone, unless I personally approve it. Let's keep a lid on all of it, from the fact that it's a different killer to the very real possibility that someone in or close to law enforcement could be the killer."

"Honest to God, Art, don't you think that's a stretch? I can't believe any one of these cops—" Malone began, and the D.A. stopped him.

"I can't believe it, either, Chris, but the fact remains that someone is leaking information, and we're going to have to deal with that." He turned to Evan. "Give this the best you've got, Detective. Find whoever killed these girls. And if it's a cop, God help him. I personally will nail him to the wall."

"I'll hold him down." Malone nodded.

"Well then, since we're all in agreement on that point, let me just add that I'm still waiting to hear about the tattoos," Annie told them. "I think if we can match them to other similar tattoos, we'll be on our way to identifying the girls."

"How much longer do you think before you have something?" Sheridan asked.

"I can't estimate how long it will take," Annie said. "I'll check in later today with my office to see if anything has turned up."

"One thing." Evan spoke up. "About the tattoos. I'd like to keep that from the press, too. Actually, I'd like to keep that from everyone who is not in this room."

"I agree." Sheridan nodded without hesitation. "There are four of us here; how many people working on this at the FBI?"

"One," Annie replied.

"And the M.E. knows about them," Evan reminded him.

"That makes six people," Sheridan said. "If this gets out, it will only be because one of us six let it out."

"You think it's that important to keep it under wraps?" Malone asked.

"I think it could prove to be. I think the less we talk publicly about this second killer, the better off we'll all be." The D.A. stood, signaling the meeting had come to an end. "Let him think he's fooled us."

"Anything else? Dr. McCall? Anything else to add?" he asked.

"I think we covered it all today." Annie stood also and gathered her notes from the end of the desk. "You have my card if you need to get in touch with me. My cell phone number is there. You can also get to me through one of the agents assigned to the other case. Agent Cahill can always find me."

"We'll look forward to hearing whatever you find out about those tattoos." Sheridan opened the door for her, and she stepped into the hall. "I assume you'll give the information to Detective Crosby."

"As soon as I have something to give him."

Annie and Evan walked to the stairwell together, careful not to walk too closely to each other.

Once they were outside the building, she asked, "Where are you headed now?"

"I thought I'd take a ride out to visit the places where my three girls were left."

"May I go with you?"

"Sure. May not be much to see, but sure."

"I can call Will from the car. I wanted to check in with him, just in case he's got something to tell me."

"I want so badly to solve this one, Annie," he told her as they walked down to Fourth Street, where he'd parked his car. "Jackie can have the big-profile case, she can have the publicity and all the glory. I'll be more than happy if I can find out who these girls were and what happened to them."

"What about the book deal?" she teased.

"She can even have the book deal." He smiled. "Someone has to make it right for these kids. I'd like it to be me."

"And the possibility that a cop is involved has nothing to do with your wanting this case all to yourself."

"It won't be all to myself. I'll have help if I ask for it. But yeah, if a cop's involved, I want to bring him in."

They turned the corner on Fourth and crossed the street to Evan's car, which he unlocked with the remote. He opened Annie's door for her, pausing to nuzzle the side of her face.

"You smell good," he whispered.

"Now, Detective," she said sternly. "What would District Attorney Sheridan have to say about such a public display of affection?"

"He wishes he were me, don't kid yourself." He kissed her neck.

"Save it." She smiled as she slid into the front passenger seat. "I'll be here at least until tomorrow."

"Yippee." He slammed the car door and walked around to the driver's side. By the time he opened the door and got behind the wheel, she was holding the phone to her ear.

"Hey, Will, it's Annie. Got anything for me on those tattoos yet?"

Evan started up the engine, but she put a hand on his arm, silently asking him to wait. He turned off the engine.

"Can you send me all this via fax to . . . Evan, what's the number of the new fax machine at your house?"

He told her and she repeated the number for Will.

She listened to Will for a few minutes longer, then said, "Would you repeat that?"

She scribbled quickly on a piece of paper she found in her purse.

"And you're sure?" She hesitated, then said, "I wish I could remember why that sounds so familiar. I guess it'll come to me. Give me a call if you find anything else. And thanks, Will. This is great. I owe you. Yeah, another one . . ."

"He's identified the tattoos?"

"He found several other similar victims in Chicago. Three girls, all Hispanic. Cause of death was different from yours, though. These girls all died from gunshots to the head. All from the same gun."

"More executions."

"That's what I thought, too, when he first said it. I'm wondering if these girls of yours would have been shot had there not been a serial killer in the same general geographic area. Making the kills look the same could have been simply a way to camouflage the hits."

"What did he have to say about the tattoos?"

"This is really interesting. These girls in Chicago all had those little stars in the same place, top of the hip, left side. None of them had any identification, but one of them had some kind of dried bean seeds in a small vial on a cord around her neck."

"Dried bean seeds?" Evan frowned.

"Right. The cop handling the investigation found that these beans apparently are grown in Central America."

"Could he be more specific?"

"He mentioned a small country called Santa Estela as a possible source."

"Never heard of it."

"I have. And it took me a minute, but I just remembered where I heard the name."

"You going to share that with me?"

"Connor was there, a few years ago. I remember overhearing him and Dylan talking about it."

"Maybe he has a contact there who could help us to identify the tattoo."

"I'll ask him. I'll e-mail him tonight." She leaned back against the seat. "We can go now."

"Thank you." He turned the key in the ignition.

"Sorry. I didn't mean to be rude. I'm just thinking."

"You're thinking that if the kids from Chicago were from Santa Estela, maybe these girls—my girls—are, too."

She nodded. "And wondering why they're here, how they got here."

"Want to skip the tour of the crime scenes for today and go straight to my place so you can use your computer?"

"Do you mind?"

"Not at all. I'm itching to find something concrete on this case."

"Will is going to fax over everything he has, including the name and phone number of the cop in Chicago who worked this case."

"I can't wait to talk to him."

"I had a feeling you'd say that."

Once they were back at the townhouse, Evan went directly to the fax machine and Annie to her laptop. She turned it on, and typed her message.

```
TO: CShields00721
From: AMMccall00913
Re: Santa Estela
Connor, strange development on a case here in PA.
Tattoos on the vics found to be identical to those found
on three vics in Chicago. Young girls, one of whom
appears to have a connection traced back to Central
America, possibly Santa Estela. Do I recall correctly
that you had spent some time there? Any contacts remain?
    A
```

She hit *send* and waited, but the immediate response she'd hoped for didn't come. Maybe tonight, maybe tomorrow.

In the meantime, she wanted to see the fax Will had sent Evan. Maybe the Chicago cop had found answers to the very questions Evan was now asking. Maybe he could give them a lead. Maybe this was the thread that, once pulled, would help Evan to send the girls home.

12

"What's on your agenda for today?" Evan asked Annie over breakfast early on Monday morning.

"First thing I want to do is try Will again." She sat across from
him at the small table next to the only window in his narrow
kitchen.

"Checking to see if he found out anything else about the tattoos?"

"No, he'll contact me as soon as he has something on that. I want
to ask him about Melissa Lowery." She sipped at her coffee. "Have
I mentioned her to you before? She's a former agent who was on the
scene the night Dylan was shot. She wrote an account of the events
of that night, but the report isn't in the file."

"I think you did mention her. Did you ask around the Bureau?"

"No one seems to know where she went after she left. Which is odd in itself, since she was with the Bureau for seven years. She must have had friends."

"I guess you didn't ask the right people. Someone knows where she is. Did you check with HR? Wouldn't they have a forwarding address?"

"Privacy issues. They don't give out anyone's home address."

"So how would Will be able to find her?"

Annie laughed. "No one really knows how Will finds out anything. He just has a knack with computers and uncanny instincts. If anyone can track her down, it will be him."

She rested her elbow on the windowsill and gazed out.

"You need a little help finishing that deck?"

"Maybe. Depends on who's volunteering."

"I could work on it with you next weekend, if you get the boards that go across the frame." Her left index finger tapped on the window glass.

"Decking."

"What?"

"Those boards that go across the frame are called decking." He downed the last of his coffee and stood. "If you really want to, we can work outside next weekend. If it rains, we can work inside." He leaned down to kiss her neck.

She smiled and reached up her hand to touch his face.

"Either way, we win."

"Either way," he agreed.

"What's that I see going on out there by the fence?" She tapped on the glass again. "Looks as if someone has been digging."

"I started to dig up that garden bed for your roses, but I didn't get around to finishing it."

"Maybe we could put that on the list for next weekend, too."

"Hmm. Build the deck. Plant the garden." He grinned as he

walked to the sink to rinse out his cup. "Sounds like what the married guys in the office call a 'honey-do' weekend."

"It'll be good for both of us to spend some time outside, do a little manual labor. I'm up for it."

"I'll make a point next week to pick up the rest of the material for the deck. We'll start early on Saturday and just work through until it's finished. Or until one of us falls over."

"That would have to be you. I'm in great shape." She tilted her head to one side. "Is that my phone ringing or yours?"

"Mine. And it's upstairs on the dresser." He bolted from the room and took the steps to the second floor two at a time.

Annie cleared the table and stacked the breakfast dishes in the dishwasher. As small as Evan's townhouse was, she loved it. It was cozy and homey. With just a little paint on the cabinets, maybe lose that old wallpaper and add some textured paint to the walls, put in a new tile floor, the kitchen could be absolutely charming. She smiled to herself, knowing that such a kitchen would exist only in her mind. Evan would never think to do it on his own, and she'd never suggest it to him. It was, after all, his house.

She went to the back door and looked out onto the small yard. The deck would take up almost all of the space, but there was still room for those roses. She opened the door and stepped out, careful to avoid the box of nails and scraps of wood he'd left on the porch, and walked to the back of the yard where she'd planted the peonies. They hadn't bloomed this year, might not bloom for a few more years. She'd heard they were temperamental and didn't like being moved. She was thinking about making a stop at the local nursery to look for something that might bloom now when she heard the back door slam.

"That was Sheridan," Evan told her as he made his way across the yard to where she stood. "I have to go."

"Please don't tell me they found another girl . . ."

"No. But they did get another letter from the killer. Apparently, he's really pissed."

"Sheridan or the killer?"

"The killer. He'd expected Sheridan to let the media know that he was not responsible for the deaths of the three unidentified girls. He wants everyone to know there's a copycat killer out there, and he wants the media to start referring to him as the Schoolgirl Slayer. He thought Malone was going to take care of these issues for him after he'd written that letter, but as you know, we thought we'd sit on that for a few days."

"What's he done?"

"He wrote a second letter. Only he sent this one to Fox News. They aired it about ten minutes ago, right at the top of the seven a.m. show." He gave her a long kiss on the mouth.

"I miss you so much when you're not here, Annie."

"I miss you when I'm not here, too." She leaned her forehead against his.

"Sooner or later, we're going to have to talk about that."

"I know." She nodded. "It's getting a little crazy, all this back-and-forth."

"If I didn't have this case, I'd be able to come to you."

"You can't not be here when something like this is going on. You have to be here."

"Still . . ."

"It's not something we're going to resolve right now, Evan. We'll talk about it. Maybe next weekend."

"Okay. Gotta go." He kissed her again before heading toward the door. "I'll catch up with you later."

"What's Sheridan going to do?"

"Damage control, he says. Whatever the hell that is at this point." He waved and went through the garage as a shortcut to his car, which was parked out front.

Annie walked back inside, locked the door, and went upstairs to gather her things. Back downstairs in twenty minutes with her bag and laptop, she decided to check her e-mail before leaving. She set up the computer on Evan's desk in his study and turned it on. There were e-mails from the office—including one from John asking her to meet with him later that afternoon about the Michigan cases—but nothing from Connor. She turned off the laptop and slipped it into its case, then called the airport to see if there was an earlier flight she could catch back to Virginia. There was one, at 12:45. She booked herself on it and called the office to let John know she'd be there.

She hung up just as her watch beeped the hour. It was nine o'clock. If Will was running true to form today, he'd already been at his desk for several hours. She dialed his cell phone, just in case he'd had a late start and was still in transit or in the field.

"Hey, Annie. Did Evan get my fax?" Will answered, having recognized Annie's number on the caller ID.

"He did. He's going to follow up with the investigating officer from Chicago this morning. Thanks so much. That might prove to be the information he needs to crack that case."

"I hope it helps." He paused, then asked, "What else is on your mind this morning?"

"You know me all too well." She sighed, a long deliberately dramatic sigh, and he laughed.

"You just don't make social calls, Annie. None of us do. Way too busy. So tell, what's on your mind?"

"Melissa Lowery."

"What about her?"

"You know her?"

"I did know her. Not well, but I knew her."

"Everyone says that." She frowned. "Everyone seems to know who she was, but I can't seem to find anyone who really knew her. And no one seems to know why she left the Bureau or where she went."

"Who needs to know?"

"I do. I need to speak with her." Annie explained about the missing report from Dylan's file. "I want to ask her if she remembers what she'd observed that night, if she remembers what she wrote."

"I'm trying to remember if I know anyone who was friends with her." He was silent for a moment. "I saw her in the lounge once or twice with Mia; maybe she knows something."

"Mia Shields?"

"Yes. Give her a call. In the meantime, do you want me to see if I can find an address for Melissa?"

"Would you mind?"

"Not at all. I live for these little intrigues. Let me see what I can do. I'll call you when I have something."

Annie smiled. Not *if,* but *when.*

"Great," she said. "I'll give Mia a call now. You wouldn't happen to have a number for her, would you?"

"Sure. She's in the directory." Will read the number off to Annie.

"Great. I love you, Will."

"Of course you do. Just don't tell Cahill. She has a nasty temper."

Annie laughed and hung up. Miranda Cahill, their fellow agent and Will's live-in love, was as well-known for her even disposition and good humor as she was for her statuesque beauty and her smart-aleck mouth.

Mia Shields answered her phone on the third ring.

"Mia, it's Annie." Annie greeted her and made small talk for a few moments, then said, "I'm trying to track down an agent who left the Bureau about two years ago. Someone said they thought you were a friend of hers."

"Who's that?"

"Melissa Lowery."

"Oh, Melissa. Sure, I knew her."

"Do you know where she is now?"

"No clue. I didn't know her all that well, I just knew her because of Grady."

"Grady?"

"He went out with her a couple of times, then when he stopped calling her, she'd corner me and want to know what was up with him, was he seeing someone else, that sort of thing."

"Grady dated Melissa Lowery?" Annie digested this. "Funny, when I asked your other brothers about her, they claimed not to know her."

"They may not have. I don't think they dated for all that long. If neither Brendan nor Andy was around at the time, they may not have been aware Grady'd taken her out. It was never a serious thing, not that I know of anyway, just a few dates. At least, that was my impression."

"You think Grady knows where I can contact her?"

"You can ask him. I think he's in his office. Want me to transfer you?"

"That would be great, thanks."

"Annie, did she do something . . . ?"

"Oh, no, no. I just wanted to ask her about a report she wrote a few years ago, that's all."

"Oh, okay. She didn't seem like the type to be involved in anything shady."

"I'm sure she wasn't."

"I'll transfer you now. Take care, Annie. I hope to see you soon."

"Me, too. Thanks, Mia."

Annie listened to Grady's phone ring and ring. Finally, his voice mail picked up and she left a message for him to call her about Melissa Lowery. She was on her way to her car when her phone rang.

"Annie, hi." Grady sounded rushed, as if he was hurrying off someplace. "What's this about Melissa Lowery?"

"I wanted to talk to her, but no one seems to know where she is."

"What makes you think I'd know?"

"Mia mentioned you used to date her."

"I wouldn't say I used to date her. We grabbed a movie together a time or two, had dinner once or twice, no big deal." There was a long silence on the phone. "Why do you need to talk to her?"

"Because, as you know, Evan and I were looking over Dylan's file, and there are several items missing, one of which is a report written by Melissa."

"Oh, it probably slipped out of the file or got misplaced. It happens all the time."

"That's what one of your brothers said."

"Well, it happens . . . By the time a file is retired, who knows how many times it's been read through. Things fall out and get tucked back into the wrong file by accident."

"This isn't a retired file, Grady."

"Sorry, Annie. Look, I don't mean to make light of this. It's just a fact of life that papers fall out of files. It happens all the time."

"I guess." She set her bag on the ground next to her rental car while she unlocked the driver's door. "So you don't know where Melissa went after she left Virginia?"

"No, sorry, I don't."

"Any idea where she's from, where her family might be?"

"No, it never came up in conversation."

"You wouldn't happen to know anyone who might know where Melissa is now, would you?"

"No, sorry. We didn't keep in touch, and I didn't go out with her long enough to find out who her friends were. Sorry."

"Yeah, me, too. Thanks, Grady." Annie disconnected the call and tossed her purse onto the front passenger seat. The conversation with Grady had left her dissatisfied. It wasn't that she thought he was lying as much as she felt he'd brushed over certain things. Who dated someone and didn't ask where they were from? Wasn't that part of that whole small-talk thing, like where you went to college? When you're just getting to know someone, wasn't that just basic?

She tucked the overnight bag behind the driver's seat along with the case holding her laptop. Her phone rang again just as she turned the key in the ignition.

"Annie, it's Evan. Would you have time to stop in at Sheridan's office before you head out?"

"Not really. My flight leaves in two hours. What's up?"

"All hell's breaking loose around here. Our killer apparently was very busy last night. Writing letters, including one to the local paper," he hastened to add. "Which is preferable to some of his other nocturnal activities. Sheridan is calling a press conference at noon and was hoping to have you there."

"For what purpose?"

"Between you and me, I think he just wanted to parade his bevy of FBI personnel so that county residents could see that all the big guns are out on this one."

"If he wants me to look over another letter from the killer, I'm happy to do that. He can fax it to my office. But I don't have time to take part in a dog and pony show today. John wants to meet with me later this afternoon, and since he's going to be out of the office all of next week, I can't put him off. There are things he wants to talk about before he leaves tomorrow."

"Hey, no apologies necessary. I agree with you. I'll tell him your plane took off already, I couldn't reach you. No big deal. Frankly, I'd like to take a bye on this myself."

"He wants you there, too? Even though you're not working the case anymore?"

"He wants everyone there. But as soon as he's done talking, I'm outta there. I called the cop in Chicago, and I'm still waiting to hear from him. That's my priority today." He paused. "I don't suppose you heard from Connor?"

"No, but that's not unusual. He'll get to me when he can. I'll let you know as soon as I hear from him." She stole a look at the clock on the dashboard, then turned the key in the ignition. "I need to get going."

"I'll give you a call tonight."

"Maybe we'll have news to exchange by then." She thought of the conversation she'd just had with Grady. "Oh, speaking of news. Guess who used to date Melissa Lowery?"

"Art Sheridan."

She laughed as she pulled away from the curb. "Grady Shields."

"You're kidding?"

"Nope. Of course, he tells me it was just a casual thing, just a few movies and dinners."

"Does he know where she is now?"

"No. He claims to not even know where she's from."

"You say that as if you don't believe him."

"I thought there was something slightly evasive in his responses. I mean, how do you go out with someone and not know where they're from? That's the type of thing you ask when you first meet someone. But maybe that's me. And maybe he just felt it was none of my business who he dated. And of course, it isn't."

"Well, maybe Will can come up with something."

"I'm counting on it." She made a left at the light and headed for the highway. "I have to go. I'm moving into heavy traffic. I'll talk to you tonight."

Annie dropped the phone into her lap and set it to voice mail, then eased onto the four-lane highway that would take her to the airport.

She sped along, reflecting back on the morning's events. The Schoolgirl Slayer had revealed more of his hand by sending yet another letter, which she was eager to read. Evan had a solid contact in his case, and she was a step closer to Melissa Lowery. All in all, it had already been quite a day.

She hoped that the officer in Chicago would have something that would shed light on the deaths of the three young girls—his girls, as Evan had started referring to them. She knew he'd work this case until he solved it, and she loved him for that, for caring about three nameless girls who seemed to go unnoticed in death. What they had been in life had yet to be determined.

There would be no glory for him in the resolution of that case, unlike the case of the Schoolgirl Slayer, which would undoubtedly land Sheridan, Malone, and Weller on CNN and *Good Morning America*. It was more than likely that Sheridan wouldn't even bother to call an all-out media conference once Evan found their killer. Since they were lumping these deaths in with the others—at least for now—there'd be no band playing for Evan, no recognition of his dedication and hard work.

Unless, of course, there was a cop involved. That would be news.

Spoken like a true cynic, she thought wryly.

As far as her own search was concerned, Will would come through for her, of that she was certain. God only knew where that trail would lead, or what she'd find, once she finally found Melissa.

13

It was almost 6:00 p.m. when Annie closed the door of John Mancini's office behind her. She was stiff from sitting, earlier on the plane on her way back from Philadelphia, later in the day for the two-hour meeting that had just broken up. She rolled her shoulders while she walked to her own office, then stood next to her desk as she listened to her voice mail. When she'd heard all the messages, she smiled, snapped off the light, and took the elevator to the floor below.

"I just got your message." She stood at the doorway to Will Fletcher's office. "I'm glad I caught you before you left. You have something for me?"

"I was just getting ready to close up shop. I wasn't sure if you were in the building. Someone said they'd seen you earlier." Will leaned back in his chair. "Come on in, and I'll—"

"Will . . . oh, hi, Annie, I didn't know you were here." Brendan Shields stood in the doorway. "We're all heading over to Pike's. It's my brother Andrew's birthday. You should come, too, Annie."

"That's the best offer I've had all week, since my girl is still in Pennsylvania and I've got nothing better to do." Will stood and stretched. "I was just getting ready to leave anyway. How 'bout it, Annie? Come with us to Pike's?"

"I think I'll pass. I've been away all week and have to leave town again tomorrow. I have a lot of work to catch up on and a presentation to prepare. But thanks, Brendan. Next time."

"I'll hold you to that." Brendan looked back at Will. "You ready now?"

"I was just packing up. You can go on. I'll meet you there."

"I don't mind waiting," Brendan told him.

"If you're sure . . ." Will piled some papers into his briefcase, hesitated momentarily, then folded one and handed it to Annie.

"Before I forget, here are the directions to that restaurant you and I talked about," he said.

"Thanks." She stuck the paper in her pocket without looking at it.

"Which restaurant is that?" Brendan asked.

"Oh, a crab place on the other side of the bay. In Rock Hall. It's a favorite of Miranda's and mine," Will told him.

"Hey, I'm always up for crabs," Brendan said. "What's the name of it?"

"I'll tell you about it while we're walking to Pike's. We are walking, right?"

"Sure, why not? It's just a few blocks." Brendan waited at the door for Will, then held it open for Annie before closing it. "Sure you don't want to come down for a quick beer and a burger?"

"I'm sure, but thanks."

"Catch you next time, then." Brendan paused, then asked, "Say, you still unofficially working on Dylan's case?"

"The file's still open, so yes. I'm still taking a look at it."

"Find anything we missed?"

"No. Nothing yet." She smiled pleasantly in spite of the fact that Brendan's attitude seemed annoyingly patronizing. "But then again, I haven't had much time. It's been a busy week. I promise I'll let you know if we learn something new."

"Were you able to find that agent you were looking for? What's her name . . ."

"Melissa Lowery."

"Yeah, her. You find her yet? Has her report turned up?" He stuck his hands in his pocket and struck a casual pose.

"No." She glanced at Will, but as he gave no indication of having any knowledge of Melissa's whereabouts, she followed his lead. For whatever reason, he didn't seem inclined to share whatever information he'd found.

"I'll keep asking around. Maybe she's been in touch with someone. I can let you know."

"Thanks, Brendan. I'd appreciate it."

Annie fingered the piece of paper in her pocket. "And thanks again, Will, for the directions."

"Anytime, Annie." He slapped a friendly hand gently on her back. "Anytime . . ."

Annie walked with the two men to the elevator, her patience put to the test while the car stopped three times on the way to the lobby. She wanted nothing more than to open the folded sheet of paper and see what Will had found for her, but was forced to wait until she'd said good-bye to her coworkers. Once in her car, she opened the paper and read eagerly.

Grinning, she refolded the paper and stuck it in the top of her purse. She'd known Will wouldn't let her down.

Melissa Lowery was living in West Priest, Montana, as Mariana Gray. Will hadn't found a phone number, but he'd found an address.

The minute Annie arrived at her apartment, she checked the travel website for flight connections from Seattle, where she'd be at a conference from Tuesday afternoon through Wednesday night, to the airport closest to West Priest.

"Looks like that would be Great Falls," she murmured as she studied the flight schedules.

The Wednesday-night flight wouldn't get her in until late, and she'd still have to find a place to stay. But if she booked the 6:00 a.m. flight on Thursday, she'd be in Great Falls by 12:30. She could rent a car and be in West Priest—thirty-five miles according to a map she located through Google—by three. West Priest didn't appear to be a very big town. Surely someone there would know Melissa.

A few clicks of the keyboard later, she'd booked the flight to Great Falls, a room at the closest motel for Thursday night, just in case, and a flight to Philly on Friday morning. Satisfied with her arrangements, she checked her e-mail before logging off the computer, hoping for some word from Connor, but there was nothing.

She showered and dried her hair and wrapped herself in her favorite robe, then went into her small bedroom she used as an office. She sat on the edge of the desk to listen to her phone messages.

"Annie, it's Will. I didn't want to say anything about Melissa in front of Brendan—no particular reason except that I figure if she's taken such pains to disappear—and believe me, it wasn't easy finding her—well, she must have a reason. Makes you wonder what she's hiding, doesn't it? Or from whom?" Will took a deep breath. "Anyway, you missed a hell of a party. All the Shieldses were out in force—except Connor, of course—though it started breaking up earlier than I'd have expected. Andrew apparently has a late date, and Grady has already downed his limit and has gone home, so that leaves me with Brendan, Mia, and Chloe Snyder, you remember her?

Well, keep in touch, hear? Have a safe trip to the West Coast, and good luck connecting with Melissa. Let me know what you find."

The line went dead and she erased the message. The next was Evan. "Annie, give me a call when you get in."

One hang-up, and another message from Evan.

She dialed his number and counted the rings. On the fourth, right before the answering machine picked up, he answered.

"How was your meeting?" he asked.

"Long. How was the press conference?"

"Pretty much what we expected. Did you have time to look over the letter from the killer to Fox News?"

"I don't have a copy."

"I faxed it to you."

"Oh." She crossed the room and took several sheets from her machine's in-tray. "There are a couple of faxes here . . . wait . . . yes, it's here. Want me to look at it now?"

"If you have a minute. But hurry up, I have news I'm itching to share."

"The fax can wait, then. Did you hear something from Chicago?"

"I thought you'd never ask." She could hear the smile in his voice. "This cop—he's a detective now, Don Manley—has been looking into the case for months. He said he has several files he thinks I should take a look at."

"Are you going to meet with him?"

"I'm flying out first thing tomorrow morning. He said he didn't want to discuss it on the phone, but if I came out there, he'd tell me everything he knows."

"Sounds intriguing."

"I am so antsy to talk to this guy, Annie. It sounded as if he's got some really hot information."

"Sheridan's okay with you going out of town for a day or so in the middle of the investigation?"

"Sheridan's attention right now is on Jackie Weller's case."

"How's that going?"

"They've interviewed everyone at the country club and the pool company; no luck there. Apparently, there was some mix-up in scheduling with the owner of the landscaping company, but I understand they're on for first thing tomorrow morning to talk to his crews."

"I'm starting to feel they've pushed the limits on this, Evan. This guy's gone what, over a week without another body turning up? He's got to be due. He's got to be jonesing for a kill right about now. If they don't get him within the next twenty-four hours, they're going to have another dead body on their hands."

"Unfortunately, I think you might be right."

"What information did they release to the press?"

"Only that they had traces of carpet fibers, years, makes, models of possible vehicles. Nothing about the grass clippings, though."

"Good. That's how they'll nail him, you know."

"You FBI types think you know it all, don't you?"

She knew he was teasing but felt compelled to defend herself anyway.

"Hey, you study behavior, sometimes patterns emerge. Sometimes you read the patterns correctly, sometimes you don't. It's part science, part art. Neither is exact. You just do your best to read the signs and hope you're interpreting them correctly."

"Annie, I was joking."

"I know." She sighed. "I guess I'm just giving you the speech I wanted to give Sheridan the other day."

"Why didn't you?"

"I guess because ultimately, he's your boss."

"Don't ever let that stop you. I'm a big boy."

"Okay, then, how about I felt it would have been unprofessional and borderline rude to correct him in front of the others."

"That's much more acceptable."

"I have news, too." She curled up in the chair and pulled her legs up under her. "Will found Melissa Lowery."

"He really is good, isn't he?" Without waiting for an answer, he asked, "Where is she?"

"Montana, living under the name Mariana Gray. I'm going to fly there on Thursday morning. I'm praying she'll talk to me, and that she remembers what she put in that report. If I'm really lucky, maybe she'll have kept a copy." Annie bit her bottom lip. "That's assuming she'll talk to me."

"Why wouldn't she?"

"I don't know. She's gone to such lengths to conceal herself out there, even changed her name. That's pretty extreme."

"Maybe she just got stressed out with the whole routine, you know? It wouldn't be the first time someone opted out of law enforcement and just tried to start their life over. And you know, she could have gotten married, which would account for the name change."

"That would explain the last-name change, but not the first."

"You think she's hiding from something?"

"Or someone. Yes, it's possible. She might just slam the door in my face once I tell her who I am."

"Assuming that she does speak with you, do you think there's anything in that report that will tell you something you don't already know?"

"Probably not," she admitted, "but it bothers me, that her report disappeared, then she disappeared. Then the other agent whose report is missing, Lou Raymond, is killed in a freak car accident. It's making me uneasy, the more I think about it. It just seems . . . weirdly coincidental."

"And anyone who knows you, knows you don't believe in coincidences."

"Have you ever met an FBI agent who did?"

"Now that you mention it, I guess I haven't."

He was silent for a moment, and she could almost see him, one elbow leaning on the desk in his office, the other resting on the arm of the chair. He'd have his shoes off and his shirt unbuttoned to the third button and his shirttails out. The familiarity of the image brought a smile to her face.

"So what are you going to do now?" she asked.

"Right now, I'm going to bed and praying to God the phone doesn't ring so that I can get one good night's sleep this week. Then, at the crack of dawn, I'm going to go into the office and copy the file on my girls, make an extra set of photos and lab reports to take to Chicago. I want to give Detective Manley a copy of everything I have on this guy. I'm hoping between the two of us . . ."

"You're hoping to find what you need."

"Exactly. I want to find whatever it is we need to catch this bastard. Bastards, I should say. There are obviously several at work here."

"In the long run, that should make it easier to solve. The more of them there are, the more likely it is that one of them will screw up eventually."

"One could only hope." He yawned. "Sorry, babe."

"No apologies necessary. Get some sleep, Evan. I'll be turning in, too, in a few minutes."

"Wish you were here, Annie."

"So do I." She stifled a yawn of her own. "But I'll be there by Friday afternoon, Friday night at the latest. We should have a lot to talk about while we're working on that deck."

"Well, here's hoping we both find the answers we're looking for. You in Montana, me in Chicago . . ."

Annie hung up the phone and looked for her glasses so she could read the fax. The letter was exactly what she'd been led to expect.

DEAR FOX NEWS PEOPLE:
I THINK YOU NEED TO TALK TO D.A. SHERIDAN IN AVON
COUNTY AND ASK HIM WHY HE DIDN'T TELL YOU

ABOUT THE LETTER I SENT TO HIM EARLIER IN THE WEEK. I TOLD HIM THAT I DID NOT KILL THOSE OTHER THREE GIRLS—YOU KNOW ABOUT THOSE THREE GIRLS, RIGHT? THE ONES NO ONE KNOWS WHO THEY ARE? I DID NOT KILL THEM AND DO NOT LIKE THAT EVERYONE IS SAYING I DID. THERE IS A COPYCAT KILLER IN AVON COUNTY AND NO ONE IS LOOKING FOR HIM. THE GIRLS HE KILLS ARE NOT LIKE MY GIRLS. ANY IDIOT COULD TELL YOU THAT.

ALSO, I TOLD D.A. SHERIDAN THAT I WANTED TO BE REFERRED TO AS THE SCHOOLGIRL SLAYER. DID HE TELL YOU THAT?

I DIDN'T THINK SO. SINCE HE DIDN'T TELL YOU ANYTHING, I AM FORCED TO TELL YOU MYSELF. I THINK HE THINKS HE IS PLAYING A GAME WITH ME. HE SHOULD KNOW THAT THIS IS NOT A GAME.

I THINK YOU ARE SMARTER THAN HE IS AND WILL CALL ME BY MY NEW NAME.

THANK YOU.

THE SCHOOLGIRL SLAYER

More posturing, more of the same demand for attention. Interesting that he hasn't mentioned any new kills, though, and has made no threats.

Annie read through the letter again.

He has to know that the police are closing in on him. Maybe that's why he's not being too cocky. He's just setting the record straight, as he sees it, and trying to take full advantage of his fifteen minutes.

"Your days as a free man are coming to an end, buddy," she murmured as she folded the fax and tossed it onto her desk.

In the morning, she'd call Sheridan and discuss the case with him, give him the benefit of her thoughts on the matter. Don't react publicly. Don't do anything, because he'll be in custody within twenty-four hours. That was the reaction of both her gut and her intellect, but Sheridan would do whatever he felt was in his best interest. Only he knew what that was.

Annie locked up her house and turned off the lights. She got into bed and searched for the remote control for the TV on the stand opposite her bed. She found it under her pillow and tried to remember when she might have put it there. She watched the news until she fell asleep.

She slept later than she'd intended the next morning, and when she awoke, the television was still on. She turned up the volume while she washed her face in the bathroom steps away from her bed, and had just started to brush her teeth when she caught scraps of dialogue. She stuck her head around the corner, her toothbrush still in her mouth, in time to see a handcuffed man being helped into a police car.

". . . who, according to detectives here in Avon County is the self-proclaimed Schoolgirl Slayer, apprehended early this morning by county detectives . . ."

The camera zoomed in for a close-up of a man with thinning brown hair and glasses, wearing a polo shirt with some kind of logo on it. Annie got as close to the screen as she could, but still couldn't make out the writing.

When the phone rang, she knew it would be Evan.

"Do you ever get tired of being right?" he asked.

"This one wasn't so tough. I figured once you narrowed the field, he'd be easy to spot."

"Can you guess who spotted him?"

"Cahill."

He swore softly under his breath and she laughed out loud.

"Miranda has a lot of experience. This is far from being her first serial-killer case. They sent her because she has an uncanny knack for seeing things that other people miss," she said. "Are you going to tell me who and how, or do I have to hang up and get the details from the TV?"

"His name is Albert Vandergris. He is, just as you had predicted, thirty-five years old and he works for the landscaper who did the lawns for all the victims' families. Has worked for them, cutting lawns, for twelve years."

"Sounds good so far," she told him, "but it wasn't a prediction."

"Right. Anyway, Jackie called the owner of the landscaping company yesterday, set it up to talk to his employees before they started for work around seven this morning. All the crews report in by six, get the day's assignments, pick up the trucks and their equipment. So Jackie shows up with the three from the FBI and a few other detectives, and the owner explained to his crews what was going on. He had all the guys waiting there in the barn and starts calling the men up, one by one, to speak with Jackie. And while she's talking to workers, Cahill wanders out of the barn and around the back. Who do you think she finds trying to slip out the back door?"

"Albert."

"You're really good at this, aren't you."

"Yes, I am. So Miranda nabs him and brings him in?"

"Not until she and Albert had a little chat."

"And she managed to get him to confess."

"Yeah, she did." Evan's voice held a touch of awe. "She told him she'd read the letter he'd written to the news station and pointed out the grammatical errors."

"And he got his back up and began to argue with her?"

"How do you know all this? You already talk to her this morning?"

"No. But she did this once before, in Indiana. Almost the exact same scenario." Annie laughed again. "But let me guess, Jackie is going for the credit here?"

"I'm betting there will be a press conference by noon this morning, complete with a carefully worded statement, prepared and read by the district attorney, praising the work of the county detectives, especially lead detective Weller, and thanking the FBI for their cooperation. I'm almost sorry I won't be here for it."

"That little weasel."

"Yeah, well, at least they got one killer off the street."

"Which leaves your case. Is Sheridan going to make the announcement that Albert is not the killer of these girls?"

"I don't know what he's going to do. I'm hoping he doesn't. I'm hoping whoever is involved with this thinks he's gotten away with it."

"I agree. Keep him guessing. Even though Vandergris has already said he hasn't killed those girls, I think it's best to keep everyone guessing on that point. I wouldn't address it until I had to."

"Yeah, maybe the killer—killers—will do something stupid. And it's not as if anyone seems to care much, one way or another, about my girls. Their deaths haven't gotten too much attention these past few weeks. All the focus has been on the other girls, the kids from the nice families and the good neighborhoods."

"Unfortunately, you know that makes better press. And like it or not, this was a story that had strong emotional appeal and a certain amount of built-in sensationalism. But the lack of focus on your vics may work to your advantage."

"Well, either way, I imagine the D.A. will find a way to keep Vandergris in the foreground for a few more weeks so he can wring every potential future vote out of it."

"Cynic."

"Oh yeah. My middle name."

"Well, with luck, Detective Manley will be able to give you some insights that could help lead you in the right direction."

"I'm afraid that might be too much to hope for." Someone spoke in the background, and Evan covered the phone with his hand. When he came back on the line, he said, "Gotta run. They're calling my flight. See if you can catch some of the press conference this morning."

While she finished packing for her trip, Annie surfed the channels hoping to find coverage of the conference, but apparently it was being carried only locally at the time. Perhaps later in the day, one of the networks would broadcast it, but she was likely to miss it.

Already running late, Annie turned off the TV and closed her suitcase. The Schoolgirl Slayer was in custody, her interest in him on the wane. Her attention was focused now on those who still escaped detection, those who, somewhere, were waiting to strike again.

14

Evan sat on a metal folding chair in the cramped windowless room
that Detective Donald Manley called his office, and read through
the reports that had been copied for him.

Manley, a tall gaunt man with long fingers and a long sharp
nose, went about his business of making calls on a battered-looking
phone from a desk that appeared to have been abused at the hands
of many. Occasionally, Evan would ask a question or two between
Manley's calls, but other than that, there had been little conversation between the two men.

Each was following his own agenda. Manley's focus was on
tracking down a witness to a shooting the night before. Evan's was
on following the story Manley had laid out for him.

According to the file, eight months earlier, the bodies of three young girls, each killed by a single bullet to the back of the head, had been found in Bonsall Park in the city. For a while, it appeared the case—the press had dubbed it the Bonsall Park Murders—would be retired to the cold-case room, since there were no witnesses and no suspects. But through networking and scanning the Internet, Manley had located other cases that had a similar feel to them. So far, after having made endless phone calls, he'd found that victims in two other cities—Boston and New Orleans—had little stars tattooed on the upper part of their left hips. Boston's two, Chicago's three, and New Orleans's four accounted for nine young girls with tattooed stars. Evan's three made it an even dozen.

"Why do you suppose it took New Orleans so long to put this together?" Evan asked when Manley had ended his phone conversation.

"Only two of the bodies were found in the city. The others were found in two other parishes and appeared to be unconnected. It wasn't until a curious detective in New Orleans noticed the tattoos that he started looking for cases where the vics were similarly marked."

"How did you find him?"

"I went state by state on the computer, looking for young girls who'd been killed execution style. These cases stood out." Manley rubbed a hand across the stubble on his chin, a telltale sign he'd been on the job since early that morning.

"Then there's a possibility there could be more," Evan said softly.

"Sure." Manley nodded wearily. "We can only track what's been entered. We both know that there are departments that aren't up to snuff when it comes to using computers. Some of the smaller departments don't have personnel who can spend time entering the data. Others just aren't comfortable with the technology, don't ask me why."

Manley removed his glasses and rubbed his eyes slowly.

"Come on." He stood and stretched. "Let's take a ride."

Evan drove his rental car because the air-conditioning in Manley's department-issued vehicle hadn't worked for the past two summers and he hadn't gotten around to getting it fixed. The day had been hot and humid, and the sun had several hours to go before it set. Following Manley's directions, Evan wended his way through busy city streets, then pulled into a broad parking lot when they reached their destination. Somehow, Evan had known they'd end up here. It was exactly where he'd have taken Manley if their positions were reversed.

They got out of the car without speaking, and Evan followed his host along a winding path that led to a stream that tumbled over a rocky bottom.

"Man-made." Manley pointed to the stream as they crossed over it on a wooden footbridge. "They brought the rocks in, stocked it with fish and other water creatures. Those trees along the banks? All brought in by some big-time landscaper from back east. Designs city parks. The city spent a fortune to make the place look as natural as possible."

They continued along the path until they reached a fountain that sat in the center of the convergence of four paths.

"They were all found there, in the fountain. Draped over the wall, facedown in the water." Manley walked closer, pointing as he spoke. "My victim number one right here. Number two, eight, ten feet to the right. And over here, my vic number three." His jaw clenched almost imperceptibly. "She didn't look like she was older than thirteen, fourteen."

"Which one of them was wearing the seeds around her neck?"

"Little number three. That's the only clue I had, going into this. Those bean seeds. It was curiosity that led me to send them over to the university to have them analyzed. I never dreamed they would prove to be the lead that could eventually help us to find her killers."

He turned to look Evan in the eye.

"And I will find them. It may take a while longer, but I will find them. I like to think she brought those seeds with her so she'd always have a part of her home with her. It would be fitting, don't you think, if those seeds are the connection that helps us to find that home so we can take her back?"

"Have you thought of circulating her picture and those of the others, through the press down in Santa Estela?" Evan asked.

"I did send the girls' photos down to the police in Cortés City, the capital. I got an acknowledgment by way of a phone call." Manley kicked at the side of the fountain. "The Cortés police informed me that many kids from those poor countries—such as Santa Estela—go missing every day. Some of them are from villages well beyond the city limits. We'd have to get very, very lucky to get an ID on any of these kids, he tells me. Chances are, anyone who'd recognize them doesn't read the papers. He says some of those villages are pretty damned remote."

"In other words, don't waste his time."

"Pretty much, yeah, that was the impression I got. He said that it was likely, if the girls were from one of those remote towns, the families have stopped looking for them already."

"Thinking, what, that the kids are runaways to the city? That they've been eaten by alligators or whatever swims in the rivers down there? Where do they think their daughters have gone?"

"Kidnapped by the slavers. A huge percentage of the kids that go missing are sold into slavery. In some cases, the parents, or other family members, have sold the kids to the middlemen, the ones who obtain the kids through whatever means—kidnapping if not outright purchase—who then deal with the slavers. The traffic in slaves—particularly children—is a big business in some countries right now.

Some child-advocacy groups are saying as many as two million children could be involved worldwide. Others are more conservative, but still . . ."

"Yeah. One is too many. How does a parent think his or her kid was caught up in this and not make any effort to find her? Wouldn't you be moving heaven and earth to bring her back if she were your kid?"

"Or he. As many young boys as girls are sold into slavery. There's a huge market for little boys, especially overseas, which is where a lot of these kids end up."

"So you think our girls were sold to slavers in Santa Estela and brought to this country . . ."

Manley nodded. "And branded with those little stars so there's no mistaking whose property they are. Then they're sent up here, to the US, by boat, by car, by truck. Sometimes they're literally walked across the border. A buddy of mine in immigration told me that anywhere from fifteen to twenty thousand are smuggled into this country every year." Manley paused, then added, "Most of them are just out-and-out kidnapped, but so many others come voluntarily, under false pretenses."

"Promised jobs that will pay enough that they can send money back to support their families at home. I read something about that recently."

"Right, except they have to pay off their transportation expenses first. These bastards charge them thousands of dollars to get to this country, then make them work off the fees in the brothels. Of course, they're rarely released, even after their supposed debt is paid off. Very few ever go to the authorities because they're afraid they'll be killed or their families back home will be killed. For the most part, they don't trust authority because the authorities all along the way have turned a blind eye and have let these terrible things happen to them because they're on the take. Sometimes, the kids have been told that their families were the ones who sold them in the first place, so they figure they have nothing to return to." He smiled wryly. "In a lot of cases, they're right."

"You figure that's the case with these girls?"

"I hate to even venture a guess with these kids. On the one hand, I know that Santa Estela and the surrounding countries are really poor. Some of the big banana plantations have been sold and the monopoly has driven wages down, so we're talking about real hardships here. Poverty that you and I can't really comprehend, so there's a good chance a family member turned the girl over for some cash. On the other hand, kidnapping is so rampant in Mexico and South and Central America, your guess is as good as mine as to how these kids got here."

Manley stood for a few long quiet minutes, deep in thought, in front of the spot where the body of the youngest victim had been found.

"This little girl had cocaine in her system. Sometimes, when a girl's uncooperative, they force her to take drugs, get her addicted. Cocaine, crystal meth, whatever it takes. That way, they can control her, through her addiction. She isn't likely to try to leave as long as she's dependent on her captors for her drugs." He averted his eyes, absently scuffing one shoe in the dirt at the base of the fountain where the girl's body had lain. "I like to think that this one fought hard; that's why they had to drug her. Because she wouldn't give up the fight."

"You know there have to be federal agencies involved here. Have you contacted Immigration, the FBI, the CIA . . . ?"

"All of the above. I've spoken to every one of them, and they tell me they're working on it, but that tells me nothing at all." He swore under his breath. "More accurately, it tells me there's a massive cluster fuck going on over this. They're all so damned territorial, you know? No matter what they say, no one wants to share. That's never going to change, no matter what they tell us. Which means that except in maybe an individual case here and there, no one is talking to anyone else. And of course, that just opens the door for more of the same."

Manley shook his head slowly.

"Frankly, I don't see where it's ever going to end."

Manley turned abruptly and walked back toward the parking lot. Evan followed, a thousand times more depressed than he had been when he'd arrived in Chicago early that morning. He found Manley waiting at the car when he found his way back to the parking lot.

"So what do you do about this?" Evan held the keys to the car in his right hand, but made no move to unlock the door.

"I don't think that anything can be done, frankly. I think it's way too big."

"Then why did you call me out here if you're convinced you'll never solve the case?"

"I didn't say I didn't think I could solve this case. Sooner or later, someone will have information to trade. I've got the word out; someone will step up to the plate when they're getting hauled off for possession with intent to deliver and their back is against the wall. It may take me a while, Detective Crosby, but I have every intention of solving my case. If it's the last thing I do on this earth, I will find the sons of bitches who murdered these kids. But the overall thing, this traffic business, that's something else. But my girls . . . I want to take care of my girls."

"That's how I feel," Evan told him. "I want to solve this for their sakes."

"I know." Manley met his eyes across the roof of the car. "That's why I wanted you to come out here."

"Sorry?" Evan asked.

"I needed to know there was someone else who really cared about what happened to these kids. That someone else is willing to keep on this, even after everyone else is convinced that it was a waste of time."

"No one's told me it's a waste of time, Detective Manley," Evan said as he unlocked the car doors.

"Someone will." Manley swung the passenger door open. "Sooner or later, someone will . . ."

15

Annie topped off the tank of the rented Ford Taurus sedan at the station advertised as the last gas for 167 miles. She had started out from the airport with a full tank, but wasn't sure how far she'd have to drive to find Melissa Lowery and figured that "Last Gas" sign must have been put there for a reason.

*Mariana Gray,* she corrected herself. She'd have to assume that Melissa was known around West Priest as Mariana Gray.

The last road sign told her that Priest lay twenty-four miles up the road, but Annie had driven in the west before and had found that sometimes the mileages weren't exactly accurate. It appeared from the map she'd picked up at the airport that West Priest lay just a few miles beyond Priest. She should be able to make the drive in well under an hour.

She was pleased to find herself arriving at Priest a mere forty minutes later. She went straight to the post office, where she was given directions that would take her three miles outside of town on Old Fort Road. When she reached West Priest, the postmistress assured her, she'd know it.

The road between the two towns consisted of two skinny lanes of flat gravel with no shoulder on either side. The scenery, however, made it worth the caution one was forced to take in maneuvering the roadway. In the distance rose the East Front of the Continental Divide, with its scraggy plateaus and rolling grassy hills. Annie stopped once, pulling off onto the edge of the hard-earthed field to photograph the landscape. She would want to share its beauty with Evan, and knew words alone could not do it justice.

The tiny town of West Priest grew on both sides of the highway, two blocks in either direction from the intersection with Main Street, which, as its name implied, was the primary thoroughfare, with one bank and three churches. A post office shared a white clapboard building with an insurance agent and a flower shop. Next door a sign advertised guns and ammunition, and across the street was a general store with a "Help Wanted" sign in the window.

Annie parked in front of the post office and, as she'd done in Priest, asked directions from the sixtysomething man behind the counter.

"I'm looking for Big Creek Road," Annie told the postal clerk.

"South or North?" the man asked.

"I don't know." Annie frowned and searched her pockets for the paper upon which Will had written Melissa's address. "It only says Big Creek Road."

"Who you looking for?"

"Mel—" She corrected herself: "Mariana Gray."

"She's out on East Big Creek."

"I thought you said South or North." Annie frowned again. "How could it be East, too?"

"Different creek." He returned to whatever it was he'd been doing when she came in. To Annie, it looked as if he'd been counting stamps.

"Could I get directions?"

"Not from me." He shook his head. "We're not allowed to give out anyone's address."

"You're not giving me the address," Annie said patiently. "I have the address. You only have to tell me how to get there."

"I don't think we're supposed to do that. You could probably get directions from Sullivan's, though. Someone there will know."

"Sullivan's?"

"Little restaurant around the corner. Only restaurant in town."

"Thanks."

Sullivan's was, as promised, just around the corner. Set in a little building made of ugly rough stone, it had a tinny bell that rang when the door was opened and a chalkboard right inside listing the day's specials. Annie took a table and ordered the soup of the day—black bean—and a small salad. The waitress appeared to be assessing her—hair to clothes to jewelry—even as she took the order.

"By the way, the man at the post office told me you might know how I could get to Mariana Gray's place," Annie said when the waitress returned with her salad, an uninspired pile of lettuce adorned with three ragged slices of cucumber and some anemic-looking tomatoes.

"You a friend of hers?"

"Friend of a friend. I know she's on Big Creek Road, but I don't know the address."

"Out there, there are no addresses, not like we have here in town."

"How do I know which house is hers?"

The waitress continued her silent evaluation, and apparently decided Annie looked harmless enough.

"To get to Mariana's place, you just go straight back there at the intersection, then go right at the bridge, then straight for about four, five miles. Mariana's is the house you come to on the left side of the road."

"Thanks."

"Welcome. You ready for your soup?"

Annie nodded, and checked her voice mail for messages while she waited for the soup to arrive. She hoped it would prove to be tastier than the salad had been.

It was excellent, a rich spicy broth filled with dark beans, tomatoes, small pieces of beef, and topped with a dollop of sour cream. After three days of hotel food, Annie savored every spoonful.

She bought a Diet Coke in a to-go container and a brownie to take with her in the car. On the way out of town, she passed the motel where she'd made reservations for that night. She debated whether or not to stop, then decided against it. She was anxious to meet Melissa, curious to see what the woman remembered and what light, if any, she could shed on Dylan's death.

Melissa Lowery's mailbox stood at the end of a wide driveway that cut through a dusty front lawn and bore the name GRAY in blue letters that looked hand-painted. Wavy green vines bearing yellow flowers wrapped around the white metal box. A double garage sat off to the left by itself, and Annie walked over to peek through the windows. A dark blue Ford Explorer was parked inside next to a John Deere riding mower and a workbench upon which rested some garden tools. A hoe stood next to the bench, and a collection of various shovels leaned against the side wall. Behind the garage was a barn that appeared to have seen better days, and a small empty paddock. Across the back of the property ran a dense hedgerow, and

Annie wondered as she walked back to the house if it marked the back boundary. If so, depending on how far to either side the property stretched, this would give Melissa several acres.

The house itself had once been painted yellow, but over the years had faded to a pale dull ivory. There were no plants around the foundation, but a pot of dark pink begonias stood on the bottom step of the concrete porch that led to the front door. Annie looked for a doorbell, but there was none, so she knocked instead. When there was no response, she knocked again, louder.

Leaning her ear to the door, she listened for sounds of life. All she could hear was a faint sort of humming. It took a moment before the sound registered with her. She stepped back from the door, then peered into the nearest window. Inside, the glass was covered with flies.

"Oh God, no . . ."

She reached for her phone and dialed 911.


The sheriff arrived in less than ten minutes. It wasn't every day he got a phone call from someone identifying themselves as an FBI agent who was standing on the front porch of a house that appeared to be filled with blowflies. They both knew what that most likely meant.

"I take it you didn't go inside," Sheriff Al Brody said as he got out of his car.

"No. If there's a body in there, as I suspect there might be, it could be a crime scene."

"Do you mind showing me some identification?" he asked.

Annie dug in her purse and pulled out her badge as he reached for the doorknob. "You must suspect it, too, or you wouldn't have gotten out here so quickly."

"Let's just say I was intrigued." He glanced at her credential, appeared satisfied, then turned the knob.

The door did not open. "Let me run around back, see if some-thing's open back there . . ."

A minute or two later, Brody opened the front door from the inside, holding a hand over his mouth.

"Do you have something to cover my shoes with? Paper boots, maybe?" she asked.

"Not with me. You sure you want to come in? This ain't pretty," he told Annie, and blocked her entry into the house.

"It never is." She stepped inside, careful to watch where she walked lest she step on evidence.

"Well, I guess this won't be the first time you've seen a body after the maggots have gotten to it." Brody moved to the left to permit her to pass.

"Not by a long shot."

"She's in there, between the living room and the dining room." He followed her, his hand still covering his nose and mouth. "At least, I'm assuming it's a she, going by all that hair. It can be tough to tell sometimes. I've known men with long hair, but none who wore pretty little flower barrettes. You know whose place this is?"

"She was going by the name Mariana Gray." Annie knelt a foot from the body and studied it carefully, looking past the writhing mass that was the second generation of maggots and focusing on searching for an obvious cause of death.

"Going by?"

"Her real name is Melissa Lowery. She's a former FBI agent. At least, I'm assuming that's who she is. You're going to need to con-firm that." Annie looked up at him. "What do you think, two weeks, give or take?"

"Judging by the condition of the body, yeah, I'd say she's been dead around two weeks."

The body was dressed in jeans and a red sweatshirt worn over a white cotton turtleneck. A thin gold bracelet circled what was left of her right wrist, and about her neck hung a small bezel-set diamond on a gold chain. On the third finger of her left hand was a wide gold ring. As the sheriff had noted, her long brown hair was held up on one side in a barrette fashioned out of a yellow silk flower.

"Driver's license says Mariana Gray." Brody stood in the doorway holding a tan leather wallet.

"There's no sign of blood," Annie murmured to herself as much as to the sheriff. "No sign of trauma to the head that I can see, but with all the insect activity, it's going to take an autopsy to determine cause of death."

She looked up at Brody and asked, "How's your M.E.?"

"He's good. He's real good." He reached in his pocket for his phone. "And I guess now's as good a time as any to bring him in. I'll be right back, Dr. McCall. I'm going to have to step outside for some better reception. I need to call in the troops."

Alone with what was left of the woman she assumed was Melissa Lowery, Annie tried to ignore what part her inquiries into the woman's whereabouts might have played in her death.

We don't know if she was murdered, Annie silently protested against the first twinges of guilt. She could have been ill, she could have had . . .

What? Annie asked herself. What could she have had that might have caused her to die at the same time as I was looking for her? How coincidental could it be?

Annie just hadn't seen enough true coincidences in her life to start believing in them now.

She stood and began to take note of her surroundings. The house was small but neat and well kept, the walls freshly painted, the furniture relatively new. She walked from one room to the next and found the entire house had a just-decorated feel to it. However long Melissa had been in Montana, she'd only just recently started to feather her nest.

A few family photos stood in a line across the mantel over the living-room fireplace. The same young, dark-haired woman appeared in several of them, and Annie thought that might be Melissa. In one photo, she appeared with a younger woman and an older man, a large black dog on the ground in front of them. In another, there was just her and the dog. In a third, she sat on a large outcropping of rock, with two other young women, all of whom bore a strong resemblance. Sisters, maybe, Annie thought. The older man might be the dad.

Annie went into the living room and straight to the dark green leather bag that had spilled from a chair onto the floor. She looked over the contents—makeup case, cell phone, a small address book, several keys on a brass chain from which a large letter *M* dangled. Her fingers itched to pick up the address book and the phone, but she hesitated, not wanting to add her prints to the surface or to smudge those already there.

"You wouldn't happen to have a pair of rubber gloves I could borrow, do you?" she asked Sheriff Brody when he came back into the house.

"I might have, in the trunk. I can check," he said, but made no attempt to go back outside to his car.

"Was there something you wanted to ask me, Sheriff Brody?" Annie stood and folded her arms across her chest.

"I'm wondering what your interest is here. What brought you here. What business you had with Ms. Gray. She wasn't a friend of yours, judging by your reaction." His eyes narrowed. "You've had no visible emotional reaction to seeing her body, the way you would if you knew the deceased. So it's got me wondering why you're here."

"Agent Lowery was involved in an operation that took place a few years back. Recently, some questions about the operation itself have come up, and in reviewing the file, it was discovered that the report she wrote is missing. I needed to ask her a few questions about what was in the report."

He nodded slowly, as if mulling over the information.

"It just occurred to someone in the FBI that her report was missing? After a couple of years?"

"I don't know when the report went missing."

"And you came all the way out here to ask her about it?"

"Yes."

"Why didn't you just call her?"

"I had a presentation to give in Seattle this week, so I thought I'd make a stopover and speak with her in person."

He went silent again, thinking it through.

"Still seems like a long way to come, when a phone call would have gotten you the same information."

He paused, as if waiting for her comment. When none was forthcoming, he said, "Unless for some reason you thought she wouldn't speak to you."

"There's a good chance she may not have," Annie told him.

"What are you basing that on?"

"She's gone to great lengths to change her identity. You don't go to all that trouble unless you don't want to be found."

"Maybe she was being stalked. Maybe she just needed some peace and quiet." He leaned back against the doorjamb. "I grew up back east. Can't say I'd blame anyone who felt like they needed to escape."

He folded his arms across his chest and appeared to be waiting for her to say something more.

"Look, I don't know why this woman came out here or why she changed her name. I don't know for certain that she was hiding out here, but I feel very strongly she was trying to get as far from someone or something as she could. I'd be real interested in knowing who that person was." Annie turned to look over her shoulder at the corpse that lay fifteen feet behind her. "It has to make you wonder, doesn't it? What brought her here under a phony name? Why she'd leave a career with the FBI and just disappear?"

"I'm sure she wasn't the first FBI agent who decided to quit."

"True. But many former agents leave the Bureau and join local law enforcement agencies. Private security, that sort of thing. Any idea what she was doing for a living?"

"No idea." He shook his head. "Maybe someone in town will know, maybe one of the neighbors."

The sound of car doors slamming drew their attention to the driveway, where several sheriff's vehicles and a beat-up black sedan had parked, their occupants filing up the walkway to the house.

"Looks like the gang's all here," Brody observed. "Let me get you those gloves, Dr. McCall, so we can put you to work along with everyone else. I could see you're interested in the contents of that purse there. Let's see what's what . . ."

The first thing Annie did was start to check the numbers of the last calls that had been made to Melissa's cell phone, but one of the sheriff's deputies made a point of looking for that item, so she had to hand it over. While doing so, she tucked the address book under her leg as she knelt on the floor next to the spilled purse. When the deputy walked outside to start calling back the numbers, she took the small red book and stepped around the M.E. to walk into the kitchen. There she opened the back door and sat on the top porch step to skim through the pages.

For some reason, Melissa seemed to prefer listing some of her contacts not by name but by initials. Annie went page by page, studying the entries, but none were recognizable. Until she came to the *S*s.

*G.S.*—followed by a number Annie did not recognize.

Grady Shields?

She tapped the book against the palm of one hand. Could be an old phone book. Could be a number Melissa hadn't called in a long time. Annie took her cell phone out of her pocket and checked the number she had for Grady. It wasn't the same as the one in Melissa's book. Annie dialed the number and listened to it ring.

"Hello?" A familiar male voice answered.

"Grady?"

"Yeah, who's this?"

"It's Annie."

He hesitated, then asked, "How did you get this number?"

"I found it in Melissa Lowery's phone book."

"What are you doing with Melissa's phone book?"

"Looking for someone who might have had a reason to kill her."

The silence that followed was so long and so complete, Annie thought Grady had hung up.

"Melissa . . . ?" he whispered, his voice little more than a rasp.

"She's dead, Grady."

"But . . ." Another silence, then finally, a click.

"Grady?" Annie asked, though she knew he was no longer on the line. She disconnected the call and slid the phone back into her jacket pocket.

"You find anything interesting in that book?" Sheriff Brody asked from the top of the steps.

"Not really," she said, handing it to him.

"Well, we got two of the neighbors out front, just drove by and saw all the cars, so they stopped in. I'm just about to go on out and talk to them, thought you might want to come out with me."

"I would. Thank you."

Brody came down the steps and walked toward the corner of the house.

"Too much going on in there," he told her. "I want to stay out of everyone's way as much as I can."

"So we figure she's been dead approximately two weeks." Annie fell into step beside him.

"Yeah, that's what we figured." He nodded.

"And no one missed her in all that time?"

"From what I gathered, from the folks out front, she didn't work. Went into town for food and supplies every two weeks or so. Stopped at the library to pick up a couple of books while she was there, maybe had lunch at Sullivan's. Other than that, it seems like she kept to herself."

"Well, let's see if the neighbors remember if she's had any company lately . . ."

The neighbors did.

In particular, Mrs. Owens, a widow in her midseventies who lived half a mile up on the other side of the road, distinctly recalled having seen a tall, good-looking dark-haired man with the deceased on several occasions.

"Recently?" Annie asked.

"Last time, maybe a month ago. Maybe a little less."

"Within the last two weeks?"

"Not him, but there was a car parked here week before last."

"How do you know it wasn't him?"

"He always came at the end of the week, stayed till Sunday or sometimes Monday morning. This was in the middle of the week, and the car was only here for the one day."

"Do you remember what day of the week it was?"

"It was a Tuesday."

"Are you sure, Mrs. Owens?" Brody spoke up for the first time since Annie had engaged the woman in conversation.

"I'm positive. I was on my way into town to the dentist. Dr. Jacobs. He's only in West Priest on Tuesday's. Rest of the week, he's in Priest or over in Tall Trees."

"This tall, dark-haired man . . ." Annie began.

"Good-looking. Don't leave out the good-looking part."

"How often did you see him? Twice a month? Once? Every two months . . . ?"

"Maybe once a month, sometimes twice, close as I remember."

"Do you think you'd recognize him if you saw him again?"

"Oh yes. He really was a looker."

"Thanks, Mrs. Owens. If you remember anything else, you just give me a call, hear?"

"Will do." Mrs. Owens nodded but made no effort to leave. "What do you suppose happened to her? You got any suspects?"

"Now, now, don't go talking about suspects. We don't even know what she died from. Could be natural causes. Let's not go jumping to conclusions, Mrs. Owens. That's how rumors get started."

"Well, you know I'm not one to gossip," she said to the sheriff and to Annie.

"That's good, then. We don't need any speculation going around town until we know for certain what happened here. And we might not know that for a few more days. Gotta give the medical examiner some time to do his thing."

Mrs. Owens nodded her understanding and turned to leave.

"You don't suppose someone killed her deliberately, do you, Sheriff?"

"Mrs. Owens, I thought we just agreed we would not be speculating," Brody said sternly.

"Just wondering." The older woman resumed her walk to her car. "She was such a lovely thing, so sweet. Always waved when you went past."

"Mrs. Owens," Annie called to her. "Would you happen to know where Mariana worked? What she did for a living?"

"Oh, she didn't work. I think she had some sort of family money or something, some inheritance, maybe it was." Mrs. Owens opened her car door. "But she sure didn't work. Up all hours of the night; I used to see lights on down here all the time. I said something to her once, about her staying up late and was she reading or watching TV, and she said most nights she didn't sleep well, that she slept better during the day. Which I thought was strange, you know. The way she said it, made me think that she was afraid to sleep at night, like she was safer sleeping during the day."

"Why do you say that?" Annie asked.

"Just a feeling I had. She had that house lit up like a Christmas tree all night, every night, and the one night I stopped by to drop off some mail that got put in my box by mistake, it took her like a full minute to unlock all the locks."

Annie and the sheriff looked at each other.

"Did you notice a lot of locks?" Annie asked the sheriff.

"No, but let's go take a look . . ."

An inspection of the inside of the front door proved there to be a dead bolt, a slider, and a regular bolt.

"The only lock that was on when we first got here was the slider," Brody told Annie. "I unlocked that to open the door for you. I guess I missed the others because they were unlocked, and because I was so busy at the time covering my nose and mouth and dodging the swarming flies."

"Let's check the back door," Annie suggested.

There were three locks on the back door as well. Locks on the windows. A dead bolt on the basement.

"Sheriff, what's the crime rate out here?"

"Zilch. I can't remember the last robbery. Murders? None in the three years I've been sheriff. We had a few hunting accidents, and last year an old man died of a heart attack up the road, a little higher up in the hills. But crime rate? I gotta say we don't have one."

"Then why would she have all these locks?" Annie bent closer to inspect them. "Fairly new, too, all except the slider. The dead bolts were installed more recently. Certainly within the past year or so."

"Well, we've only got one place in town that sells locks. Larsen's Hardware. They sell, they install."

"Maybe someone should drive down there and talk to them."

"Just as easy to call Hank Larsen on the phone, have him come on up here and identify the locks as his."

"Maybe he'll remember chatting with her. Maybe she told him what she was trying to lock out."

"Maybe. It's a good place to start," Sheriff Brody agreed, but made no move toward the house.

"Were you going to call him today?" Annie asked.

"I thought I'd wait until the body was moved out, Dr. McCall. Not everyone can walk past a partially decomposed body and appear not to notice."

"I notice, Sheriff Brody." Annie started back into the house.

"Dr. McCall," Brody called to her as she stepped over the threshold. "May I ask who you called earlier?"

"Excuse me?"

"You went out the back a little while ago with that little phone book of the deceased's. Looked to me like you called one of the numbers."

"I called a fellow agent who was an old friend of Ms. Lowery's."

"That friend of a friend you mentioned earlier."

"Yes."

"That friend have a name?"

"Grady Shields." She hated having to give up his name, not knowing what Grady's involvement with Melissa might have been, but she couldn't lie, either. "Special Agent Grady Shields."

"And his relationship with Ms. Lowery—or Ms. Gray—was what, do you know?"

"Former coworker. Friend."

"That number for Agent Shields, it's in the address book?"

"Yes. Was there something else, Sheriff?"

"Not right now."

She closed the door and went back inside, hoping for a moment with the medical examiner. While she waited for him to finish preparing the body for transport, she stepped out onto the back porch to make one more phone call.

"Evan, I'm afraid there's been a change in plans . . ."

16

Connor leaned on the iron railing that enclosed the balcony over-looking the Atlantic coast of Morocco and watched the gulls circle overhead. An occasional protesting scream pierced the tranquillity of the morning as a coveted morsel of fish was snatched from one beak by another. The sky was as blue as he'd ever seen it, and the breeze as gentle as a caress. Coming on the heels of the past few weeks spent in a Middle Eastern desert, the peaceful morning was balm to his soul.

There was a rap on the door, and he answered it without hesitation.

"Your breakfast." The dark-eyed woman carried a rectangular

tray in both hands and headed straight for the balcony. "You should eat here, in the sun. It will relax you."

"Magda, you're more like my mother than my mother was."

"Someone has to watch out for you," she said without smiling. "It might as well be me."

She placed the tray on the small glass table and removed the napkin to reveal a plate of warm croissants, figs, a thinly sliced pear, and a small mound of white cheese.

"Sit and eat. I'll be right back with your coffee."

"You're way too good to me," he said as he sat at the table.

"I certainly am." Magda went through the double doors into the room and disappeared into the hall. When she returned, she brought a second tray, upon which stood a tall carafe and two cups. She poured coffee into both cups, placed one before Connor, then sat opposite him at the table.

"Nice of you to join me." He offered her the croissants, but she waved him off.

"I eat early, at dawn. You know that. I need an early start if I'm to take care of you and the rest of my guests in the manner in which I've made you accustomed."

"There is no finer hotel in Essaouira. It's the reason I've come to love this city. The reason I spend any available free time right here." He tilted his cup in her direction before taking a sip. "And besides, there's no better coffee anywhere in Morocco."

Satisfied, Magda leaned back in the chair and raised her face to the sun, her eyes closed.

"There's a new guest who checked in two days ago. An American woman. She's an archaeologist, she says, on holiday."

"So?"

"So you should make her acquaintance. She's very pretty. Blond. Soft-looking. She doesn't go out much."

"So maybe she's tired. Maybe she sleeps a lot."

"Maybe she's lonely. Maybe she'd appreciate a little companionship from a fellow countryman."

"Why are you always trying to set me up?"

"Because you live like a mercenary."

"I'm not a mercenary."

"I know what you are. But you still need a nice girl in your life."

"I have a nice girl in my life. I have you."

"I'm old enough to be your mother, and if you ever looked at me that way, Cyril would slit your throat." She smiled, but her eyes remained closed.

"Your husband should be jealous of you. You're one in a million, Magda."

"I know." She tucked an errant strand of graying hair into the bun at the back of her neck.

"Magda, if I wanted to make a phone call"—he placed his cup on the table to refill it—"there would be a secure line?"

"Of course. All of my lines are secure." She lifted her head and opened her eyes. "I myself check them every day, just like you showed me. Do you think I forget such things?"

"I was just wondering if you were still in the habit."

"You need not worry. This is a small hotel, most of our business is repeat. Same people, over and over. Many of them, like you, require that extra measure of security." She drained the coffee from her cup and rose. "For you, there will always be security here. Whatever you need. We don't forget, Cyril and I."

She patted Connor fondly on the arm and walked past him.

"The American woman takes tea in the courtyard every afternoon at four," she said without breaking stride. "Today she'll be seated at one of the tables for two, in the corner near the palms."

Magda closed the door behind her.

Two gulls were battling on the top of the courtyard wall, and Connor watched idly as he finished his meal and thought over the e-mail he'd gotten from Annie. It had been dated the previous week, but he'd only just received it last night, after checking in to his room and turning on his computer for the first time in days. He'd known there'd be no electricity where he'd been headed, so he'd left the laptop locked in a safe deep in the basement of the hotel. He'd had no qualms about leaving it there. Magda and Cyril would guard it with their lives.

There was something to be said about having someone in this part of the world in your debt, he acknowledged, though that had never entered his mind the day he dove off the prow of a fast-moving pleasure boat to rescue a young boy who'd fallen over the side. Without a life jacket, the panicked child would have quickly drowned. The boy's horrified parents had watched helplessly from the dock as the tall dark-haired stranger reached their son and carried him back to the boat, whose captain had circled back around and cut the engine, the other passengers calling encouragement. From that day, the best room in Villa André had always been available to Connor. He knew that he could always count on the most comfortable accommodations, the best food, the best service—and some motherly fussing—from Magda.

He leaned back in the chair, his face to the sun much as Magda's had been, and went back over Annie's message in his mind. He hadn't thought about Santa Estela in months.

He moved the tray out of the way and set up the laptop in its place. He booted up and scanned his incoming mail before opening the saved e-mail from Annie.

Connor, strange development on a case Evan is handling in PA. Tattoos on the vics found to be identical to those found on three vics in Chicago. Young girls, one of whom appears to have a connection traced back to Central America, possibly Santa Estela. Do I recall correctly that

you had spent some time there? Any contacts remain? Am
looking for source and/or significance of the tattoo.

He drummed his fingers on the table, thinking back to that night
in the alley in Santa Estela, of the truck filled with terrified children.
Any connection between dead young girls in two cities and Santa
Estela was way too coincidental. He'd thought that business had
been shut down two years ago. His cousin had personally worked
on that and had assured him the trafficking of children had been
dealt with.

He brought the phone from the room onto the balcony and
plugged it in, then dialed the familiar number. When the answering
machine picked up, he said, "Hey, it's Connor. Hope all you guys
are doing well. Just wanted to ask you a quick question. About Santa
Estela and that report I asked you about a few years back, you remember? Do me a favor and take another look at that situation,
would you? I'll check back in with you in another day or two, hope
you have something to tell me."

Connor started to hang up, then said, "And hey, if you see my
brother, tell him I said hey, all right? Your brothers, too. Take care,
cuz . . ."

He disconnected the call and stood up to stretch. From the balcony he could see into the courtyard, where, right at that moment,
a woman in a gauzy white dress had stopped to put a large hat atop
her head. Before her hair had disappeared under the hat, he'd noticed it was blond, cut short in a choppy style, as if done without
artistry or skill. She was tanned, almost as tanned as he was, and
even from a distance, he could see she was very well put together.

The American Magda had told him about?

Tea in the courtyard at four might be interesting after all. He
watched her disappear through the courtyard gates and hesitate, as
if unsure of her direction. He was tempted to join her, to offer her a

tour of the marketplace, but he had a meeting in twenty minutes with a man who had information Connor's superiors were eager to obtain.

He turned off the laptop, located his sunglasses, and locked the door behind him, the memory of the events of a dark night in Santa Estela and all thoughts of the pretty blond American put aside for a while.

17

Annie lay spooned beside Evan, her eyes open in the dark, watching the rain splat against the bedroom windows. She'd arrived late the night before and had deferred any discussion by climbing into bed next to him and keeping him otherwise engaged for nearly an hour.

She knew him well enough to know that he knew she was not asleep. When she felt him pull the sheet up over her bare arm, she knew that sooner or later, the concerned questions would begin.

She didn't have to wait long.

"So, you want to talk about it?" he asked softly.

"I thought maybe you might want to tell me about Chicago."

"Ladies first."

"Melissa had a number in her phone book listed to a G.S. I called it. Grady answered."

"That was the only number in the book?"

"No."

"Why'd you pick that one to call?"

"Because of the obvious—the initials. I knew Grady had dated Melissa, but when I asked him about her, I got the feeling he wasn't being truthful. Something told me it wasn't as casual a relationship as he tried to pass it off. No matter how casual a relationship is, there are certain things you have a tendency to talk about when you first meet someone, and for him to claim to know nothing about her, nothing about her background, it just didn't ring true. So when I saw those initials with a Virginia area code, I thought I'd dial it and just see what happened."

"Did you tell him Melissa was dead?"

"Yes."

"And . . . ?"

"And he hung up on me. He sounded genuinely stunned. Stunned, and upset."

"Which plays back to him having more of a relationship with Melissa than he'd wanted you to know."

"But why? Why would he lie about that?"

"Why was she hiding in Montana?" he asked. "I think if you answer one of those questions, you'll have the answer to both."

"I guess the only one who knows is Grady. And the only way to find out is to confront him."

"Have you heard yet from the M.E. in Montana as to cause of death?"

"I'm still waiting. I expect they should know by today. God, I'm hoping it was natural causes."

"What difference would it make?"

"The difference between her dying a natural death or one that I possibly led someone to—"

"Whoa. Hold up there." He sat up partially and turned her to face him. "Where is this coming from?"

"It's coming from the fact that Melissa seemed to be living quite happily in Montana until I started looking for her."

"Annie, please don't tell me you think you are in any way responsible for her dying."

"If she was murdered, yes, I have to question why now. The thought that somehow I could have brought this on her is making me physically sick."

"You can't be serious?" One look at her face assured him she was. "Okay, let's take a look at this, shall we? Let's assume for a moment that Melissa was murdered. You found her, Annie. What makes you think that someone else couldn't have found her, too? Someone who maybe started looking for her long before you did."

"I've been looking for her for a few weeks. My search and her probable date of death are suspiciously close, Evan."

"That is supposition on your part."

"No, that is fact. Shortly after I started asking about her, she died."

"Who knew you were looking for her?"

"Just about everyone in the Bureau. I asked so many people, and some of them probably asked some other people . . . Evan, if I hadn't been so adamant about finding her, she might still be alive."

"I think that's a long shot, Annie. I think it's way too soon to start beating yourself up over something that may not even be true. Let's put it aside until we find out what caused her death. It could have been any one of a number of things. Before you blame yourself, let's get the facts."

She lay silent for a long time, then turned in his arms and said, "All right, then, it's your turn. Tell me what you found in Chicago."

"This detective, Don Manley, is quite a guy. You know he's devoted the past eight months of his life to finding the killers of these girls? He's totally committed to this case, even though it's been shelved. No leads at all."

"How likely is it that he'll find a lead now? Realistically?"

"He says he has a lot of feelers out. He thinks that sooner or later, someone will have some information to deal. He's willing to wait."

"How does this help you in your case?"

He lay silent for a moment, as if he hadn't considered the question before.

"It helps me to know that there's someone else out there who isn't giving up. It helps me to know that when the day comes that Manley gets his lead, he'll pass on whatever he learns to me."

"In the meantime . . . ?"

"In the meantime, for me, it's back to the evidence. Avon County isn't Chicago, and I don't have the network that Manley has. If I'm going to find our killer, it will have to be through the evidence."

"Unfortunately, there isn't much of that, as I recall. Or did something turn up while I was away?"

"Nothing new," he admitted. "And you're right, there isn't a lot to go on."

"You had some dirt," she murmured. "Did a full analysis come back on that?"

"Not that I've seen."

"I can follow up on that for you, have our lab break it down as far as it can go. Maybe that could lead somewhere."

"Oh, and the dog hair. Let's not forget about the dog hair."

"Do I detect some sarcasm there?"

"I keep thinking the lab report will come back with a match to a golden retriever. 'Cause there are so few of them around, it would be real easy to track the owner."

"Hey, you've been in this game long enough to know that you don't discount anything."

"Yeah, I know. It's just a little frustrating. The Schoolgirl Slayer is in custody. Seemed awfully easy to solve that case."

"Not to the parents of the girls who died."

"True enough. Oh, hell, I think I'm antsy after meeting with Manley and wanting so badly to make this right for these girls, to find out who they were and take them home. You look at what's happened to these kids—sold or kidnapped or lied to in order to get them under control, sent to work in brothels. Forced into prostitution before they're even in their teens. Then tossed aside for whatever reason—executed." Evan made no attempt to disguise his anger and disgust. "And let's not lose sight of the fact that as long as he's still out there, other girls could be at risk."

"You're thinking there are more girls in the area?"

"Why not?" She could hear his wheels turning. "Let's assume for a minute that there was in fact a working brothel in the area. A brothel with only three girls? Not likely." He shook his head. "So there would be others . . . but would they all be from Santa Estela?"

"How do you find out?"

Annie felt his body tense slightly and smiled to herself, recognizing that he was onto something and, in minutes, would be out of bed and getting dressed, in anticipation of going wherever the thought would lead.

"A few years ago, the D.A. started this program where whenever they picked up a woman for prostitution, they picked up the john and printed his name in the paper. It caused a lot of grief for a lot of guys. After the third arrest, you not only got your name in the paper, you got jail time. Light time, but time all the same. Imagine being some big executive type, or some big lawyer down in Philly, having to take a month off to do time. The program sort of fell to the wayside after a while. Not a lot of guys actually served any time."

"So, you're thinking if you had a list of the men with two arrests, you could check in with them, see if any of them knew or heard about some young foreign girls in a house."

"Right." He had slowly disengaged himself from her and was sitting on the edge of the bed.

"And they would speak with you now because . . ." She began to mentally count the seconds before he stood and started looking for the clothes he'd earlier discarded.

"Because maybe if they thought the program was being reactivated, they might appreciate a heads-up before such a sweep—and a possible third arrest—might take place."

. . . twenty-two, twenty-three, twenty-four . . .

"Twenty-five," she announced.

"What?" he asked as he retrieved his jeans from the floor.

"It only took you twenty-five seconds between the time you sat and the time you stood. You beat your own best time of thirty-seven by a mile."

"You really think you have me pegged, don't you?" He laughed softly.

"Absolutely, I do. I can see right through you."

"Like what you see?" He pulled a T-shirt over his head and started to tuck it into his jeans.

"I love what I see."

He hesitated, then asked, "Annie, are you sure you don't mind if I just look a few things up—"

She cut him off. "Of course not." There was no point in making him explain. She knew his heart, and knew that he'd do what he had to do. Just as she would. "It's an excellent idea. You need to follow up on it."

"It may lead nowhere."

"Or it may lead to your killer." She sat up and wrapped the sheet around her.

"Will you be here when I get back?"

"Actually, I probably will not. I need to talk to Grady, and I don't think a phone call is the way to do that."

"Want me to go with you? It's Saturday. I could drive down with you later this afternoon, we could go see Grady, then I can drive back tomorrow night."

"I would love to have you come home with me. But I think I'll get more out of Grady if I'm alone. I don't think he'll tell me anything if you're there."

"Okay." He leaned over to kiss her. "But I can still drive down later today, if you want."

"Why don't you wait and see how many names you come up with, and see how many are willing to talk to you. If I know you, you'll be up to your neck in this for the rest of the day."

"God, I hope I can get a break." He looked under the chair for his shoes, then remembered he'd left them downstairs. "I need something solid on this."

"So go for it."

"You're sure you don't mind?" He hovered over her, studying her face.

"Go." She glanced at the clock on the nightstand. It was 4:30 in the morning. "Actually, I think I'll get up now, too. The earlier I get back to Virginia, the sooner I'll be able to sit down with Grady and see if I can get some of the truth about his relationship with Melissa."

"Good luck, babe." Evan kissed her one last time. "Maybe I'll see you later tonight . . ."

"And maybe I'll wake up tomorrow and be my longed-for height of five-eight," she murmured as he went down the steps. "Neither is likely, but one can always hope . . ."

———

Annie stood in the vestibule of the building that housed Grady's condo, along with five others, all of which had mailboxes lined up along the wall to the left of the front door. Junk mail overflowed from the black box bearing a label that read, *G. Shields, 2B.*

Interesting he hasn't picked up his mail in a few days, she thought as she rang the bell for his unit, but his car is in the parking lot. She went outside and looked up at his apartment. There were air conditioners in two of the three front windows, and she could hear their faint humming. She went back into the vestibule and rang the doorbell again. She rang it over and over, until finally, she got a response.

"What." It wasn't so much a question as an expression of exasperation.

"It's Annie, Grady."

"Not now, Annie."

"I'm not leaving until I talk to you."

"You're talking to me now."

"Let me come up, Grady. We need to talk about Melissa."

"I did not kill her. And I don't know who did. What else do you need to know?"

"Do you really want me to go into that right here, right now, where anyone could come along and—"

He buzzed her through the locked front door, and she crossed the lobby to the stairwell that rose directly in front of her. She climbed the steps and found Grady waiting for her in the doorway of his apartment. From his appearance, she guessed that the mail had been piling up in the box because he hadn't left the apartment in several days. It had certainly been that long since he'd shaved.

He stepped aside and motioned for her to come in, then closed the door behind her.

"So tell me what it is you're looking for, then you can go and I can get back to the business of getting myself good and drunk." He walked into the living room, and she followed.

"Looks like you've made some progress there." She noted the empty bottles of wine that formed a circle on top of the coffee table. "Odd choice, though. Most men drink themselves into a stupor on beer or hard liquor. Merlot doesn't seem to fit."

"What is it you want?" He flopped onto the sofa but did not offer her a seat.

She pushed some newspapers onto the floor and sat anyway.

"Why were you so secretive about your relationship with Melissa Lowery?"

He appeared to be trying to formulate a response.

"Come on, Grady, just say it."

He still searched for words.

"All right, let's try this approach. Why did Melissa change her name and move to Montana?"

"Free country." He picked up the nearest bottle and checked its contents. Finding it empty, he moved on to the next one and refilled his glass.

"Cut the bullshit," she said softly. "We both know she was afraid of something. Or someone. Was it you?"

"Me?" The question took him off guard. "God, no."

"What was your relationship with her?"

"She was . . . my best girl." His eyes filled with tears. "She was . . . my wife."

"Your . . . ?"

He nodded slowly. "We were married in Reno eight months ago."

"Why all the secrecy? Why was she hiding, Grady?"

He exhaled slowly, a long breath fraught with pain.

"Someone scared her."

"Who?"

"Now, don't you think if I knew that, I'd have dealt with it?" He lifted his head and met her eyes, and she understood exactly how he would have dealt.

"She gave you no information, she never told you why—"

"Yeah. That much I know. She was on a job, she saw someone who shouldn't have been there, and included his name in her report."

"Who wasn't she supposed to have seen?"

"I don't know. *She* didn't even know who it was. All I know is that after she wrote the report, someone contacted her by phone and told her she was to forget that she had been there, forget who else she'd seen there, and to destroy any copies of her notes. He left a bag with a lot of cash—a *whole* lot of cash—on her doorstep and suggested she resign from the Bureau and take the first train out of Dodge."

"Or . . . ?"

"Or he'd kill her."

"Why didn't she go to someone at the Bureau?"

"Who would do what, Annie? Protect her from someone she couldn't even identify? Someone who obviously *works* for the Bureau?" He got up and ran a hand through his dark hair. "Believe me, we went through all of this. Whoever was threatening her works for the Bureau. He's supposed to be one of the good guys. He could have been anyone. How do you even begin to figure out who you can trust?"

"Well, what about the job she'd been on, start with that. Look at the people who were there, figure out—" She stopped short, staring at him. "Grady . . ."

"Annie, please don't even ask."

"Tell me it wasn't the job where Dylan was killed."

He was agitated and drunk. He swayed when he stood, then sat slowly back down.

"And that's why Melissa's report was missing, because someone took it deliberately and made sure she wouldn't replicate it?"

"Yes."

Annie digested the information.

"I'm sorry, Annie. I'm really sorry."

She waved away his apology, past that now. "Why," she asked, "didn't he just kill her?"

"I don't know." He took a long swallow of wine, this one straight from the bottle. "I've asked myself that same question a dozen times. Why didn't he just kill her."

He wiped tears from his face with the hem of his shirt.

"I guess the question really is, why did he kill her now?"

"I have a call in to the sheriff in Montana. As soon as I've heard about cause of death, I'll let you know."

He cleared his throat. "Appreciate it."

"In the meantime, why not put the wine away? Take a shower, get something to eat. Get some sleep."

"Merlot was the only thing she ever drank." He held up the bottle and studied the label as if it held some weighty truth.

"Grady, I am so sorry about Melissa. I don't know what to say." She swallowed hard. "I'm more sorry than I can say, if my looking for her, for her report, was the catalyst—"

"Don't, Annie. There's no point . . ." He shrugged helplessly.

"Still . . ."

"Just . . . don't, okay?" He looked away.

"I'll call as soon as I hear anything." It was the only thing she could think to say.

"Okay."

She wanted to go to him and put her arms around him, but she knew that nothing would comfort him. Instead, she walked to the door to let herself out. She opened the door to leave, then turned and asked, "Did anyone know that you and Melissa were married?"

"Only my brothers."

"You didn't tell your sister?"

"Nah." He smiled weakly. "You know Mia, she talks to everyone. But my brothers, well . . . you know how they are. They're both so closemouthed, you never know what's going on with either of them."

18

Evan took a sip of coffee and grimaced to find it had gone cold during the course of his telephone conversation with john number twenty-seven on the list of seventy-four he'd gotten from the D.A.'s files when he arrived at the courthouse at 5:30 that morning. To say the guard at the front door had been surprised to see anyone at that hour—least of all on a Saturday—would have been an understatement.

"Early day, Detective?" The man had yawned as he unlocked the front door.

"Yeah." Evan shifted the cardboard carrier holding the three large cups of coffee he'd picked up at the local convenience store. As he passed through the metal detector, he handed one Styrofoam cup to the guard. "Thought you could use a wake-up this morning, too."

"Thank you, Detective Crosby. Nice of you to think of me."

"Nice of you to let me in." Evan smiled and walked the dimly lit hall to the stairwell, and took the steps down to the basement, where the county detectives and some of the assistant district attorneys were housed.

The hallway was darker here, and it had taken him several tries before he managed to open the main office door. He locked it behind him and walked through the common area, lit only by an "Exit" sign on either side, and went directly to his small office at the end of the hall. He'd placed the coffee on one side of the desk and turned on his computer. He searched the files until he found what he was looking for, opened one of the coffees, and sipped at it while he scanned the screen, occasionally making notes on a yellow legal pad he'd pulled from the bottom drawer. By the time his list was complete, the sun had come up and enough of the morning had passed that he could begin making his calls without risk of having anyone complain that it was too early.

By noon, he'd called almost one third of the names on his list and had spoken with twelve. The others had either not answered or were no longer at the number he had on record. Out of the twelve, only five were willing to speak with him about their prior arrests. He'd left telephone messages for several others but was not optimistic that many—if any—of his calls would be returned.

Of the five he'd spoken with, none of them admitted to knowing anything about any young Hispanic girls working in an area house in which they might be held against their will.

"I wouldn't go for none of that, man, none of that young stuff," one of the johns had told him. "That's disgusting, man . . ."

"There are a couple of Hispanic chicks working the corner at Seventh and Warwick," another had offered when pressed, "but they ain't no kids."

"I don't usually ask to see ID, you know what I mean?" another had snorted.

Evan rubbed his eyes and stood to stretch. His legs felt cramped and his shoulders stiff, and he thought a walk outside, even just around the courthouse, might be refreshing. He opened his door and noticed lights on in several of the other offices. He'd been so engrossed in his research that he hadn't heard anyone else come in.

He stopped at Cal Henry's door to chat for a moment, but left when Cal's girlfriend called. Their verbal feuds were legendary, and Evan had witnessed more than enough of them in the past. He waved to Cal and continued on his way outside.

"You take care, Detective," the guard at the door called to him, barely looking up.

"I'm just running out for a minute. I'll be back."

Evan stepped into the sun and shielded his eyes from the glare. He took a deep breath, and deciding he was as much in need of food as of exercise, he walked two blocks to Main Street, where he picked up lunch from the deli on the corner. He returned to the courthouse and took a seat on one of the benches on the front lawn and proceeded to eat his ham and cheese on rye while mentally replaying the conversations he'd had that morning, hoping to find some inadvertent comment that might lead him to something concrete.

Reluctantly, he had to admit he hadn't missed anything the first time around. There'd been no slip of the tongue, nothing he could use as an excuse to call any of the men back to confirm. He rolled up his lunch trash in the bag it had come in and started toward the trash can when he heard someone calling his name.

"Hey, Joe," he called back to his former partner, who was walking up the sidewalk with a large brown file folder under his arm.

"Evan. Good to see you." Joe Sullivan met Evan in the middle of the sidewalk.

"What brings you in on a Saturday?"

Joe held up the file.

"I just got a call at home from Shelley Stern telling me this case is going to trial on Monday and she needed whatever materials I had that she didn't have." He shook his head. "How am I supposed to know what she has?"

"I'm going back in, want me to drop it off for you?"

"Nah, I'm going to need to talk to her anyway."

Evan tossed his trash in the direction of the open can and missed.

"I see moving up to county detective hasn't done anything to improve your aim," Sullivan noted.

"It'll take more than a new job to do that. What's new in Lyndon?"

"Not much. Things have quieted down a lot since the slayer was brought in. Nice job Jackie did with that case, wasn't it?"

"Nice job that *Jackie* did?" Evan scoffed.

"What's that supposed to mean?"

"It means Jackie had a lot of help from the FBI."

"That's not the way I heard it."

Evan shook his head in disgust and waved to the guard, who was already on his way to unlock the door.

The two men went through the procedure to enter the building, then walked together down to the D.A.'s office. Joe stopped off at Shelley Stern's office—the third door on the left—and Evan continued on to his office. Fifteen minutes later, he looked up to find Joe in the doorway.

"So you working all day or what?"

"Most of it. I'd hoped to finish up early enough to make a trip down to Annie's for the rest of the weekend, but I guess that's not going to happen."

"What are you working on?" Joe asked. "That the other killer case?"

"What other killer case?" Evan looked up from the file.

"Word around is that the Slayer didn't pop those last three girls, the Hispanic ones." Joe came in and plopped himself in the seat near the door.

"Where'd you hear that?"

"Just around. Don't remember where, exactly."

"Good thing it wasn't supposed to have been kept under wraps or anything," Evan muttered.

"So if you're not going to see the old lady, want to meet up later for a few beers and a burger down at Taps? I'm meeting a couple of the guys at six."

"Rosemary is letting you out alone on a Saturday night?"

"She's off with her sister this weekend. She and Joey. They'll be gone through tomorrow afternoon."

"How's he doing, your son?"

"He had a better year in school this year." Joe nodded. "He had a rough time for a while. You know, he's small for his age, isn't real good at sports. It's tough for a boy like that. We finally did find something he liked doing, though, so he's doing better."

Evan was about to ask what that thing was when his cell phone rang. He checked the number and found it to be one of the men for whom he'd previously left a message.

"Sorry, Joe, I've got to take this."

"Hey, no problem. Stop down at Taps later, if you can. We'll all be there. It would be great if you could join us. Like old times. If not, we'll get together sometime soon."

"Sounds like a plan. Thanks."

Joe waved and left the office as Evan answered his call.

"Yeah, Manny, thanks for calling me back. I appreciate it. Listen, about that incident a few years back . . . yeah, that one. Hey, I hate to bring that up, but there's a rumor going around the D.A.'s office that they're thinking about bringing back that three-strikes-and-jail-time thing again, and I just wanted to see if you were keeping clean . . ."

It was almost eight by the time Evan finished the last of his calls. He was starving and for a moment considered Joe's offer. Then he looked at the pages of notes he'd made, all the information he wanted to enter into the computer before Monday came around, and decided he'd do takeout on the way home instead. He'd enjoy a night out with his old friends and coworkers, he acknowledged as he packed up a few files to take home. They had a good bunch of guys down there in the Lyndon Police Department, and there were times when he missed working with them, missed the companionship and the familiarity of having the same partner every day.

Well, maybe he'd have time for a beer or two. He turned off the overhead light on his way out of the office and dialed Joe's cell phone as he walked up the steps. When there was no answer after six rings, Evan disconnected the call without leaving voice mail. Tonight he was tired and had a lot of reading to do, none of it light, he told himself as he waved good night to the guard, so it was just as well he hadn't been able to hook up with Joe. He'd catch up with the guys later in the week.

Maybe by then, Joe would have remembered where he'd heard about the second killer. The one whose existence wasn't supposed to have been discussed outside the D.A.'s office.

He wondered who'd been talking, and how the information had made its way to the Lyndon PD.

He stopped for pizza on the way home and ate standing up at the kitchen counter while he listened to his voice mail. Then he locked up the house and took his files to his second-floor office, where he read until he passed out. Sunday morning he showered, shaved, and started all over again, making calls and taking notes, crossing names off one list and adding them to another.

At four in the afternoon, he looked out the back window at the dirt patch that was Annie's garden and hoped that by this time next week, they'd be together, working on it. He put the thought aside and went back to his phone calls. He worked until midnight, then closed up shop and went to bed.

At four o'clock Monday morning, the phone rang, and he answered it groggily.

"Crosby? Sargeant Crocker, Broeder police department. Got someone here who wants to talk to you."

There was a soft rustle as the phone was passed from one person to another.

"Hey, Detective, Perry Jelinik, remember me?"

"Sure." Evan pulled himself up onto one elbow and tried to stifle a yawn. "I busted you for possession two years ago."

"And four years before that."

"You get picked up more recently by someone else, Jelinik?"

"Yeah, actually, I was." There was a pause. "I was wondering if you could help me out with that. Talk to the arresting officer or the D.A. for me or something."

"Why would I do that?"

"Well, I hear you're looking for an address . . ."

19

After two solid days of reviewing police reports to prepare a profile for a D.A. in Florida, Annie was almost happy to be going back into the office again. She felt as if she'd been in solitary confinement since she arrived home on Saturday morning. She was trying to recall when she had ever welcomed a Monday quite as much when she heard her fax beeping to signal that something was being sent to her machine.

She went into her office and leaned over the desk to pull the sheet of paper from the incoming tray and was surprised to see a copy of Melissa Lowery's autopsy report.

Annie scanned it quickly, skipping over the sections she deemed inconsequential to cause of death (". . . the liver has been removed and upon examination is found to weigh . . .") and going straight to the chase.

Cause of death: Exsanguination due to gunshot wound to the chest.

Melissa had been shot and left to bleed to death.

Not something Annie was looking forward to sharing with Grady.

She was still wondering how to handle that when the phone rang.

"Dr. McCall?"

"Yes."

"Sheriff Brody."

"Oh, Sheriff. I was just about to call you to thank you for faxing the autopsy report on Melissa Lowery."

"Told you I would do so. Glad I caught you on your home phone. Your cell phone wasn't picking up."

She searched her purse and found the cell at the bottom. She'd turned it off the night before after she spoke with Evan because the battery was running down, the charger was in the car, and she hadn't felt like going out in the rain to get it.

"So now that we know for certain she did not die a natural death," he was saying, "you have any thoughts on that?"

"Not just yet."

"I was just wondering if maybe your reason for coming all the way out here to see her might have something to do with her being murdered."

"Sheriff, with all due respect, at this time I cannot discuss the reason for my visit." Annie bit her bottom lip, wishing she'd been able to talk to John before she had to have this conversation with Sheriff Brody. "I'm not trying to be evasive, and I apologize if it sounds as if I am, but my visit had to do with an FBI investigation, and I really can't discuss that with anyone at this time. Please keep in mind that my position with the Bureau is primarily as a profiler. I try to stay out of the bureaucratic aspects. I can give you the name of the special agent in charge to whom I report, if you'd like to give him a call."

"I'd appreciate that." Brody didn't sound at all surprised to hear that he wouldn't be getting information from Annie.

She gave him John Mancini's office number, knowing John would be out of the office for another few days. Having called John on Saturday to bring him up to date on Grady Shields' involvement with Melissa, and Melissa's involvement in Dylan's case, Annie knew John would want to avoid Sheriff Brody for as long as possible.

"Just a few other questions for you, Dr. McCall."

"I'll answer what I can, Sheriff."

"Any thoughts on why an unemployed former FBI agent might have a few hundred thousand dollars stashed away?" Before she could respond, he added, "Ms. Lowery had a savings account with a little over six hundred thousand dollars in it."

"Wow."

"That was pretty much my reaction. Lot of money just sitting there, can't help but wonder where it came from. And this is after some substantial outlays of cash. Seems Ms. Lowery paid cash for that spread she was living on, only eleven acres, not much out here, but still . . ." He cleared his throat. "Paid cash for that new SUV, cash for a bunch of new furniture. Any idea how she could have done all that?"

"No. None." Annie hated lying, but now wasn't the time to tell Brody about the nameless someone who had given Melissa what Grady had described as a lot of cash in exchange for her resignation from the Bureau and her disappearance. "Maybe she had some family money."

"Her father was a bus driver and her mother retired with a twenty-five-year pin from the local school district. They have no idea where the money came from."

"I'm sorry, Sheriff, I just can't help you."

"You wouldn't have any thoughts on who this gentleman friend might have been?"

"No, sorry. Did you ask her parents if they knew who she was involved with?"

"They said they thought she had someone special in her life, but she didn't talk about it. You think that's strange, not to talk to your mother about your boyfriend?"

"Since my mother died before I was old enough to have boyfriends, I wouldn't know."

"Sorry about that, Dr. McCall."

"And a lot of women just don't discuss their personal lives, especially if it's not a serious relationship, you know?"

"Maybe." He sighed heavily. Annie could tell he was frustrated, that he knew she had information that could help him, but he'd apparently dealt with the Bureau in the past. He didn't push, and that made her feel that perhaps he'd pushed before and gotten nowhere.

"Oh, one more thing," he said. "I spoke with the locksmith in town. He said Mariana Gray had come in one day about seven months ago and asked for all new locks, doors and windows. He thought it was unusual at the time—nobody out here locks up like that, there just has never been a cause for it in the past. That could change, in light of this murder. Anyway, the locksmith said he went out to her house, and she had him double-dead-bolt all the doors and put locks on every one of the windows. Said he never saw anyone so worried about her house being broken into."

"Well, she did live around D.C. for several years. We have our share of crime out east, you know. Maybe her place here was broken into, maybe she'd been the victim of a crime in the past and it made her skittish."

"Or maybe she was afraid of someone." He cleared his throat again. "Guess she was right about that, eh?"

"It does look that way, doesn't it?" she replied, momentarily distracted by the call-waiting signal. She walked to the phone base to check the caller ID. It was an overseas number she didn't recognize. Connor?

"Well, I guess I'll give your agent Mancini a call, see if he'll throw me a bone or two and give me a few leads."

"If he has any, I'm sure he'll be more than happy—"

"Please, Dr. McCall. I've been down this road with the FBI before. We both know that you know what's at the bottom of this. I just hope that if you find Melissa Lowery's killer, you'll at the very least let me know so that we can stop wasting our time looking for him—or her—out here."

"Sheriff Brody, you have my word. If we find the killer, you will be the first to know."

" 'Preciate that, Dr. McCall. Hope it's soon. We've got some nervous people out here." He hung up without waiting for any further comment.

Annie immediately placed a call to John, but had to leave voice mail detailing her conversation with Brody. She was relieved that he was away for a few more days. At least he had a legitimate excuse for ducking the sheriff.

Annie started to return the phone to the cradle when she remembered the call that had been coming through while she was speaking with Sheriff Brody. She sat on the end of her desk and listened to the message.

"Hey, Annie, it's Connor. Sorry I missed you, but I wanted to get back to you about Santa Estela. When you get into the office, ask John to give you clearance to look over a report that would have been written, oh, I guess around the end of 2002, maybe early 2003. It concerns our successful efforts to shut down some traffic. I tried to get in touch with one of the agents involved, but I haven't heard back. I'm guessing he's in the field or undercover somewhere and hasn't gotten the message. I don't know who was in charge of this at a supervisory level, or who else was involved, but it must have been a fairly big op. If you see the report, you'll know who the agent is, and you can probably get the green light to talk to him directly. But until you're cleared, I can't give you any other information. All I can say at this point is that there is a report, and it should contain names and places. Read the report—you'll know where to go from there. Sorry I missed you. Get back to me if you have any other questions. See ya."

Annie listened to the message two or three times before hanging up the phone.

There was a report. The Bureau had a report. Names, places . . . contacts. Maybe they'd even be able to locate the families of the girls who'd been killed. She practically danced into her room to finish getting dressed. She couldn't wait to tell Evan, couldn't wait to see the report.

She put in another call to John, but there was no answer. She pulled on a pair of linen pants and slipped her feet into flat shoes, searched her dresser for earrings, a bracelet, all the while thinking of how wonderful it would be if she could find the evidence that could lead to the resolution of these killings.

She went back into her office, picked up the autopsy report on Melissa Lowery, and tucked it into her briefcase. She tried both John and Evan one more time, but wasn't able to reach either one of them. No matter, she told herself. She'll get through to both of them before the day was over.

Buoyed by the turn of events, she turned off the light and headed off to work.

20

"She was my brother's wife, Luther."

"She was a loose end. Another of your loose ends," Luther said calmly.

"She wouldn't have gone back on the deal."

"You don't know that. And with Annie McCall right on her heels, there was too big a risk. She knows how to work a witness. I don't think Melissa would have had a chance."

"Melissa didn't even know I was involved. I was really careful. She had no clue as to which name on her report was the one that wasn't supposed to be there."

"All she had to do was give Annie the names of the agents she remembered seeing that night—and we know she would have remembered having seen you—and sooner or later, McCall would have been able to put it together."

"There were a lot of agents there that night."

"Only one of whom wasn't assigned to the op." Luther spoke as if explaining something tedious to a child. "And let's not even bother to talk about the fact that you were *family,* Shields, and never mentioned to anyone in your *family* that you were there that night? You think that wouldn't seem odd to anyone?"

His comment was met with silence.

"I saw the report, Shields," Luther continued. "She saw you with the rifle case."

"About fifteen people were carrying rifle cases, Luther."

"Only one of them was noted coming out of the building. A building that no one had been assigned to enter."

"I explained that to her. I told her I'd gone upstairs after hearing the shots fired. I told her I was looking for the shooter. She believed me."

"She might have, but someone less trusting, someone trying to put the pieces together—someone like Annie McCall—might not be so quick to accept your explanation."

"Melissa wouldn't have told Annie anything."

"Look, this whole thing has been stupid on your part since day one. It was stupid to even try to deal with her. You should have just pushed her in front of a train or something."

"We could have moved her, we could have—"

"Enough, all right? It's done. I did what you should have done in the first place."

"Luther . . ."

"Yeah, yeah, I know. Your brother was in love with her. I heard it before. I never should have let you handle that yourself. You just let your emotions get in your way. You're pretty much useless to me at this point."

Another silence.

"But you can still redeem yourself. I'm going to give you one chance—but only one."

"Connor." The name was said with a sigh.

"Forget about Connor. I'll deal with him myself. You've already proven that you cannot be trusted when it comes to your own family."

"Are you kidding? Didn't we just talk about Dylan?"

"That was two years ago, you killed the wrong man, and you came close to being caught." Luther laughed out loud. "Besides, what have you done for me lately?"

"Not funny, Luther."

"I wasn't trying to be."

"What is it you want me to do?"

"As I said, Dr. McCall is getting a little too close."

"You want me to kill Annie?"

"I want you to help me set it up. Just get her to the right place at the right time, and I'll take care of the rest."

"You know what, Luther? I'm out. You can keep the money from the last shipment, you can keep the contacts. I want out."

"You just can't walk away from this, Shields. You owe me."

"I don't owe you jackshit, Luther. I did my job all along. I handled the security in Santa Estela, I handled the cops down there. I did everything you needed me to do. But I'm done."

"This one last thing, and we'll call it even."

"I can't help you kill Annie."

"It's her, or it's you, Shields. You make the call."

The pause on the other end of the phone had been laughably brief.

"What do you want me to do?"

He'd listened to Luther's plan, and his stomach had turned. He'd known Annie for years, they'd been friends. They'd worked together, socialized. How in the name of God could he let this happen?

And yet Luther had made the consequences very clear.

He crossed the room and gazed out the window, wondering how his life had gotten so crazy.

Oh, he knew the answer; there was no big mystery there. Back in the beginning, it had all seemed so easy. He was just the lookout, back then. That's all. It was just an easy way to make some extra cash. Enough for a new car—nothing flashy, of course. No one in the Shields clan went for the flash. Expensive cars, expensive jewelry, designer clothes—none of that was understood. He'd never have been able to explain a Mercedes, not even one of the smaller ones. In his family, work was honorable. You worked for the sake of the work itself, not for the rewards.

And that had been his downfall, going for the rewards.

The irony of it was that he'd barely spent any of it. The single largest purchase had been to buy Melissa's silence. He knew he'd gone overboard there, had given her way too much, but he figured she'd given up a lot. Her job, her home, and, he'd thought at the time, her relationship with Grady. He'd felt obligated to give her more than enough to help her start and maintain a new life. It had never occurred to him that Grady would miss her, would find her. Would fall in love with her.

Would marry her.

All he'd really wanted was to keep her quiet, to keep her in the background.

And, he admitted now, to keep her off Luther's radar.

He was sweating profusely and pacing like a caged animal.

He went into the bathroom and stripped, dropping his clothes thoughtlessly on the floor. He turned the shower on high and stepped in, letting the hot water beat against him until his skin was red. Even then, he didn't want to leave the steamy shelter.

It all went back to that moment when Luther had asked him to do a little side job for him—to serve as a watch while Luther conducted a little business. There, in Central America, everyone, it seemed, was on the take. It hadn't seemed like such a big deal.

Then he'd run into Connor in the alley in Santa Estela.

His life had been all downhill from there.

He'd murdered his own cousin, for Christ's sake. Worse, he'd murdered the *wrong* cousin.

Killing Connor would have been one thing. They'd all grown up in his shadow, and since Connor was older than the rest of them, he never really felt he'd known him at all. But Dylan . . . oh, they'd had their differences growing up, sure, but shit, he hadn't wanted him dead.

When he saw what had happened in the aftermath, how the family had crumbled, how his own old man had sobbed uncontrollably, well, it had made him sob, too. He cried as he served as one of Dylan's pallbearers, cried through the funeral mass, and wept like a child as the coffin was lowered into the ground. Every detail of that entire day had been etched into his brain so deeply that even now, two years later, he could recount every minute.

He woke up many nights shaking, having relived the entire thing. At those times, only his own cowardice had kept him from shoving his Glock down his throat and pulling the trigger.

He hadn't dared tell Luther that Connor was now asking about the report. The report that didn't exist, about an op that never took place. If he knew anything at all about Connor, it was that he was tenacious. He wouldn't let go of this until he got what he wanted.

He stayed in the shower until he couldn't stand the sound of beating water any longer. He got out and used a towel to wipe the steam off the mirror. He stood and stared at his reflection, and realized he barely recognized himself anymore.

He forced himself to shake it all off, to get control of himself. He couldn't think about Melissa anymore, couldn't think about Annie.

He put both women from his mind, wiped their names from the slate as if neither existed. They were no longer of consequence.

He dried and went into the bedroom to dress. He glanced at the clock on the bedside table and realized most of the afternoon was gone. He picked up the pace and dressed as quickly as he could. He hated to be late, especially today, when he was expected at Grady's, where he'd offer his condolences to his grieving brother.

21

Outside the Broeder police station, it was a typical early August morning in eastern Pennsylvania, with temperatures and humidity in the eighties and rising. Inside, the faulty air-conditioning system pumped a steady warm breeze into the small room. Evan stood behind the glass for several minutes, wiping the sweat from the back of his neck and watching what was happening on the other side to get a feel for the way things were going with Perry Jelinik. Apparently, they were going okay.

Jelinik sat in a high-backed plastic chair in the Broeder PD interrogation room, his hands folded on the tabletop, his head down. Every once in a while, he'd look up at the clock, but he pointedly avoided making eye contact with the Broeder detective who was leaning against the wall, his arms folded, a look of disgust on his face.

Evan rapped on the door with his knuckles, then let himself in.

"Detective Carr, good to see you," he said as he stepped into the room.

Carr nodded without smiling. He clearly was not happy with the way things were playing out.

"So what's going on here?" Evan asked Carr.

"Here we have Perry Jelinik, who we picked up at three this morning selling coke out of the back of his station wagon," Carr said without expression.

"Who was he trying to sell to?"

"Detective Olensky."

"Not smart, Perry." Evan shook his head. "Not smart at all."

Perry wisely said nothing.

"So, where's your lawyer?" Evan asked.

"I only got one call," Jelinik told him, "and that was to you."

"Really? I'm flattered." Evan sat on the edge of the table.

"I figured you were a better bet. Last time, my lawyer didn't do such a great job keeping me out of jail."

"Maybe it's time to get another lawyer."

"Maybe it's time for you and me to talk." Jelinik addressed Evan, then turned to look pointedly at Detective Carr.

Carr raised both hands in front of him, as a gesture of surrender, and walked backward to the door.

"He's all yours," he told Evan as he left the room. "Chief Mercer said to let you do your thing."

"You and Mercer must be tight," Jelinik said.

"We know each other." Evan wasn't about to share the news that his sister, Amanda, and Sean Mercer had recently become engaged. "Lucky for you he believes in professional courtesy."

"Yeah. Lucky for me."

"So let's cut to the chase, Jelinik. What do you have—or think you have—that's good enough to serve as a Get Out of Jail Free card?"

Jelinik lowered his voice. "I got an address. The one you're looking for. That whorehouse in Carleton."

Evan stared at him without reaction. Carleton was a small middle-class town a few miles away, and might have been one of the last places Evan would have looked.

"Maybe it's old news."

Jelinik just smirked and said, "Do we have a deal?"

"What exactly do you want?"

"I want out of here."

"No can do, Perry." Evan shook his head. "You're looking at a mandatory sentence."

"We both know you got pull with the D.A." Perry sat back in his chair and folded his arms over his chest, his smile replaced with thinly disguised impatience.

"No one has that much pull, Perry." Evan slid off the side of the table and started toward the door. "I could maybe help get your sentence reduced, but I can't make it go away."

"How much?" Jelinik asked as Evan opened the door to leave.

"Depends on how good the information is and what kind of mood the D.A. is in when I talk to him."

"The information is good." Jelinik was less cocky now, but still confident.

Evan turned and gestured for Jelinik to continue.

"You're gonna do the best you can for me, you promise? You give me your word?"

"I give you my word, I will do the best I can for you."

"The house is on Lone Duck Road, just past where it goes into a Y with Franklin, you know where I mean? There's that small lake there, the one with all the geese around it?"

"I know it, sure." Every kid who'd grown up in Avon County had, at one time or another, swum in that lake in the summer or skated on it in the winter. Evan had almost drowned in that lake as an eight-year-old when he fell through the ice. He knew it well.

"About a quarter mile down the road, past the lake, on the opposite side, is a driveway. It's one of those half-circle things, goes in on one side, comes out on the other."

"That's it?"

"That's it." Jelinik nodded.

"And you know this because . . . ?"

"Because I was there, man." He paused, then shook his head. "No, no, not for that. Those girls out there don't even speak English. Well, no more than they have to, to do their jobs, if you get my drift. At least, that's what I heard. I was only there to tow a car; this was back when I was working for Stock's, you know the repair place? I drove their tow truck."

"Whose car needed to be towed?"

"The lady who was in charge, I guess she was. Older lady, maybe fifty or so. Short dark red hair, kind of on the skinny side."

"What was her name, you remember?"

"Dotty something. I didn't need to know her name, I only needed to tow her car. Calvin might know, though. He owns the shop."

"You still work there?" Evan glanced in the mirror but was unsure if anyone was there on the other side, listening.

"No, man, I got canned about six months ago."

"How long ago was it that you towed this woman's car?"

"About that long. I didn't work there for long, maybe a couple of weeks, that's all."

Evan took a sip of his coffee, then made a face.

"Shit, it's cold. How's the coffee here, Perry?"

"Not too bad. It's still early, so it hasn't had time to solidify in the bottom of the pot."

"I'm going to see if I can get a refill. You okay there?"

"I'd rather have a soda. It's hotter'n shit in here."

"I'll be right back." Evan ducked out into the hall.

"You see Carr?" he asked the officer at the door.

"He's in there." The officer pointed to the next door.

"You get that, Carr?" Evan went into the room. Through the mirrored wall he could see Jelinik staring up at the ceiling, one knee bouncing nervously.

"Got it. House right past the lake."

"Would you call Chief Benson over in Carleton and ask him to send someone out to Stock's Auto Repair and see if they can get a name and address for this woman? We're going to need the exact address for the warrant, and we're going to need to check the tax records to find out who owns the property. My guess is that it doesn't belong to the woman who's running it."

"I'm on my way." Carr left the room without glancing at Evan.

Must have been something I said, Evan thought, catching the door that Carr had allowed to swing back. He went into the break room, dumped the coffee in the sink, and dug in his pocket for change. He dropped the coins into the soda machine and hit the Pepsi button, then repeated the process. After both cans had dropped, he returned to the interrogation room.

He set the cans on the table and Jelinik took his, clutching the can with both hands as if to cool them.

"So, let's go back to the house where you picked up the car that day. You said the girls there don't speak English. How'd you know that?"

"Oh, Stock's kid told me. He goes out there once in a while, spends a little time, drops a little cash."

"Which one of Stock's kids?"

"Chuck, the oldest one. He's about twenty-five or so."

"He work at the shop?"

"Him? Nah, he wouldn't work there. He went to college, he's

some kind of insurance guy. He just stops in to see his old man once in a while, and this one time, he was talking about this place."

"What else did he say about the girls, other than that they don't speak English? He say what language they spoke?"

"Spanish." Jelinik nodded readily. "Said he took Spanish in school, so he had no problem talking to 'em."

"He say anything else about the girls?"

"Just that some of them were young. Like, real young."

"You know anyone else who might have frequented that house?"

"No. But Chuck might."

"I'll be sure to ask him. Thanks, Perry. You've been very helpful."

"Wait a minute. You're just going to leave me here? I thought we had a deal . . ." Jelinik began to whine.

"I told you I would speak with Chief Mercer and with the D.A. I made no promises other than that I would do my best to get the best deal I could for you. I won't go back on my word." Evan walked toward the door. "But we both know that under the circumstances, there's no way you can just walk out of here right now. Give me a little time to talk to some people, see what I can do. But in the meantime, you're a guest here in Broeder, and there's nothing I can do about that, so I suggest you make yourself comfortable. Take a nap, Perry. Watch a little daytime TV."

"Can't blame a guy for trying," Jelinik muttered as Evan closed the door behind him.

Once he'd entered the hall, Evan's stride lengthened and he headed for the lobby, his cell phone in his hand.

"Beth, Evan Crosby. I need to talk to Sheridan . . . no, no, I'll hold . . ."

By noon, Evan had the name of the person to whom the property on Lone Duck Road was registered, though he doubted that he'd be face-to-face with Lawrence Bridger anytime soon. A warrant for the search of the premises was obtained, but by the time the county detectives, along with several officers from the Carleton police force, arrived, the house was empty.

"They can't be gone for more than a day," Evan observed. "The Sunday paper and the one from today are the only ones on the front porch. *Damn.*"

He kicked the newel post.

"I can't believe we got this close . . ."

"What do you suppose tipped them off?" asked Bob Benson, Carleton's chief of police.

"Who the hell knows?" Evan grumbled. "Guess we need to get the crime-scene techs out here. Let's go over the place, basement to attic. Fingerprints, fluids, whatever we can find."

"You want to call in the county people?" Benson suggested. "They're faster and there are more of them."

Evan called Sheridan for the fifth time that day and told him what they'd found—an empty house—and asked that he send out the best techs he had on staff.

"I want Carlin Schroeder and Mark Schultz," Evan told him.

"You got 'em," Sheridan replied without hesitation. "And I'll call Jeffrey Coogan down there in the lab and let him know this gets priority or I'm going to recommend a career change for him. Let's get every iota of evidence from that house. Let's find these bastards and nail them."

"Amen." Evan paused, then added, "I have to tell you I'm feeling real uneasy about the timing."

"You mean the fact that they folded their tents just when you're starting to ask questions on the street . . . ?"

"Yeah."

"Who knew you were asking?"

"Every john in the county who'd been busted more than once over the past two years."

"So someone tipped off someone over the past few days."

"Jesus, I just started making my calls on Saturday. How could anyone have moved that fast?"

Bob Benson walked around the side of the house, waving to Evan excitedly.

"Looks like Benson's men found something," Evan said as he walked toward the back of the property.

"Go check it out. Just keep me in the loop, Crosby," Sheridan told him. "I'll get the techs you asked for and send them out ASAP. In the meantime, we'll keep looking for Lawrence Bridger and any other properties he might own, and I'll have someone track down Chuck Stock and see what he can tell us about the place."

"Thanks. I'll be in touch." Evan closed the phone and slipped it into his pocket.

"What have you got?" he called to Benson.

"There's a small shed out back; the door's padlocked; but we got it open," Benson told him. "Lucky for us, someone had the presence of mind to include 'any and all outbuildings' on the warrant. Anyway, there's a mess in there. My officers thought it was paint at first, but it sure looks like blood. All over the walls, the floor . . . even on the ceiling."

Two officers stood silently outside the wooden shed that was set at the very back edge of the property, where it backed up to dense woods. They stepped aside as Evan and their chief approached, and held the door open for the two men to enter.

The shed was no more than twelve feet wide and fifteen feet long. Rusted garden tools lay in a forgotten heap against a back wall. There was a metal folding chair near the door, and dirty blankets were piled in the middle of the floor. One small window on each wall was covered with dark paper, and in the August heat, the room was claustrophobically still. Benson waved away a yellow jacket and pointed to the wall.

"Check out the spatter," he said to Evan. "Odd patterns, don't you think?"

Evan knelt near the door and studied the way the blood had hit the back wall.

"Lot of blood to have come from one person," he noted. "The D.A. is sending the county CSI team over, including our two best techs. Let's see what they find. First, let's get a confirmation from them that this is, in fact, blood."

Ordinarily, Evan wasn't one to speculate, but his gut told him whose blood they would find mingled in the harsh abstract work that adorned the dark walls of the shed. The thought of what had happened to those young girls—his girls—in this room made his hands shake with rage.

His phone rang, and he was grateful for the excuse to back out of the airless enclosure. He stood under a half-dead maple in the backyard and listened to the news. When the call was complete, he hung up and motioned to Chief Benson.

"The D.A.'s office has located another house registered to Lawrence Bridger."

"Nearby?"

"Between here and Reading."

"That one vacant, too?"

"No." Evan smiled for the first time since he'd arrived on the scene. "No, that one is a busy place, apparently. The sheriff has had it under surveillance for several hours. Whoever lives there has had a lot of visitors this afternoon. All of them men."

"Well, fancy that."

Still smiling, Evan headed toward his car.

"Hey, Detective, aren't you going to wait for the lab people?" Benson called after him.

"Nope. I don't need to be standing around watching them swab the stains and dust for prints. It's going to take them hours—maybe days—to process this place. You give me a call if anything comes up, but for now, I need to be down in Oakmont. The sheriff is waiting on a warrant, and I want to be there when it arrives. I intend to be the first person to speak with the lady of the house . . ."

"Dorothea Rush." Evan looked from the woman to her driver's license and back again. "That your real name?"

She nodded sullenly.

"I want my lawyer."

"There's the phone." He pointed to it. "But you haven't been arrested yet; you're aware of that, right?"

She nodded again, this time warily.

"Then why did they bring me down here to the police station?" she asked.

"We just need to ask you a few questions. Look, Dotty . . . is that what people call you, Dotty?"

"My friends do." She stared at him straight on.

"Well, maybe by the time this is over, you'll consider me a friend."

She scowled, and he amended his statement to, "Okay, maybe not a friend, but I may be in a position to help you."

"Help me how?" That got her attention.

"Look, we know you don't own that house, we know you don't bring the girls in, we know your only role is in running the day-to-day. Keep the riffraff out, keep the girls clean, that sort of thing, am I right?"

"Sure." She nodded without meeting his eyes. "That's pretty much it."

"So you have to know that you're not the person we want. We want the person who owns the house."

"I don't even know who that is."

"You live in a house, but don't know who owns it?"

She shook her head. "I never met him."

"What did you do with the"—Evan searched for the word—"proceeds?"

"Someone comes by on Mondays and Thursdays. I hand over what we took in since the last pickup. On Mondays, he pays me. On Thursdays, he pays the house."

"Pays the house . . . ?"

"Expenses for the girls. Doctor's visits, prescriptions, that sort of thing."

"How often do the girls see a doctor?"

"Only if they're sick."

"When was the last time someone was sick enough to call a doctor?"

She shrugged. "I don't remember."

"Who does the food shopping?"

"I do. Online. I order through a website once a week, the stuff is delivered to the house."

"You pay with cash?"

"Credit card."

"Credit card?" Evan frowned. "Yours?"

"No, Orlando's."

"Who's Orlando?"

"He's the one who picks up the money."

"His name is on the card?"

Dotty nodded.

"Where's the card now?"

She opened her handbag, took out her wallet, and handed over the card.

"Orlando Ortiz. This his real name?" Evan studied the card.

"How would I know?"

"Good point." Evan tapped the card against the palm of his hand. "I'll be right back."

He disappeared into the hall, where he met Dan Conroy, one of the county assistant D.A.s. He handed over the card without a word, and Conroy, grinning from ear to ear, took it happily.

"Let's see where this little gem leads us. You'll be the first to know," Conroy promised Evan.

"Okay, so, does Orlando Ortiz own this house, you think?" Evan asked Dotty when he returned to the room.

"I don't know. Honest to God, I don't know where he lives or who he works for, if that's his real name or not. For all I know, his real name is John Smith."

"Who hired you?"

"Orlando."

"How did that happen? You saw an ad in the classifieds for a madam and thought you'd apply?"

"He came to me. I used to work someplace else. He offered me a job, said someone was starting up a new house, they wanted someone with experience to run it. Said I'd be paid well if I ran a tight ship and I asked no questions. I figured what the hell."

"When did they move you out of the house in Carleton?"

"Sunday." Her eyes flickered nervously.

"How'd that come about? You lose your lease?"

"He—Orlando—came by early in the morning and told me that everyone was moving out in the afternoon. They were sending trucks and they'd be taking us to another house."

"You didn't think that was odd?"

"I thought maybe the house was sold. I was paid to not ask questions. I didn't ask."

"Did you ask questions when those three young girls disappeared about a month ago?"

"They didn't disappear. They were moved."

"Moved? Moved where?"

"I don't know." She shrugged again, a flip of her shoulders, but the movement appeared overly casual.

"Because you don't ask questions."

"Right."

"Even when you see their pictures on the front page of your morning newspaper, after they turned up dead?"

She opened her mouth, but no words came out. Her face flushed crimson, and she averted her eyes.

Evan turned to leave, then stopped near the door and turned back. "Who watches out for you?"

"What do you mean?"

"Who's your security?"

She studied her nails for a long time, and Evan knew she was trying to decide which side in the drama that was about to play out would most benefit her. Finally, she said, "There were a couple of cops who came by at night. I don't know their names, and I don't know what police department they were from, so don't ask me. I don't know. But it was just the two of them, every time."

"They were in uniform?"

"No."

"How do you know they were cops?"

"Orlando told me."

"What else did he tell you about them?"

"Only that the boss bought them to keep the peace and to protect his interests."

"Would you recognize them? These cops?"

"Maybe. Maybe not . . ." She met his gaze head-on.

Evan knew the look: *Depends. What's in it for me?*

Disgusted, he left the room, determined to find the rogue cops, with or without Dotty's help.

## 22

". . . so we put together an album with photos of every cop in the county, and she just looks at them all and goes, 'I don't know, I don't think so . . .' "

Annie could hear the exasperation in Evan's voice.

"Honest to God, Annie, to get this close and to have to play this kind of game . . ."

"She's not going to give you a thing she doesn't have to give up. Not now, anyway. She's going to hold on to every card she can get her hands on, save them 'til she needs them."

"Maybe we should turn the heat up on her, give her a reason to start talking."

"It couldn't hurt. She can only give you more at this time, right? She can't give you less."

"True. She gave us some information, but nothing that would implicate anyone other than this guy she calls Orlando."

"And that may or may not be his real name."

"Exactly." He exhaled loudly.

"Well, here's something that should cheer you up. It looks like I have a lead on the kiddie trade coming out of Santa Estela."

"What?"

"I got a call from Connor—voice mail, actually. He said the Bureau was involved in some op down there to shut it all down, about two years ago. There's apparently a report in the office. Unfortunately, I have to wait for John to get back from his vacation tomorrow to get my hands on the report, but I'm hoping it will give us something you can use."

"God, that's phenomenal! I can hardly believe it. But why do you have to wait for John?"

"It must have been highly classified. I don't have clearance to pull the case, but John will, I'm sure. That's why I called you, to tell you that you might have another thread to pull soon."

"That would be terrific. This case has been like a black hole from day one. Honestly, this job is such a pain in the ass sometimes."

"Hey, you know what John said. Anytime you're ready to make a career move, come see him."

"That would simplify things, wouldn't it?" His voice softened.

"Not if it's not what you want to do. That would only create other problems."

"But we could spend a lot more time together. This catch-as-catch-can is wearing me down, Annie. I want to be with you."

"I know exactly what you mean, my love. I get worn down, too, you know. And I want to be with you, too."

"So what's the solution? You're there, with a job you love; I'm here with a job I love. In spite of what I say sometimes, I love what I do."

"We could both move to Baltimore and commute to our respective offices."

"Hey, swell idea. Why didn't I think of that?" He tried to make light of the situation, but his retort came out flat, and he made no more attempts at humor. Instead, he said, "I'm just better when I'm with you. None of it—none of this shit—is as bad if I can come home to you."

"I know. Me, too. We'll work it out, Evan. We'll think of something."

"Damn it. Hold on, Annie, I have another call coming in . . ."

Annie walked to the front window and looked out over the small grassy section in front of her building. The sun had yet to set, but the day was already beginning to fade. She stepped out onto her small balcony and leaned on the railing to watch the sky turn colors. The geranium she'd bought early in the summer sat dried in its pot, the soil petrified, the plant almost mummified. She couldn't remember the last time she'd watered it, or what she'd been thinking when she bought it. As much as she loved flowers, she always let them die. Too much work, too much time spent away from here.

"That was the lab," Evan said as he came back on the line. "Preliminary reports show that the blood in the shed matches my girls' blood types. Of course we'll need to match the DNA, but I know that's where they were killed. I knew it the second I stepped inside. It was as though—" He stopped, knowing he'd been about to say something that would sound irrational, then decided he didn't care. "It was as if they had led me there, as if they opened that door and went inside with me. As if they wanted me to see what had happened to them there, like they were standing behind me, pointing around the room. They showed me where and how they died." He hesitated, then asked, "Does that sound crazy?"

"Not to me," she assured him. "Now all you need is for them to tell you who."

"Sooner or later, they will. I told you before that I really believe the answer is already there, in the evidence. It's like a big puzzle. I just haven't found the right way to fit the pieces together. But when I do . . ."

"When you do, you'll have the key to the whole thing, from here to Santa Estela. I'm hoping I can help you with that. I was so excited this morning, after I got Connor's message. I couldn't wait to get into the office. Then of course I got there and realized that I had to wait for John. But this is going to come together soon. I can feel it."

"God, I hope you're right. If we can find this guy, this Orlando, maybe he'll lead us to the next rung on the ladder."

"How about the girls who were in the house? Were they able to tell you anything?"

"They're all with social services right now. I won't be able to talk to them until the morning, but I don't expect them to know who's running the operation. At least they should be able to tell us who they are and how they got here. We can take them back to their homes, get a lead on the kidnappers in their part of the world. The Bureau report should help us with that. It might take a while, but we can close down this little cottage industry. Maybe not permanently, and maybe only this little piece of it, but it's something."

"And then maybe you can find out who the murdered girls were."

"I'm hoping so. Right now, we don't know if these girls were from the same villages or even from the same country. But you're right. Maybe soon we'll be able to start tracing backward to find their homes."

"That should make you feel a lot better."

"I'll feel better when I've got their killer—killers—in prison, awaiting trial."

She started to say something, then heard the click on her phone.

"That's your call waiting, Annie. Go ahead and take it. I'm going to try to get a little sleep tonight, get an early start in the morning."

"Are you sure? I can let the call go into voice mail . . ."

"Go on and take it. I'll talk to you tomorrow. Love you."

"Love you, too." She paused, then clicked off his call to pick up the incoming. "Anne Marie McCall."

"Annie? It's Brendan."

"Hey, Brendan, what's up?"

"You still looking for a copy of those reports, the ones that have been missing from Dylan's file?"

"Of course. Why do you ask?"

"Well, I'm not sure, but I might have found them."

"Are you serious?" Her heart leaped in her chest. "Where? When?"

"Well, like I said, I'm not positive these are what you're looking for, but they might be. I found them this afternoon, stuck in a file. A shooting out in Oakland the same day that Dylan was shot. I guess at some point the reports might have fallen out, and maybe someone just looked at the date and filed them in the first file that popped up with that incident date on it. Anyway, I meant to bring them home, but I left them in my briefcase, and wouldn't you know, I left that locked in my office. I thought maybe I'd drop copies off tonight, but I have a tire going flat . . ."

"I'll come for you. I can be there in fifteen minutes." Annie didn't wait for a response. She hung up the phone and grabbed her bag, marveling at her good luck that day. *I should have bought lottery tickets today.* First, I get a call from Connor with a tip that could lead to something on Evan's case, and now this. If my luck holds, maybe I'll get into the office and find that John is back and I can get my hands on that Santa Estela case.

She all but whistled all the way to Brendan's house, a neat little bungalow set back on a narrow lot on a pretty street halfway between her apartment and the office. She parked in the drive and turned off the ignition, then followed the brick walk to the front door.

She rang the bell and waited for him to answer. When he did not, she rang it again, then a third time.

"Strange," she muttered aloud. "He knew I was on my way . . ."

Annie pushed against the half-open door and called Brendan's name. She stepped inside and called again. He stepped out of the kitchen, his cell phone to his ear. He waved to Annie to give him a minute, then walked toward the back of the house. At one point, he raised his voice, but quickly lowered it. When he came back into the living room, his phone had already disappeared into the pocket of his jacket. He smiled at Annie and apologized for not having let her in.

"Sorry. I was on the phone."

"Hey, it happens. Are you ready to go?"

"Yeah, just one second."

Brendan left the room for a minute, then came back in, tucking something into his belt.

"Don't trust my driving, eh?" she asked playfully.

"What?" He frowned.

"The Glock." As her duties were primarily those of a profiler, Annie rarely carried a weapon, but she knew that many of the other agents could not step outside their homes without one. She rarely thought anything of it.

"Oh. I just . . ." He stood in the middle of the room, and for the first time since she arrived, she took a good look around. There were piles of newspapers, magazines, and mail on the floor around the sofa. An empty pizza box and several empty beer bottles stood on the coffee table.

"Brendan, is everything all right?" She turned to him.

"Sure. Fine. Why do you ask?"

"Whenever Dylan had something on his mind, he forgot to pick up after himself. I was just wondering if it was a family trait." She tried to make a joke out of it, but she knew it fell flat and had sounded more like criticism than observation. "Sorry, I don't mean to sound like your mother."

"Oh, that." He waved off the mess. "I started cleaning up earlier, didn't get to finish. I've just been so busy lately, running from one job to the next, it seems—"

"Hey, I understand. We all have weeks like that." She jingled her car keys. "Shall we go?"

He stared at her for a moment, then said, "Yeah, let's do it."

Brendan followed her out the front door and down the steps. They had just started down the walk when a man in a dark suit stepped out from behind a car parked in front of the house and called out.

"Brendan! Let her go!"

"Wha . . . ?" Brendan grabbed Annie by the arm and held her protectively.

"Put the gun down, Brendan, and let her walk to me."

Brendan stood stock-still.

"It's no good, Brendan. Let her go!" The man was shouting as he came slowly up the walk, his gun drawn.

"Brendan . . ." Annie tried to twist away from him, but his grip on her right arm tightened. When she turned, she saw the gun in his hand. "Brendan, for God's sake . . ."

"Luther, you bastard." Brendan raised the gun, but before he could get a shot off, the man on the sidewalk fired twice, striking him in the chest.

Brendan crumbled to the ground, the gun still in his hand, and Annie screamed.

"Dr. McCall, are you all right?" the man asked anxiously.

He removed his glasses, and Annie recognized her savior.

"Luther," she gasped. "What the hell . . . ?"

"Just tell me you're all right, that he didn't hurt you."

"No, no. But I don't understand . . ."

Luther Blue knelt down next to Brendan's body and sought a pulse. "He's dead."

"Oh my God . . . Brendan . . ." Annie's knees began to shake.

"Come on, here, sit." Luther led her gently to the steps and helped her to sit, even as he was calling for backup on his cell phone.

Annie began to sob. "I don't understand . . ."

"I'm sorry, I'm so sorry, but he had his gun up to your back, and I was afraid he was going to kill you . . ."

"No, no, he and I were going in to the office, he found reports I've been looking for, about Dylan's death, he left them locked in his desk—"

"Dr. McCall, Brendan didn't have these reports. I do. Believe me when I tell you, he wasn't going to turn them over to you or to anyone else."

"What are you talking about?"

"I'm talking about the fact that I believe the report implicates Brendan in Dylan's death."

"I don't believe it."

"I'm sorry, but I'm afraid it's the truth." He took an envelope out of his jacket pocket and handed it to her as the first of the unmarked cars pulled up in front of the house. "Brendan Shields shot and killed his cousin and fellow agent Dylan Shields. The proof is in that envelope. And if I hadn't arrived when I did, I'm afraid he would have killed you as well . . ."

"Isn't John here yet?" A shaken Annie met Will Fletcher in the office lobby. She'd called him because, with John out of town, Will was the acting supervisory agent in charge.

"Yeah, I called him the minute I heard. He should be back anytime now." Will put his arm around her. "What do you want to do? Do you want to go upstairs and wait in the office, do you want to get something to eat while we wait for John? What do you want, Annie?"

"Maybe we can just get something cold to drink."

"When did you last eat?"

"Lunch, I think."

"It's almost midnight. Let's walk across the street and grab a sandwich or some soup or something. You look real shaky."

"I *am* real shaky."

"Did you give a statement to anyone yet?"

"Not a formal one. They're waiting for John."

They stepped outside into a muggy D.C. night. Will took her arm to steady her and they walked across the street to the all-night deli on the corner.

"Did you call Evan?"

"Yes." She nodded. "He wanted to drive down tonight, but I told him to wait. He's right on the brink of cracking a case he's been working on for weeks, and I don't want him to distract himself from that. I'm okay, I wasn't hurt."

Will held the door for her and walked into the deli behind her. It was cool and quiet inside, and they went up to the counter to place their orders, then took a booth.

"So, you want to tell me what happened tonight?" Will asked.

"I'm still not sure I understand." Annie rested her elbows on the cool porcelain tabletop.

"Start from the beginning, maybe we can piece it together."

"Well, it started with Brendan calling me earlier tonight. He said he found the reports that were missing from Dylan's file, that he'd left them in the office. He said he was going back to pick them up, but he had a tire that was losing air, so I told him I'd come over and get him." She stopped to take a sip from the glass of water the counter waitress had brought her. "When I got there, he was on the phone. He didn't even hear me ring the bell, so I went inside. I could see him back in the kitchen area, and when he saw me he waved, you know, like 'I'll be with you in a minute.' He got off the phone, and we started out of the house. We got as far as the top of the sidewalk when Luther showed up, started to yell at Brendan to drop the gun and let me go, and something about, it was all over, not to hurt me . . ." She rubbed at her eyes. "The next thing I knew, Luther was shooting at Brendan and Brendan fell . . ."

"Had you seen a gun in Brendan's hand?" Will asked quietly.

"Not outside, but then again, I wouldn't have. He was behind me. I knew that he had one with him, though. I saw him put it in his belt."

"He needed a gun to go to the office?" Will frowned.

"A lot of agents don't go anywhere without their Glocks; you know that, Will."

"True enough." Will stirred a packet of sugar into his iced tea. "Had you felt threatened, did you know that Brendan had pulled the gun?"

"I had no clue." She shook her head vehemently. "I had no idea there was anything wrong until Luther showed up and started shouting at Brendan."

"You said Luther was yelling at Brendan to drop the gun, to not hurt you, to let you go . . ."

"Right."

"Did Brendan yell anything back at Luther?"

"It all happened so fast, I don't . . ." She rubbed her index finger across her chin, a gesture he'd seen her use when she was deep in thought. "He called him a bastard. 'Luther, you bastard.' That's the only thing I remember hearing him say."

"That's an odd thing to say, don't you think? Under those circumstances?" Will frowned.

"I don't know. He might have said something else. I was just so stunned, so startled, I was having a hard time figuring out what was going on. Everything happened so fast, Will . . ."

His phone rang, and he took it from his pocket.

"Fletcher." He listened for a moment, then said, "I'm with her right now. Sure. No problem."

He folded over the phone and returned it to his pocket.

"That was John. He's on his way in from the airport."

"Does he want me to meet him at his office?"

"No. He wants me to take you home and make sure you get some sleep. He'll give us a call in the morning."

She frowned. "You'd think he'd want to talk to me."

"He does. In the morning. Right now, he wants to talk to Luther Blue."

23

Luther sat calmly in the small leather side chair that faced John Mancini's desk and waited for the interrogation to begin. He'd been there for almost two hours awaiting John's arrival, in the company of Special Agent Harold Kimble, a man Luther considered to be stupid and without imagination. He might actually enjoy this.

"Okay, Agent Blue," Mancini was saying as he eased himself into his own well-worn leather chair. "It's been a long night for all of us, so let's get to the point. What the hell happened?"

"I shot Agent Shields," Luther told him. "I killed him."

"We know that part, Luther," John said, his face and voice both weary. "Let's talk about why."

"He was going to kill Dr. McCall."

"Why would he want to do that?" John frowned.

"I'm thinking it was because she was—"

"You're thinking? You don't know?" Kimble rose half out of his seat.

"Sit down, Harold." John motioned him back into his chair. "Let him finish."

"I think it was because she'd been asking about the reports that were missing from the Bureau file of the investigation into Dylan Shields's death."

"Why would that have been a concern to Agent Shields? He and Dylan were cousins."

"I believe it was because the reports would show that Agent Shields—Brendan—fired the shots that killed Dylan."

"Agent Blue, you understand the seriousness of this accusation?"

"Sir, I understand full well. That's why when I found the reports—"

"You found the reports?" Mancini's eyebrows rose in tandem. "All three of them?"

"Yes, sir, Agent Lowery's report, Agent Raymond's report, and a memo from Agent Shields. Connor Shields. I found them by accident. I was looking through the McCullum file, and I found the reports in an envelope stuck in the back of the file. I immediately realized these were the missing reports—"

"How did you know about that? How did you know they were missing?"

"Sir"—Luther smiled benignly—"everyone in the unit knew about the missing reports. Dr. McCall had, at one time, asked just about everyone about them, especially the report written by Agent Lowery."

"Had she asked you?"

"No, not directly, but I heard about it from several people. And then, with Agent Lowery having been found dead so recently, I thought I'd read over her report and see what the big deal was."

"The big deal?"

"There was a buzz going around the office that there was something in her report that might have been the reason she'd been killed. So I thought if maybe I looked over the report, something might jump out at me."

"And did something?"

"Not at first. I had to go back to the old file—the original file. It took me a few hours, but I figured it out."

Mancini gestured for him to continue. It was all Luther could do to keep from grinning like a fool. He had the man eating out of his hand.

"The file contained the customary list of FBI personnel assigned to the op. It's stapled in the front of the file. So that's where I started. With the players. I heard that's what Dr. McCall had done, so I did the same. I read through the file, read all the reports, to put the entire op into perspective. Then I read the other three reports again, in context. That's when I realized several things." He paused for effect. Mancini and Kimble were hanging on every word. He let them hang for as long as he could. "Agent Lowery's report mentioned seeing Agent Brendan Shields leaving the building identified as Building A on the diagram."

He looked from one to the other, then asked, "May I show you?"

"Please do."

"If we could get the file in here? I left it on my desk, with the original reports." Luther smiled weakly at John. "I made a copy of the three reports, but I gave them to Dr. McCall."

"Why?"

"Because she'd been looking for them."

"When did you give her these reports?"

"Tonight. After I . . . after the . . . after the shooting at Agent Shields's."

"You took them with you?"

"Yes. I wanted to confront him about why—"

Mancini held up a hand to stop him. "We're getting ahead of ourselves."

"I can run down and get the file, if you like."

"Please . . ."

Luther hustled down the hall to his office, buoyed by his own enjoyment of the situation. He was relishing the spotlight, loving the script he'd written for himself. It was, he thought, quite simply brilliant. By the end of the night, he'd be hailed as a hero. He could hardly wait to get to the part where he'd explain how he'd saved Annie McCall's life.

He returned with the file and opened it on Mancini's desk.

"Okay, here's the list of personnel, in front, then the list of documents in the file. I think everyone agrees that all the documents were here except for Agent Lowery's report, a memo from Agent Shields—that would be Connor Shields—and a sketch of the scene from Agent Lou Raymond." He looked up first at Mancini, then at Kimble, and said meaningfully, "Interesting, don't you think, that both Agents Lowery and Raymond died suspiciously? She, murdered just last week, and he, a one-car accident on a dark stretch of highway?"

"How do you know Lowery was murdered?"

"Sir, everyone in this unit knows she was murdered."

"And you found all three of those items in the McCullum file yesterday? Doesn't that strike you as odd?" John leaned back in his chair, and Luther could feel his eyes bore through him.

"Yes, of course it does." Luther nodded calmly. "I was thinking, if someone had gone to the pains to remove the reports in the first place, why didn't they just destroy them? It makes no sense to hide them in another file, where they could be found, but who knows what this person was thinking? Maybe he'd just stuck them in there to get rid of them when someone else came in the room, and meant to go back to get them . . . I don't know. I wasn't the one who put them in there in the first place. I only found them."

He flipped open the cover of the file and took out the three documents under discussion. He handed them in turn to Mancini. "Here's the sketch Lou Raymond made of the scene, showing where everyone was at the time of the shooting. Here's the report from Melissa Lowery, and the memo to the file from Connor Shields."

He gave John a minute to look over the documents, then said, "You'll notice Brendan Shields is not listed on the personnel list, and his name does not appear on the diagram Lou made showing where everyone was standing. But Lowery notes that she saw Brendan exiting the building—the building from which the shots were fired that killed Dylan Shields and badly injured his brother Aidan—right after she and the others arrived on the scene." He leaned over the desk to point to a section on the back of the report. "As you can see, Brendan was noted carrying a high-powered rifle in one hand and a rifle case in the other. Lowery's report notes he told her that he'd gone into the building to see if he could apprehend the shooter, but found the building empty of all except Bureau personnel at that time."

John studied the sketch.

"Here you see who all went into the building; Lou places them all right here." Luther pointed to the sketch showing six stick figures representing each of the agents who had gone into the building after Dylan had been shot. "Brendan is not represented on the sketch."

"So we have one report indicating that Brendan was on the scene, in the building, with a high-powered rifle—despite the fact that his name does not appear on the list of assigned personnel. And we have a sketch by a fellow agent that doesn't place him on the team that went into the building, yet he was seen coming out right around the time that some of the other agents arrived on the scene." John rubbed his chin thoughtfully. "It is incriminating."

"And, sir, you have the report from Connor Shields there." Luther pointed to it.

"The significance of that is . . ." John skimmed the report. "Of course. I remember. Connor was supposed to have been on this op with Aidan. At the last minute, we pulled him off to sent him to . . ." He hesitated. "We needed him someplace else that night. We sent Dylan in as a substitute because he and Connor look so much alike that even—"

He stopped in midsentence, took off his glasses, and rubbed his eyes.

"They looked so much alike, even someone in their own family couldn't tell them apart in the dark." Luther finished the sentence.

"You seem to be implying that Brendan thought he was killing Connor," John said thoughtfully.

"I think the evidence could be interpreted that way."

"Why would Brendan want to kill Connor?"

"I guess you would have to ask Connor that, sir."

"I guess I will." John nodded. "In the meantime, let's get back to what happened tonight."

"Yes, sir. I went to Brendan Shields's home with the copies I'd made of the reports."

"Was he expecting you?"

"Well, I'd called him earlier in the afternoon, and—"

"Did you tell him what you'd found?"

"Not in so many words, but I may have implied it. I probably did." Luther appeared contrite for a moment. "In retrospect, I should have kept my mouth shut about that."

"What time was that?"

"Late afternoon, early evening. Maybe around six or so."

John gestured for him to continue.

"Anyway, I called him again, just a few minutes before I arrived. I'd been to his house once before, but wasn't sure of where to turn off Capital Road. He told me he was just leaving, and that now wasn't a good time for me to come by. He tried to brush me off, but since I was almost there—"

"Did he give you directions then?"

"No . . ."

"You said you weren't sure where you were going. How did you find the house?"

"A lucky guess, I suppose."

"Lucky for Dr. McCall." Kimble nodded.

"Yes. Well, I pulled up in front of the house, and I saw Agent Shields exiting the front door with Dr. McCall. He had her by the arm, and it looked as if he was steering her along. I got out of the car and called to him. He turned slightly, and that's when I saw he had his gun in his right hand."

"Where was the gun pointed?"

"Square at Dr. McCall's back."

"So you did what?"

"I called to him to drop the gun, to let her go. But he sort of pulled her in front of him as he came down the sidewalk. By this time, he had the gun raised and pointed in my direction, and he appeared to be about to fire, so I fired first. There were civilians in the area, the woman next door had started out of her house and went back in—"

"How many shots did you fire?"

"Two."

"How many shots did Agent Shields fire?"

"None, sir. I shot him before he could fire."

"And both of your shots struck Agent Shields."

"Yes, sir." Luther lowered his voice and tried to appear sorrowful. He gave it his all. "Sir, I can't begin to tell you how sorry I am that this happened. I've known Agent Shields for years—God, we worked together—I couldn't believe what I was seeing in that file. I wanted to talk to him about it, I thought there must be another explanation. That's why I went there. I wanted him to tell me there was another reason why he'd been in that building before the rest of the team went in, why he was there at all, since he hadn't been part of that team." Luther looked up at his boss and said sadly, "I'd tried, but I couldn't think of one."

"Why do you suppose Dr. McCall was there?"

"I have no idea, sir. I guess you'll have to talk to her about that."

"Oh, I'll definitely do that."

"Just out of curiosity, why had you pulled the McCullum file?" John asked.

"Oh. Well, I was looking for the name of a CI that we used in that case. I have another case in Detroit and I could use a little inside information."

"Did you find it?"

"Yes, thanks. I already put in a call."

"Good. In the meantime, we owe you a huge thank-you. It appears you may very well have saved Dr. McCall's life. Of course we need your gun and your badge until the investigation is complete . . ."

Luther nodded solemnly.

". . . and the Director is going to want to talk to you first thing in the morning. He and the Shields brothers—that's the last generation, Thomas and Frank—go way back. This is going to be very hard on everyone; I'm sure you understand that. But God only knows what might have happened to Annie if you hadn't been there to save her."

"I only did what any of us would have done, sir."

John nodded and stood up, a clear sign that the interview was over.

Luther was half out the door when John called to him. "I'm going to ask you not to discuss this with anyone for the time being. We have the local police to deal with. We're going to try to keep this out of the press as much as possible. I don't have to tell you what a PR nightmare this is going to be. And then there's the Shields family. As I'm sure you know, they've given more than their share to the Bureau. Brendan's father is going to be heartbroken over this whole thing. We need to be sensitive and respectful of their situation. And it goes without saying that I have your word you will not be leaving the area."

For a moment, John Mancini appeared to be about to cry.

Luther left the office feeling better than he had in a long, long time.

Were it not for the fact that it would surely have drawn suspicion, he'd have been skipping down the hall and whistling a happy tune. He'd gotten rid of one horrendous thorn in his side and made himself look like a hero at the same time. Oh, sure, his original plan had been to get rid of Annie, too, but then that woman next door had come out and blown that.

What the hell, at least he'd come out of it looking good. And it was actually better for him in the long run, he rationalized as he walked to the elevator. Annie could corroborate his version of what happened, and no one would ever question Anne Marie McCall.

All in all, it had been a very good day.

24

Connor sat in the darkened room, swirling the amber liquid around in his glass until it spun like a whirlpool. If there ever was a time in his life when he wanted oblivion, it was now.

He'd been en route from his weeklong rest in Essaouira to his latest assignment when he'd gotten the call from John Mancini on his cell.

"Call me from a secure line. Now."

It had taken Connor another hour to return to the Villa André and make the call. He'd spent every minute since wishing he had not.

His cousin Brendan was dead, shot by a fellow agent who'd seen Brendan with a gun pointed at Annie McCall's back.

At first he'd been tempted to laugh out loud. How crazy was that scenario? Brendan holding a gun on Annie? Was he kidding?

Then came the bombshell.

From all the evidence, it appeared that Brendan had been the one who shot and killed Connor's own brother Dylan.

For Connor, the world had tilted and was now spinning off its axis. None of this could be true. Brendan couldn't have killed Dylan, Connor had told John. Brendan hadn't even been there that night.

"Actually, he was. His presence was mentioned on a report. A report he may have killed to have kept secret."

And then John had told him about Melissa Lowery's report, and her disappearance, and her death . . . and her marriage to Grady.

No way would Brendan have killed the woman his brother loved, Connor had insisted. This is all insanity.

"Connor. If he killed Dylan, what would have stopped him from killing a woman he barely knew?"

"What are you doing to determine whether or not he did in fact kill Dylan?"

"We've confiscated the weapons from his house. We're going to start running ballistics tests this morning."

Then came the kicker.

"Connor," John said, "can you think of any reason why Brendan would have wanted you dead?"

"Me? You think he was coming after me next?"

"No. The theory is that you might have been the original target."

"That's just crazy."

"Think for a minute, would you? I know this is all coming as a shock, but put your emotions aside and think. Is there any reason Brendan would have wanted you dead? Anything you had over on him, or anything that you knew that could hurt him, anything questionable about his actions, anything strange that struck you as odd or out of the ordinary. Anything he seemed secretive or evasive about?"

"Santa Estela." The words left Connor's lips before he'd even thought of them.

"What about it?"

"A couple of years back, I was there right before the elections . . ."

"I remember."

"On the night I was to leave, I was on my way down to the dock for the boat that was to pick me up, and I took a shortcut through an alley that ran between some abandoned warehouses. There was a deal going down; I watched from the alley. Six, seven men, a truck filled with kids. One of me. I was trying to figure out what to do when I ran into Brendan."

"You ran into Brendan in the alley?" John had been clearly surprised.

"He walked in one end while I was at the other. Almost didn't recognize him at first, it was dark, and let's face it, the last person you expect to run into under those circumstances is a member of your own family."

"What was he doing there?"

"He told me he was on the op that was just about to close down the kiddie traffic."

"What op?"

"The operation to shut down the traffic in children coming out of Santa Estela. He told me not to worry about the kids in the truck because he was part of the team that was shutting it down that night. When I asked him about it later, he blew me off as if it wasn't important, but an op like that could have had international repercussions and I . . ."

"Connor, there was no team in Santa Estela that had been sent in to work on the child-slave trade."

"He must have been working for another unit then, because he told me—"

"Listen to me. He was working for me. He's always worked for me, and only for me. There was no op. He was there to keep an eye on the rebels, to keep the political situation stable."

"John, you're wrong. They closed it down that night, he told me they did. There's a whole file on this, he wrote a report—"

"Did you see it? Did he show you the report?"

"Well, no, but he told me—"

"Connor, we're talking about the man who may have killed your brother. Why are you defending him?"

"I can't believe any of this. The Brendan I knew—"

"Just how well did you know him?"

Connor had paused to take a deep breath.

"If any of what you're telling me is true, I'd have to say I didn't know him at all."

There'd been talk after that of a memorial service to be held the following week.

"You might want to think about coming home for it, Connor."

"I don't have to think about it. I won't be there."

"I can arrange for you to come home."

"That bastard." Anger had started to take over. "The bastard. How could he have pulled the trigger on Dylan?"

"Well, like I said, he might not have realized he was shooting Dylan. It was dark, you were supposed to be there with Aidan that night. I don't think Dylan was the target."

"You think he wanted to kill me because I'd seen him in Santa Estela? You think he was part of that, selling truckloads of children? There's no way he would have been involved in something like that, John."

"Think it through. Why else would he have been there? We know there was no op to shut it down, so if he wasn't shutting it down— and we know he lied to you about that—he must have been part of it. It had to occur to him that sooner or later, you would ask about that, and there was the danger that you'd figure out what was going on."

"You really think he was involved in the trafficking?"

"I think he had to have been. And he had to know that sooner or later, you would be asking about how that all went down."

"I did," Connor had said softly.

"What?"

"I did ask. A week or so ago. I left a message on his answering machine, asking him what happened."

"Why? What made you think of it?"

"Annie was asking me about Santa Estela. She knew I'd been there, and her new guy, that detective from Pennsylvania, had a murder vic who might have had ties to Santa Estela." He had stopped to recall exactly what Annie had said. "I think it was more than one vic, young girls, and there was a question about some tattoos."

"Did you tell Brendan that Annie had been asking?"

Connor closed his eyes, trying to remember what he'd said on the message. "Honest to God, John, I don't remember if I did or not."

There was silence while each digested what had been said.

"Is there a chance that Brendan wanted to kill Annie because I told him she was asking questions? Jesus, John, I don't know."

Before he hung up, Connor had asked, "How's my dad doing? Have you spoken to my uncle Frank?"

"I spoke with your brother. Maybe you should give him a call. There was some talk about who would be the pallbearers."

"Well, they can count me out. No fucking way." The anger resurfaced. "Son of bitch murdered my brother, I'm going to carry his casket? How could Aidan even consider it?"

"I don't think Aidan is thinking about honoring the dead as much as he's thinking about honoring the living."

Connor had let that sink in. Regardless of what Brendan might have done, his father—Connor's uncle Frank—would be devastated at the loss of his son. To lose a son under these circumstances would be humiliating for a man—a family—who had served the Bureau long and well.

"Call Aidan, Connor," John had said. "And if you change your mind about coming home, just let me know. I'll clear it."

"Don't expect to hear from me."

Connor had hung up and had gone to the balcony to look out over the water, his eyes stinging with tears. He'd had a hell of a time processing the information he'd received. His cousin had wanted to kill him, but shot and killed his brother instead. Then he himself was shot and killed while apparently planning on killing Annie.

What the hell had happened to his world?

He thought of Brendan as a young boy, almost a decade younger than Connor. He'd been the quiet one, the one who always held to the background. There'd been a time when he and Dylan had been adversaries of sorts, but that had long since passed. No, he couldn't believe that Brendan could have fired that shot. Brendan, who had sobbed as he'd carried Dylan's coffin down the steps of St. Bernadette's Church, Brendan, who had comforted Connor's father as well as his own.

Connor had started drinking after the conversation with John, and hadn't stopped. Unfortunately, the whiskey hadn't made him drunk, hard as he'd tried to silence the voices in his head.

He had called Aidan and berated him for even considering bearing Brendan's coffin.

"It's not for him, Connor," Aidan had said. "It's for Uncle Frank. And for Dad. You remember how Dad leaned on Uncle Frank through Dylan's—"

"Yeah, I remember." Connor had cut him off. "But this is different. This is the bastard who killed Dylan. Of course he thought he was shooting me."

"That's what's bothering you, isn't it?" Aidan had said. "You're feeling guilty because Dylan took the shots that may have been for you."

Connor had tried to respond, but couldn't get words out.

"Con, no one is ever going to blame you for not dying that night. Jesus, Con."

When Connor still did not reply, Aidan had said, "Look, come home and be with us through this. Dad needs you, Uncle Frank needs you. Mia, Andrew . . . shit, Con, I need you."

"Sorry, little brother. You do what you want. But I'll have no part in it."

"If you change your mind—"

"I won't change my mind. Give everyone my love, though."

And with that, Connor had hung up.

There were lights from the boats that still came and went in the small harbor, even at this late hour. Connor stood by the rail, watching, wishing he was on one of them.

Maybe tomorrow, he told himself. Maybe tomorrow he'd take a boat out. Maybe he'd just keep it going until it ran out of gas. And then, maybe he'd just slide overboard and let the water take him where it would.

He went back into his room, picked up the phone, and called downstairs for another bottle.

25

"How about if I just meet you at the cemetery?" Evan rolled down the window of the rental car he'd picked up at the airport and cursed himself for not checking the air-conditioning before he'd gotten onto I-95. Now he was stuck in a massive traffic jam, the temperature had risen into the high eighties already, and the fan was blowing warm.

"That's fine, Evan," Annie told him. "The church is going to be packed to capacity, if the number of cars already in the lot is an indication."

"I'm surprised that so many people came out for him, a disgraced FBI agent."

"It's for his family. His dad has ties that go back fifty years. He and Dylan's dad were very highly regarded in the law enforcement community. Yes, there's certainly a lot of embarrassment, but at the same time, there's been a lot of support. I'm really not surprised that so many people are here to pay their respects to Frank. And to Andrew, and Mia. And the others."

"Are Connor and Aidan there?"

"Aidan was at the viewing last night. Connor apparently is having a real hard time of it, according to Mara. She said Aidan was just devastated by what's happened, and the fact that Connor refuses to come home and support the family is really bothering him."

"She's been there all week?"

"Of course. She's Aidan's wife. She'll stand by them."

"Even though Brendan was going to kill you?"

"In spite of it."

"I think you're pretty remarkable, to go to the viewing and the funeral of the man who tried to take your life. Not to mention the fact that he murdered Dylan."

"I'm too close to the family to not go, Evan. We talked about this. If you don't want to come to the services, you shouldn't feel you have to."

"I want to be there with you." He craned his neck to look out the window at the traffic that still hadn't moved. "However, at this rate, I'll be lucky if I'm out of here by noon."

"Well, since the service here is going to start in about ten minutes, why not just plan on meeting me at the cemetery." She was walking now. Evan could hear the click of her heels, the change in her breathing. "You have the directions?"

"Yeah. Assuming I ever get off 95 to use them. I'll catch up with you at the cemetery."

"Okay. Look, I'm going into the church. I'll see you later."

Evan ended the call and tossed the phone onto the front seat, then leaned heavily against the door. The car in front of him moved forward by about a foot, and all the other cars inched up behind one another hopefully.

There was nothing worse than a traffic jam on a major highway on a hot, steamy, humid August morning. Evan felt along the floor for the water bottle that had earlier rolled from the passenger seat and took a long drink once he'd successfully snagged it. The cars began to move, slowly at first, then a little steadier. With all the car windows down, there was a slight bit of breeze. He was debating whether to get off at the next exit and try to find the church, or simply go ahead to the cemetery, as he and Annie had discussed, when the car in front of him came to a halt, and the others stopped behind it. Traffic stalled once again, making the decision for him. He turned up the radio and searched for last night's baseball scores.

Luther stood alongside his car and watched the faithful flock to the tent that had been erected next to the gaping hole in the earth that would serve as Brendan Shields's last earthly home. Luther hadn't gone to the church with the others from his unit that morning—he felt that would have been too much for the family; his presence would have been more noticeable there. But here, under the open sky, where all of the family and those closest to the dearly departed had gathered together under the tent, he could hug the back of the crowd and disappear into it. He wasn't sure how anyone would feel about having the man who was responsible for the gathering mingling among the mourners, and thought his best bet would be to stay out of sight as much as possible.

But that was fine, as far as Luther was concerned. He'd rather be in a position where he could observe the goings-on. Once everyone arrived and the coffin was in place and the preliminaries dealt with, he'd stroll through the headstones off to his left and find an inconspicuous place for himself amid the crowd that spilled from the rear of the tent.

From his vantage point, he watched the procession of long black limos slowly approach, watched the bereaved family—a huge mass of black hats and black suits—walk together across the grassy expanse. The pallbearers gathered at the back of the hearse to carry the coffin, which the priest followed in the company of Frank Shields and his brother, Thomas, and their children.

Luther knew each of them by name, had worked with several of them over the years. He felt nothing for any of them, not even the beautiful Mia, who, once upon a time, had been the focus of many of Luther's fondest dreams.

Other cars eased along the drive, looking for places to park and hoping to find a spot under a tree where there might be some bit of shade. It took a full twenty-five minutes for all the cars to empty and the mourners to make their way to the gathering place. From a slight rise back near a line of trees, a lone bagpiper began to play "Amazing Grace," and even Luther was touched by the poignancy of the moment.

A fitting tribute to one who had fallen from grace, Luther was thinking as he closed the car door and started across the grass, well behind the tent and the overflow of friends and family. Once he reached his destination, he was careful to pick a spot at the very back, where no one he knew stood.

At least, he thought he had.

Then the woman in front of him turned around, and he was face-to-face with Anne Marie McCall.

She smiled, her big blue eyes brimming with tears, and patted his arm, a gesture meant to comfort him, he assumed, to show that she understood why he felt he had to be here. He smiled gently in return, as if silently communicating his thanks.

*As if I would have missed this. As if I'd be anywhere else today.* Brendan Shields had been a stone around his neck—had been for the past year or so—and had brought all this on himself. He'd screwed up just about everything he'd been asked to do.

It was beyond Luther to understand why any of these people mourned his loss.

Connor scanned the crowd, searching for his father and brother under the tent, but was having a hard time placing them. Finally, he located his dad in the middle of the first row of seats, between his cousin Mia and his brother Aidan. He'd catch up with them later. He knew they'd be happy to see him.

He regretted that he hadn't arrived early enough to be there with them now, that he hadn't been there for the past week to share the pain and the grief—and yes, the shame—with the family, especially his uncle Frank. It embarrassed him every time he realized it had taken him way too long to understand the importance of his presence here, both to himself and to his family. He hoped they would forgive him for his shortsightedness.

The crowd was huge, much larger than he would have expected, and he was wondering if the others in the family had been equally surprised at the numbers. He made his way to the back of the tent, where friends and coworkers spilled onto the grass twenty or thirty deep, and was moved by the show of support for his uncle and his cousins. He took a place in the very last row.

He nodded a silent greeting to several people from the Bureau as the priest began to pray, his words echoing through the small speakers on either side of the tent. Connor stood with his hands together, his head bowed, a sign of reverence he'd learned as a small boy in a large Catholic family. The priest finished the prayer, and the piper began to play again, a tune Connor didn't recognize. He gazed around the mourners in the crowd in front of him and thought he recognized Annie, though in that hat, he couldn't be certain it was her. She turned and saw him, then smiled and winked. As she turned back toward the front, a man behind her glanced back at him. Connor caught his gaze, and held it.

A shock went through him as he realized where he'd seen that face before.

In the headlights of a truck, in the shadow of abandoned warehouses, in Santa Estela . . .

The man continued to stare at Connor, at first almost quizzically, then, as if in recognition. He smiled broadly, stepped forward, and whispered something in Annie's ear before moving to the far side of the crowd with her, one hand on her arm, the other hidden inside his jacket.

Connor moved along with them, keeping thirty feet behind, as they stepped from under the tent and made their way around the headstones and monuments. He heard footfalls behind him and spun around, his gun drawn.

Evan Crosby was moving fast to catch up. They greeted each other silently, and Evan motioned that he'd be following from the tree line. Connor nodded in agreement, and both men took off across the gently rolling terrain in pursuit of Annie and her abductor, the identity of whom was a mystery to both Connor and Evan.

The cemetery ended at a high black iron fence capped with tall spikes. It was too high to vault over, and impossible to climb. Connor approached cautiously, his gun in plain sight, slowing his step.

"So. We meet," the man holding Annie called to him. "I've heard a lot about you, Connor Shields."

"You have me at a disadvantage," Connor replied. "I know *what* you are, but not *who* you are."

"Allow me. Luther Blue." He pronounced the name defiantly.

"Luther Blue? But you're the one who . . ." Confusion crossed Connor's face for just a second.

"The one who shot Brendan, yes. Yes, I am."

"I was going to say, the one who saved Annie." He kept his eyes on Luther, willing himself not to glance at Evan, who approached

Luther slowly from behind, as quiet and deliberate as a cat stalking a mouse.

Luther Blue laughed. "So the story goes."

"What do you mean, so the story goes?" *Keep him talking,* Connor told himself. *Give Evan time to get himself into position.*

Luther grinned.

"Brendan didn't have his gun drawn, did he?"

"Well, he drew on me."

"But not on Annie." Connor met her eyes, and silently begged her to be silent, to be still, not to give Luther any reason to react. But she was a pro. She'd know what to do.

"It's immaterial." Luther shrugged. "He was planning on killing her, not there and then, but yes, it had already been decided. However, after that was set up, it occurred to me that I could kill two birds with one stone—you're going to have to forgive that lousy pun—and still come off looking like a hero. You have to give me credit, it was pretty damned slick."

"About as slick as the back of your head is going to be if you so much as blink." Evan stood behind Luther, the barrel of his gun flush against Luther's skull.

"I can still take her out with one shot," Luther said calmly, as if they were discussing where to have lunch.

"You'll be dead before your finger twitches."

"Shall we see?" Luther remained cocky, even as he began to pale.

Evan pushed the barrel into Luther's head.

"What do you think, Shields? Who's your money going on?" Evan asked.

Luther's eyes shifted back to Connor, who had not moved from his spot twenty feet away.

"My money's always been on you, pal," Connor said.

"Nice." Luther smiled, careful not to move his head. "I think you two must be best buds."

"I'll tell you what I think," Evan said. "I think you have two choices here. I think you drop the gun and take your chances with a jury, or I put a bullet through your brain right now."

"What do you think, Agent Blue?" Connor spoke softly, evenly. "A minute ago, you were bragging about how slick you are. Think you're slick enough to outwit a jury? Slick enough to make a deal? I'll bet you know plenty about the kiddie slave trade, plenty the government would love to hear. Who knows, you could trade a little of this for a little of that."

"Or," Evan repeated, "I could put a bullet through your brain right now."

The air was thick and the sun almost directly overhead. The four stood stock-still for a full minute. Three were holding their breaths; the fourth was weighing his options.

Finally—*clunk*.

The Glock hit the ground, and Luther released his hold on Annie, who stepped away from him and into Connor's arms. Connor knew she must be aching to go to Evan, but the scene had yet to play out.

Luther held up both hands in a gesture of surrender.

"Crosby, you've got cuffs?" Connor asked as he walked toward them.

"No." Evan shook his head. "You're going to have to take him in, anyway. I don't have jurisdiction here."

"Now he tells me," Luther muttered.

Connor stood in front of Luther, the gun in his hand pointed straight at Luther's chest.

"I want to know one thing. Did you kill my brother?"

"Saint Dylan?" Luther asked. "No. No, that was Brendan."

"Do you know why?" Connor stepped closer.

"Because he thought Dylan was you." Luther smiled and pointed in the direction of the road. "Shall we go?"

"Why did he want to kill me?"

"Because of what you'd seen in Santa Estela. He was afraid you'd ask too many questions."

"What about Santa Estela?" Evan frowned.

"Our friend here was running a kiddie shuttle out of the country, sold them off to—where, Luther?" Connor asked.

"To whoever offered the most money, of course."

Evan stopped and stared at Luther's back. The man continued to walk as if he didn't have a care in the world.

"Who did you sell to in Pennsylvania?" Evan asked. He called to Connor, "Stop for a minute."

He caught up with Connor and Luther and grabbed Luther by the lapels. "Who did you sell to on the East Coast?"

"I didn't do the selling, Agent . . ." Luther paused. "I didn't catch your name."

"Who did the selling, Blue? Who did you give the kids to?" Evan persisted.

"They were brought to me by a contact in Santa Estela. I moved them out of the country. Where they went to once they left Santa Estela, I have no idea."

"Who paid you?" Evan was almost in his face.

"I don't think we're going to continue this conversation any longer." Luther turned to Connor. "If you're taking me in, take me in. Let's not waste any more time. It's hot out here . . ."

They walked between the rows of graves, an odd little parade of four. Luther first in line, Connor directly behind, his gun drawn. Still calm, Annie walked hand in hand with Evan, keeping the pace. They were within thirty feet of the tent when Connor put his hand on Luther, bringing him to a halt.

"Annie, find John Mancini. I don't want to go into the crowd with a gun drawn," Connor said.

Evan walked around in front of Luther, his hand on the gun inside his waistband.

"Just in case you're thinking about taking off into the crowd," Evan told him, "there's nothing that would make me happier than putting a bullet in you."

Annie returned in minutes, John and several other agents in tow. John walked silently around Luther, as if inspecting him.

Finally, he said, simply and without emotion, "Take him in."

Connor handed Luther over to several of his colleagues, one of whom cuffed him and started to lead him away.

"Luther," John called out, and Luther turned.

"There was no CI in the McCullum case."

"What?"

"There was no confidential informant used in the McCullum case."

"You stay up all night last night, looking for that?" Luther asked.

"Didn't have to," John told him. "I was the special agent in charge. And it was Memphis, by the way, not Detroit . . ."

26

Four nights later, Evan leaned an elbow on the bar at Taps and looked around, still dazed by all the attention he had received after his role in bringing in Luther Blue had been announced by the FBI in a statement crediting him with the apprehension of one of the major players in the international traffic in child slavery.

"Way to show up the feds." Todd Holiday slapped him on the back for at least the fourth time. "Unbelievable, man. You made us all proud."

"Hey, I heard the FBI wants to hire you; that true?" Joe Sullivan sidled up behind him.

Evan shrugged. "Hey, you know, rumors are flying around about everything this week."

It was true—John Mancini had offered Evan an assist in getting into an accelerated program—but Evan didn't feel like getting into any of that right then and there. Tonight was Disco Night at Taps, and with the Bee Gees playing, Tom singing along in a weak falsetto, and all his old friends there with him, Evan pushed all thoughts of his next career move from his mind. He waved to Sean Mercer, the police chief from Broeder, who was weaving through the crowd with Evan's sister, Amanda.

"Hey, hero-man." Amanda hugged her older brother. "I saw you on the news last night. The local stations are really playing you up big-time, aren't they?"

"There's so much focus on the arrests of the crew who was running those brothels in the county, it's a good thing. Not the publicity for me, but shining the spotlight on this trafficking in children . . ."

"I couldn't believe this was happening, right there in Carleton." Amanda frowned. "Everyone I've spoken with has reacted the same way. No one believes it could happen here."

"It's happening in a lot of places. It's good that the story's out there. People should be aware that this is going on in their own backyards; it's way more common than even I ever imagined. And I'm a cop."

Sean motioned to the bartender, who promptly set up three beers. He handed one to Amanda and one to Evan, who waved it off and pointed to a place on the bar where six or seven beers were already lined up.

"If I drink every beer that's been bought for me tonight, I'll have to crawl home. I've already had three, not counting this one. I think I'll just nurse the one I have for a while."

"I'm really proud of you, Evan," Amanda whispered.

"Thank you. But it doesn't take much heroism to save the woman you love when someone is holding a gun to her head."

"Where is said woman you love?" Amanda looked around the crowded bar.

"She's still in Virginia. She'll be here on Friday, though. We have big plans for the weekend."

"A romantic weekend away? Cape May? New York?" Amanda asked.

"West Broeder. The backyard. Just me, Annie, and a couple of rosebushes." He grinned. "I already bought 'em. They're lined up along the back fence, just waiting to be planted."

"Way to plan a getaway," Sean deadpanned.

"Hey, that's what my girl wants, that's what she gets."

"Crosby, the boss is here. He's looking for you." Johnny Schenk slapped him on the back. "He wants to kiss your butt a little. I say let him."

Evan laughed and stepped around his sister to greet Chris Malone, who, still in his dark suit and dark tie, looked out of place in the smoky, loud neighborhood bar. He was a sport to stop in, Evan acknowledged as he accepted the congratulations and words of praise Malone had offered.

An hour later, his ears ringing from too many repetitions of "I Love the Nightlife" and Blondie's "Heart of Glass," Evan slumped into a booth opposite Joe and leaned against the hard wooden back. They had a basket of chips and a bowl of peanuts between them, and a couple of beers. Just like a hundred other nights they'd shared in this booth, in this bar, after their shift together as detectives in the Broeder Police Department. Those were the good old days, Evan was thinking as he grabbed a handful of peanuts.

"Getting too old for this kind of partying, Sullivan," Evan told Joe.

"Hey, I know what you mean. Nights when I'm not working, I'm asleep by now." He glanced at his watch. "I should probably get going soon. Rosemary and Joey are leaving early in the morning, and all the commotion always wakes me up."

"All what commotion?"

"Oh, you know, getting everything out into the car, the dog starts barking . . . though I have to say, they're getting better at it. It doesn't take 'em as long to get on the road as it did when they first started."

"Started what? I'm confused. What are they doing?"

"Didn't I tell you? We've been looking for something for Joey to get into, something he could do, so on a whim back in November, we took him to this dog show down near Philly, the big one, at the big expo center. Honest to God, Evan, you never saw so damned many dogs in your life. And all of them just groomed so nice, better than a lot of the guys in here tonight, I gotta tell ya."

Joe took a sip of his beer.

"Anyway, this show is what they call benched, which means that the dogs are all up on these tables for most of the day, and you can walk back there, see them, ask questions, and learn about the different breeds. It was interesting, I gotta admit, but Joey, he was just beside himself. They have these kids, they call them junior handlers, who compete in the rings with their dogs. He started talking to a couple of them, got interested, and next thing we know, he's asking if he can do it, too. How do you like that? We spent years shuttling him to soccer, baseball, football—all that stuff he hated and didn't do well at. And here he gets all psyched up about showing dogs."

"So what did you do? How does a kid get started in that?"

"While we were there, he talked to someone in one of the local kennel clubs, who took a shine to him. This woman, she's a breeder out near Reading, she invited him over, taught him the ropes, worked with him all winter. She's a terrific lady; she and Rosie have gotten to be good friends. Anyway, she offers to let Joey show one of her dogs in one of these junior handling competitions back in the spring. He doesn't win, but he does okay. Next thing I know, it's every weekend." Joe rested his arms on the table and laughed. "It's a pain in the ass, vacuuming all that damned dog hair out of the back of the car—I had to buy Rosie one of those big SUVs to carry around the dog and the equipment, you wouldn't believe all the crap you have to cart around—but it's been worth it. The kid is happier than I've ever seen him. Doing better in school, too. It's like a miracle has occurred."

Evan felt a twitch start somewhere low in his gut, the twitch that was the equivalent of a light going on or a distant bell starting to ring. He stared at his beer, not wanting to analyze the twitch, or look into the light, or hear the bell.

"So did you buy him a dog?" Evan didn't want to look at Joe, didn't want to let his imagination take him further than he wanted to go.

"Naw, didn't have to. The breeder has an older dog she lets him show. Dog stays in our house, sleeps in his bed. This big, hairy thing. Clumber spaniel, you ever seen one of them? Rare, this breeder is the only one in this part of the state. Great dog, though, gentle as a lamb. Loves Joey, Joey loves him. It's been great for the kid."

"That's great, Joe, that you found something for your son to enjoy." Evan couldn't even raise his eyes to look at Joe. If he was wrong . . .

Evan prayed he was wrong.

He'd known Joe for fifteen years. He'd danced at his wedding, he'd held his son in his arms at the hospital on the day he was born. For years, he'd watched Joe's back, and Joe had watched his.

"Yeah, it's been real good for him." Joe nodded and popped a few more peanuts into his mouth.

"Hey, I'm going to hit the men's room," Evan told him. The gnawing at his insides was unbearable. "Don't go anywhere. I'll be right back. I might ask you for a ride home. I'm feeling a little woozy after all those beers. I'm not used to drinking so much anymore."

"I hear you, buddy." Joe nodded again. "I'll be here."

Evan walked to the back of the bar and down the short hall that led to the restrooms.

It could be coincidence, he told himself with every step. It probably doesn't mean a thing, and I'm blowing this whole conversation out of proportion because I want so badly to solve the case. The thought of Joe being involved was ludicrous, wasn't it?

Evan could think of only one way to find out.

At the very end of the hall was a door that opened to the parking lot. Evan pushed the door open and stepped outside; at the same time he was taking his phone out of his pocket and speed-dialing Annie's home phone.

"Annie," he said when she picked up, "did the full lab reports ever come back on the trace from my girls?"

"I miss you, too, sweetie," she said, yawning, her voice groggy from sleep.

"Sorry, babe, I'm in a hurry"—he tried to disguise his impatience—"and this is important."

"The trace from the FBI lab on the girls?" she asked.

"Yes. You were going to have them run a full analysis on some dog hairs that were found on the bodies."

"Oh. The dog hairs. Yeah." She yawned again. "I saw that."

"Annie, it's important. Where's the report now, do you know?"

"Probably in my briefcase. What is it you needed to know at one thirty in the morning?"

"I need to know what kind of dog the hair came from. I hate to ask you to get out of bed to look for the report, but I really need to know."

"That's all you need? The breed of dog the hair was from?"

"Yes. And I need it now. So could you please go get the report and look it up?"

"I don't need to, I remember. It was a dog I never heard of, and I actually called the lab back to double-check because I thought maybe there was a typo or something," she told him. "It was hair from a Clumber spaniel. You ever hear of that breed?"

"Yeah. Unfortunately, I just did. Thanks, babe. I'll call you in the morning."

Evan went back into the bar and slid into his seat. Joe was on his cell, explaining to his wife that he might be a little late.

He looked up when Evan sat and told him, "Rosie said to tell you hi, and that she's proud of you."

"Thanks, Rosie." Evan's throat was tight, and he wondered how in the name of God he was going to be able to do what he was about to do.

He stared at his beer while Joe completed his call, then, when he'd hung up and put the phone back into his jacket pocket, Evan asked quietly, "Why'd you do it, Joe?"

"Why'd I do what?" Joe frowned.

"The girls. Why'd you get involved in that whole thing?"

Joe's face froze for several long minutes, then he said, "What girls are you talking about, Evan?"

"Joe, for the love of God, don't." Evan closed his eyes, squeezed them tightly shut. He couldn't bear to look at his former partner, even as he accused him. "Don't even try to talk around it, okay? I know you were part of it. I need to know what part, and I need to know who else."

"Jesus, Evan, how could you even think I'd . . ." Joe tried to stand, but Evan's arm shot out and grabbed him by the throat.

"Talk to me, Joe. Talk to me now."

"I got nothing to say. Let go of me."

Evan tightened his grip.

"You raped and murdered three little girls, Joe. You—"

"No, no." Joe went white and shook his head vehemently. "No, I didn't have a hand in none of that. I would never . . . no, God no, I never touched those girls, Evan. You have to believe me."

"How did the hair from a Clumber spaniel get on their bodies, Joe? You just told me how rare the breed is, how there's only one breeder in this part of the state." Evan's voice rose to a near shout. "How did the dog hair get on their bodies?"

The music had been lowered as the crowd had thinned, and those standing close to the booth turned, wide-eyed, as even-tempered Evan Crosby pulled his former partner out of his seat and slammed him against the bar.

"How did the dog hair get on their bodies?" Evan repeated.

"I didn't kill them, I swear to you." Joe was beginning to shake. "I only moved them."

"Moved them from where to where?" Evan demanded.

"From the place where they were . . . from where I was told to pick them up, to where I left them."

"Jesus God, Joe, how could you?"

The two men began to struggle, and the startled bystanders intervened to subdue Evan and to surround Joe with questioning eyes.

"I didn't kill them, I didn't rape them. I never harmed those girls," Joe said, looking from one man to the next, wanting them to understand that his role had been limited to taking care of the girls after the fact. "I tried to help them, see? I left them where they'd be found right away, I made them look like that other guy had done them, so they'd get some press, maybe someone would recognize them and they'd go back to their families. I tried to do the best I could for them . . ."

He turned to Evan, tears running down his face.

"I tried to do the best I could so they'd be found, so they wouldn't be lying out in the rain. I couldn't stand to think of them lying out in the rain, all alone like that . . ."

27

"Here. Catch." Annie stood on the back steps of Evan's townhouse and tossed him a bottle of water.

"Thanks," he said, catching it in one hand. "The sun is brutal today."

She looked up and squinted. "I don't think this is a good time to be planting roses. We're better off waiting until later in the day, when the sun drops down a little. I read someplace that you're not supposed to plant in the heat of the day."

"Hey, that works for me." He jammed his shovel into the over-turned dirt in the flower bed they'd spent the morning preparing and wiped his brow with the hem of his T-shirt. "I'd just as soon wait until it gets a little cooler."

"We can still finish getting the bed ready, dig the holes, put in that stuff you bought that's supposed to be good for the roots."

"Or we could wait until later and do everything when it cools off." He grinned hopefully.

"I say we dig now, plant later." She walked to the side of the yard, where four rosebushes stood, still in their black pots, in the shade. "The poor rosebushes have already been waiting an extra week to be planted. It's a miracle they're still alive."

"They look awfully comfortable there, in the shade. Are you sure we should move them?" Evan opened the water and took a long drink.

"It's going to be overcast tomorrow morning, then rain for the rest of the weekend. Planting them tonight will be perfect."

He took another drink, then replaced the plastic cap and set the bottle on the fence, between pickets, where it tottered unsteadily.

"I am worried, though, about them drying out while we're in Santa Estela." Annie frowned.

"Maybe I can get Amanda to stop out a few times during the week to water them."

"Good idea." Annie pulled her hair back behind her ears and looked for the container of root food she'd left near the fence.

"How do you think that's going to go, meeting the girls' parents?" she asked.

"I hope it goes okay, at least with two of the families." He leaned on the handle of the shovel. "The police suspect that the third girl, the one who still hasn't been identified, was probably sold by her family in the first place. They aren't likely to come back now and claim the body."

"Maybe by the time we get down there, they will have." She pulled on her gardening gloves and tossed a handful of granules into the first hole Evan had dug.

"I still can't get over John pulling all those strings, getting the locals down there to start showing the girls' pictures around until they located the families. Arranging for the bodies to be transported back to Santa Estela, and for us to accompany them . . ."

"John understands how important it is for you to take them home, sweetie. And if you want to look beyond that, I think it's important for the new government down there to assure the people that every effort is being made to find their lost children and to bring them home. It's a brilliant PR move on the part of the new president of Santa Estela, and a goodwill gesture on the part of our government."

"For whatever reason, I'm grateful. And I'm really happy that they're sending Don Manley as well. He's so grateful for the chance to go, to take his vics back. It was good of John to suggest it. If it weren't for Don's girl, and the little vial of bean seeds around her neck, we never would have been able to put this all together."

"That's what happens when everyone pools their info. Things get done." She smiled and added, "I'm really looking forward to the trip. I just know this will be something I'll always remember."

"Yeah, real romantic vacation." Evan stopped digging and looked at her almost apologetically. "Ten days in a hot, steamy, third-world country whose most lucrative export is its kids. With luck, maybe we'll even get some mosquito netting for our tent. Maybe the piranhas will be migrating and we'll be able to get in a swim."

"It'll be the best vacation either of us ever had, you wait and see." She wrapped her arms around his waist. "We'll still be talking about this when we're old and gray. You will always have the memory of having returned those children to their families, to be buried with love and respect. I'm proud of you, that you cared enough to take that on when no one else seemed to give a damn about them."

"John said something like that when he offered me the job."

"Are you still thinking about that?"

"No. Right now, I'm thinking about planting a garden with my best girl, and taking a trip with her through a snake-infested jungle. I'll think about the job offer when we get back."

"Fair enough." She gave him a tap on the butt before getting back to work, measuring another spoonful of fertilizer and dumping it into the next hole.

"Two more," she told him, pointing to the rest of the plot, where holes had not as yet been dug.

"Here?" he asked, the shovel poised to dig, and she nodded.

"Hey," he said, "while I dig these last two holes, why don't you plant those geraniums in that big planter at the end of the deck?"

"Wouldn't you rather wait until you finish the deck?" She frowned. "If I plant this up now, you'll have to carry it up onto the deck, and it's going to be heavy."

"No big deal." He shrugged. "Just go on and plant the flowers, we'll worry about moving it later."

"Okay, if you say so."

Annie carried the pot of geraniums and ivy to the large planter Evan had left at the foot of the deck, and poured in a bag of potting soil. Next she pulled the plants from their pots and started to transplant the ivy. When she started on the geraniums, he heard her exclaim, "Oh."

She looked at him from across the small yard.

"There's a little box in the bottom of the geranium pot."

"Is there, now?" He stuck the shovel into the dirt and started walking toward her. "Well, maybe you should open it."

She shook the small dark blue box from the pot and opened it.

"Evan," she said softly, meeting his eyes as he walked toward her. "Evan."

"What do you think, Annie?" he asked. "Think it's time to make it legal?"

She nodded.

"Well then, let's see if it fits." He took her hand, then took the ring from the box and slid it onto her finger. "What do you think? Does it fit all right?"

"It fits perfectly." She had not taken her eyes from his face.

"Do you like it?"

"I love it."

"You haven't even looked at it."

She looked at her hand, at the simple gold band with the round diamond and nodded. "It's perfect. I love it."

"So, I guess this means yes?"

"This means yes."

He gathered her in his arms and kissed her.

"Will this get me out of digging for the rest of the afternoon?"

"Probably not"—she laughed—"but it might get you a bonus at the end of the day."

"I like the sound of that." He kissed her again, then said, more seriously, "I'm thinking a Christmas wedding might be really nice, you know? All those red flowers they always put in the church—"

"Oh! Bad timing on my part. Sorry, guys."

Annie and Evan looked up to see Grady Shields walking down the drive that ran behind the house.

"Hey, Grady," Annie called to him. "This is a surprise."

"Yeah, well, I just wanted to drop by to see you before I left. I wanted to thank you and Evan for what you did to bring that bastard Luther Blue in." He turned to Evan. "The only thing I'm sorry about is that you didn't blow his head off when you had the chance. He's still trying to make deals, you know that? Still offering to give up other members of the kidnapping and trafficking ring in exchange for a reduced sentence."

"Maybe the feds will offer him something on the kidnapping, but he'll still have to face murder charges in Montana," Annie assured him. "I spoke with Sheriff Brody a few days ago. I had promised I'd call if we found Melissa's killer. He understands the situation very well, but he's willing to wait his turn to prosecute Luther for

Melissa's death. He won't be getting away with it, Grady. It may take a while, but he will stand trial in Montana."

"That's the first good news I've had since this started," Grady said. "Maybe I'll still be out there when that day comes."

"You're going to Montana?" Annie asked.

"Melissa left the property to me. At first I thought I couldn't live in the house where she died. Then I started remembering all the good times we had there, and I was thinking maybe it would help her spirit to rest if I went back for a while. Maybe it would help my spirit, as well, to be with her." He shrugged. "I can't think of any-place else to go right now."

"Are you taking a leave, then?"

"I talked to John yesterday, he told me to go. He'll take care of the paperwork for me, send me what I need to sign. Told me just to keep in touch, let him know when I want to come back."

"I hope you do, Grady," Annie told him sincerely. "I'll miss you."

"I'll miss you, too." He gave her a quick hug, then offered his hand to Evan. "Take care of her, Crosby."

Evan merely nodded.

Grady took a few steps backward, then let himself out of the gate. He walked to the end of the drive, then turned once to wave before disappearing behind the corner house.

"He looks terrible," Annie said.

"He's lost the woman he loved. I'd look terrible, too, if anything happened to you. It just reminds me to cherish each day, to never take it for granted." He paused, then said, "If I take the job John offered, the main reason would be so that we could be together every night, instead of this crazy commuting back and forth."

"You're not going to think about it until we come back from Santa Estela, remember?" Annie reminded him. "I think you should stick to that. Besides, there are other things we need to talk about, as far as the trip is concerned."

"Like how to tell the parents what happened to their daughters." Evan grew sober again. "How to tell them why they had to die."

"Maybe it will give them some solace to know that they never accepted the horrible things that had been done to them, that they'd been unwilling participants. And that they died because they would not stop fighting, they would not cooperate, isn't that what Joe Sullivan told the D.A.? That these girls were killed as an example to the others?"

"Bastard. I still can't get over him getting involved in something like this. I can't reconcile the Joe Sullivan I knew all these years with the man who participated in any way in prostituting young girls . . ." Evan shook his head. "And for the worst of reasons."

"It's not the first time a man sold his soul for money, and it won't be the last." She put her arms around him. "Just be grateful you were able to put a stop to it."

"This was just the tip of the iceberg, Annie. You know that."

"But at least that tip was cut off," she told him.

He appeared to be about to say something when his phone rang.

"Crosby," he answered, listened for a few minutes, then said, "Give me fifteen minutes."

He snapped the phone shut and turned to Annie. "That was Malone. They found two bodies in a boarded-up house down on Longwood. A couple of transients, it looks like, and I—"

"Go. I'll be here when you get back."

"Annie, I'm sorry."

"Don't be. Go."

"I guess I should run upstairs and get cleaned up, get out of these dusty clothes." He looked around the yard, at the half-dug bed and the plants sitting here and there. "I hate to leave you with this mess."

"Don't give it another thought. I'll finish up out here."

"Are you sure? I'll probably be gone for at least the rest of the afternoon."

"It's okay. Go on and do what you do." She kissed him and

turned him in the direction of the house. "I'll be here when you get home . . ."

She watched him take the steps two at a time, knowing that his mind was already on the crime scene and what he would find there. It was what he did, and who he was.

Annie wouldn't have had him any other way.

# ABOUT THE AUTHOR

MARIAH STEWART is the bestselling author of numerous novels and several novellas. She is a RITA finalist for romantic suspense and is the recipient of the Award of Excellence for contemporary romance, a RIO (Reviewers International Organization) Award honoring excellence in women's fiction, and a Reviewers' Choice Award from *Romantic Times* magazine. A native of Hightstown, New Jersey, she is a three-time recipient of the Golden Leaf Award and a Lifetime Achievement Award from the New Jersey Romance Writers, and has been inducted into their Hall of Fame. Stewart is a member of the Valley Forge Romance Writers, the New Jersey Romance Writers, Novelists, Inc., the Romance Writers of America, and International Thriller Writers. She lives with her husband, two daughters, and two rambunctious golden retrievers amid the rolling hills of Chester County, Pennsylvania.

## ABOUT THE TYPE

This book was set in Sabon, a typeface designed by the well-known German typographer Jan Tschichold (1902–74). Sabon's design is based upon the original letter forms of Claude Garamond and was created specifically to be used for three sources: foundry type for hand composition, Linotype, and Monotype. Tschichold named his typeface for the famous Frankfurt typefounder Jacques Sabon, who died in 1580.